S0-BRV-700

WITHDRAWN

THE SCORPION

Also by Albert Memmi

The Pillar of Salt
Strangers
The Colonizer and the Colonized
Portrait of a Jew
The Liberation of the Jew
Dominated Man

The Scorpion

or The Imaginary Confession

BY ALBERT MEMMI

TRANSLATED FROM THE FRENCH BY
ELEANOR LEVIEUX

A Howard Greenfeld Book
J. Philip O'Hara, Inc.
Chicago

First published in 1971 by Grossman Publishers.

Manufactured in the United States of America.

J. Philip O'Hara, Inc. 20 East Huron, Chicago 60611.
Published simultaneously in Canada by Van Nostrand
Reinhold Ltd., Scarborough, Ontario.

LC: 79-114950
ISBN: 0-87955-908-X (trade)
ISBN: 0-87955-906-3 (paper)

What are you going to think of my book? Will you find that it follows my true bent? I lived it for four years and I wrote it in order to overrule my own objections. I come down with books the way other people come down with diseases. I don't have any use for any book unless its author nearly died.

André Gide

Whoever confesses lies and flees the veritable truth, which is void, shapeless, and generally blurred.

Paul Valery

Contents

The Scorpion

The Four Thursdays

The Scorpion (continued)

The Cellar

Chronicle of the Kingdom of Within

Author's Note

As the reader will realize, the type in this book should have been printed in several colors. I will explain this in my *Dialogues on Colored Writing*. Because the publisher objected on technical grounds, arguing that the cost of such a book would be out of reach, we have had to make do with typographical variations. We rely on the reader to make an additional imaginative effort. That will be his contribution to this joint work.

THE SCORPION

The Scorpion

He moved ahead with a jerk, turned about, started up again as suddenly, stopped short. Now there could be no doubt about it: the unheard-of thing, the wall of embers was everywhere, without a breach. He remained motionless in the midst of the monstrous trap and made no more attempt to rebel in that sudden savage way that drove people wild with joy.

With their eyes riveted on the circle of fire, the spectators fell silent. The end was near, it could not fail; they had been told it would come; they had seen it for themselves; there was no other way out. Now he was moving his head slowly in dreamlike despair. And every time his changing shadow was projected onto part of the crowd, there was a ripple to avoid that horrible caress.

At last the weapon rose slowly, hugely, absorbing every bit of equilibrium in that body, every gaze turned onto that strange armored monument glistening under the lamps, the weapon ending in an atrocious blade, curved and keen. And suddenly, so fast that some people, distracted for one minute fraction of time by the fatigue of fixed attention, admitted sadly that they hadn't seen anything—the weapon had struck the head. The crowd howled, unbearably wounded and delivered. A single ruddy flash, perfect in its brutality and neatness, and the extraordinary pyramid had collapsed in a still tumult of carapaces.

The game of death was finished. The crowd had just relived what it had known already but which no recital, no rehearsal would ever make it believe.

Before leaving the enclosure, the spectators filed out before the little arena, rapidly growing dark as ashes gnawed away the embers. Although the cadaver had become astonishingly tiny, now that it was deprived of movement and the eeriness of shadow, no one dared go too near the chaotic little black mass, for fear perhaps of the still-fresh poison but also out of respect for the great lesson: reduced to his sole self, certain of not finding any other solution, the scorpion had killed himself.

Fine, only it's not true: scorpions do not commit suicide. That's a legend that circulates in Moorish cafés and old wives' tales. Emile must have heard it in our father's store, where he continues to find half of what he tells his readers; there's not one of his stories that doesn't give me the feeling I know it already. But, the DREAMLIKE DESPAIR of the scorpion! The scorpion REDUCED TO HIS SOLE SELF! That's Emile's own mythology. The truth is not so sublime as all that. Sometimes, just for the fun of it, children, and occasionally tourist guides too, it seems, will place a scorpion in the middle of a ring of embers. Half-burned, panic-stricken by the heat, the poor thing does in fact end up wounding itself and dying of its own venom—but only because it's been thrashing around, not because of some noble decision or some metaphysical discovery. This childish mania for giving the least little thing an echo, a significance which is less clear than the thing itself! But maybe that's what lit-er-a-ture is all about?

One good thing anyhow is that it must be part of that novel of his. Let's come back to the problem at hand:

"Would you be willing to take the responsibility of putting Emile's notes in order? I can't think of anyone else who could do it or who would be better qualified than you. You know your brother better than I do. The publisher would also like the finished pieces to be separated from the rest, especially the novel, he's very insistent about that. Everything should be in the top right-hand drawer, 'the cellar'; I haven't touched it since."

Just a few lines, but then the whole letter is short, as neat as her neatly drawn-back hair, and as sharp as her own gaze; a letter in which my sister-in-law says the important things about her children, about the house, about her future legal and even sentimental relations with the family. In two pages, everything is said, except about Emile, her husband, about whom there is not a word, nothing about the past, nothing about what may have become of him. All right, never mind. That, too, perhaps I'll understand as I go through these papers. The publisher and I are not looking for the same thing.

Yes, everything must be in "the cellar." I used to kid Imilio about it often enough, and he would smile without answering. The drawer that was always open, the top right drawer of his desk where, day after day, he used to toss in those sheets of paper (always the same kind, a schoolboy's notebook, the only reassuring thing) pell-mell without ever taking them out again, except that from time to time, by some magician's trick, he would pull a book out of it all. And now I'm the one who's supposed to do the magic! The trouble is that I don't know the rules, I don't know how to make books. And if I'm to "put things in order," I'll need a key, or maybe several. Who has them, now that Imilio is not there? Marie? That's not even certain, and anyhow she'll never talk. . . .

Six o'clock. Mahmoud's noble bow and silent smile, Juliette's "Good night, Doctor, see you tomorrow," and here I am alone again except for the noises in the rue Zarkoune. Ever since this morning the same unending procession of people that has become twice as big since Boulakia left: "Keep your eyes open. It doesn't hurt. The left eye, one drop, two drops; the right eye, one drop, two drops. There. All done. There. All done." No matter what happens, I'll never leave this country. It's my country, I was born here, I'm more useful here than anywhere else, I have no right to abandon these people, especially now. When the Center was inaugurated, the Minister told me again how grateful he was that I am staying; he even repeated it. I answered him almost aggressively, saying I didn't see how he could even think of thanking me for that. I couldn't live anywhere else or any other way, without this marvelous profession that has no mystery about it. Being a doctor is a prosaic, day-to-day business, but that's why I like it. A tiny little sliver, hardly visible, and a man as big and strong as a horse is suffering, terrified, overwhelmed; the doctor makes a single gesture and the patient is relieved, grateful, transformed. That's the real miracle. How can anyone deliberately prefer dreams, inefficiency, and questions without answers?

I've warned Marie-Suzanne I'll be coming home a little later than usual. I want to do a little work every evening in the quiet of the Dispensary. But where should I begin? Imilio, Imilio! How can I make out anything at all in this tangled heap? What belongs to the novel, the Journal, and the rest?

The Cellar

Periodically my father emptied and cleaned out the cellar, I don't remember why, maybe because of the dead mice and rats, or even cats or dogs, that we always found there. At the same time, with Peppino's help, he gathered an extraordinary harvest from it—toys, dolls that were broken or intact but always faded, pale and cold, as if they had come back from another world, balls of all sizes and kinds, enough of them for a magician, shoes, clothing, kitchen utensils, and also the most unexpected or incomprehensible objects, parts of things, I suppose, and once even a revolver. We never found out how it got there.

We were still living in the Impasse Tarfoune, in a perfectly quiet district filled with the ceremonious scorn of each person for all the others; this carefully defined ritual of mutual mistrust and politeness was enough to keep everyone in his place. Yet apparently people were in the habit of throwing things they couldn't manage to get rid of any other way furtively through the air-hole of our cellar. But still, how did they do it without being noticed? The Impasse was narrow and, after all, despite the silence and calm that filled it, they were visible from every window. The fact is that every year brought a harvest, and that it had to be gathered regularly or else there would have been mountains of things, up to the air-hole perhaps, mingled with the bodies of small animals that came to die there and slowly rot—or that were also thrown into our cellar deliberately and had to be taken out before the heat set in.

My father borrowed big leather boots for the occasion from Camillieri the sewerman, a neighbor from outside the Impasse, and repaired them afterwards free of charge; without them, my father explained, he would get sick. Peppino went down in his canvas shoes; Italians are sturdier, and where could he have found boots? Then for two days the mammoth unpacking went on, literally blocking the Impasse, and everyone came to see, but from a distance, curious and on the defensive, as if it concerned them of course but indirectly, as if they were making an effort not to recognize these objects even though they had been theirs, because to do so would have been to announce that it was they who had thrown them into our cellar, or simply because they would have been ashamed to admit that they had owned such wretched property. They merely looked at the things from afar, as at a dubious part of themselves, and never protested against the very strong odors that pervaded even their bedrooms. "That proves it," my mother would say. At most, a child would come from time to time and delicately pick out—having genuinely mislaid it—a flattened and withered ball that had lost its colors and lost its soul as well through a slit in the rotten rubber; he would look at it pensively for a minute before putting it gently back on the heap without showing any of those extreme feelings before this plaything, which had belonged to him, which are peculiar to childhood, enthusiasm at finding it again or anger at seeing that it had become unusable.

Never, in any case, did anyone ever offer to help my father carry out this grand collective clean-up. Not even myself, I must admit, originally because I didn't dare tackle that great black hole, later because I could not vie with him for the privilege which went with this annual solemn event. So I kept putting it off until we had moved out of the Impasse and it had become foreign to me. I regret it now that I have to make such a great effort to imagine what the inside of our cellar was like—the only cellar I ever had after all; apparently it took up the whole lower part of the house and even, people whispered, was connected with the oven where the dismembered body of little Salem had been burned.

Once the cellar had been emptied, my father carried down large pails of quicklime and burned the floor and the walls with it. But the cart that was to take everything away to the lake sometimes came late and meanwhile the Impasse, cluttered up by this boneyard of little animals unduly swollen from having stayed in the dark and damp, by all these toys, scraps of metal, bits of wood, and rags, topped off by enormous flowers of green and yellow mold, was turned into an astonishing and useless bazaar that everyone feigned to overlook. Only my mother, who always dared everything in the same innocent way, would prowl around that putrid avalanche a little, looking with disdainful irony at the common entrails of our district, and from time to time, lifting up some object even odder than the others, she would mutter, "And what about this? Who threw this away? Nobody? Absolutely nobody." Then, mock conciliatory, she would add, "All right, either the house has given birth—or else I'm dreaming."

No, she wasn't dreaming. But what is this story about the cellar? It's not that it isn't true; our father did carry out a clean-up like this but only from time to time, every two or three years, I think; irregularly, anyhow. And what's this solemnity, this mystery? It was actually a game for us children to wade through the mess; there was nothing silent or frightening about it. I was younger than Imilio, it's true, but I don't recall that our father placed such importance on this task or derived any special satisfaction from all the smells it let loose. He must have dreaded them really, because of his asthma. . . .

Or rather, our father brought this slightly theatrical gravity to everything he did. He wanted to keep his role, but that went without saying; no one would have thought of challenging him for it, not even in fun, and he didn't need confirmation of it. And later on, long before our father began to withdraw into the background, wasn't it Emile himself who took over that role in his own way? It was only natural, for him and everyone else, for our mother of course, for our sisters and even for the boys: he was our eldest brother, and our father was nearly blind. Besides, he had always had a natural bent for the role. Even when he was very young people used to say—ironically, of course, and somewhat enviously, perhaps—that he spoke the way one should write. The implication being that there was something deliberate, artificial, and stiff about him; and it is true that he spoke little, slowly, and precisely, always seeming to look for the definitive way of phrasing something. In addition, he always appeared to be straightening the folds of some imaginary toga and held his head as if leaning back, probably because of his near-sightedness; no wonder he annoyed people and was respected but not liked.

You might say that Emile officiated. . . . How awful! Inadvertently, I've used the past tense. Emile officiates, lofty and sure of himself, over life and death, the way Father used to discuss them every morning with God. . . . No, that's not being very fair. It's strange, after all these years, even now, under the present circumstances, I can't manage to shake off my mistrust, my—yes, let's be frank—my resentment of Emile completely. And what about myself? Haven't I caught some of my father's and my elder brother's play-acting? What else am I doing, so many times, with my patients? Is it really fair to call it play-acting? Isn't it more a sort of ceremony or rite? Don't I officiate too, in my own way?

Come on, Narcissus, let's get back to our puzzle: where does this passage belong? With the Journal, or the novel? Nothing to do with poor *Scorpion,* in any case. The Journal then? But why is Imilio bringing up this childhood memory? In connection with what? Maybe the best thing to do at first is just to go ahead without looking for any explanations. After a while the guidelines will begin to stand out—if there are any!

Who's to say whether he was writing with any definite plan? and with only one plan? The publisher assumes he was, but only because that would suit him. "What are you working on now, Imilio?" He always answered that kind of question evasively or jokingly. Once he said to me, "I'm working up several batches of dough at the same time; the first batch that's ready I'll put in the oven." And another time he said, "I take part of the dough and shape it; then if the shape doesn't please me, I throw the abortive thing back and knead it again."

I'd better stop for tonight, or else I'll be going around in circles, I can tell. I have too much on my mind as it is. It's a hard and fast rule, I must not tire myself out the day before a difficult day, and tomorrow I have to do a detached retina! I've been doing surgery for ten years and I still have to force myself not to think about it the day before. I make myself go to bed early. I don't like working that way, right to the limit, running an extreme risk. Doing a detached retina is like operating at the bottom of a well on a piece of moldy cloth, an old lace curtain that's been burned. It's such an underhanded illness, I hate it, and the disaster is so unexpected. Suddenly the patient's whole life, his family, his livelihood, everything is upset. He's come in about something that's nothing really, and all of a sudden, there he is, arrested at the hearing, sentenced, punished! And I'm the one who has to break it to him. It's a horrible feeling. One day, in the eye of a pretty, lively girl of eighteen, I saw a brain tumor: I felt as if I had to hand down a death sentence. Tomorrow, it's poor Fredj Sebbah, a patient of mine for years, but never anything serious. He was part of the routine—glasses, irritations that were more or less imaginary. And then it happened, and right away I offered him a bed, I suggested that "he spend a few days with us." At first he didn't understand, then he panicked and began to cry, begging me to let him go home first to warn his wife and children, as if I had some power to prevent him, like a jailer. So tomorrow the operation will have to be a rush job, the kind of desperate move it always is in a nasty case like that, and I can't promise the patient or myself anything. That part of my profession I don't like at all. It still frightens me a little, despite my ten years of experience.

That cellar was just a little cubby-hole that didn't communicate with anything, at least so far as I know, and certainly not with the oven cellars in the rue des Terrasses, several hundred yards away. Anyhow, I never heard of any connection between our cellar and the horrible stories that were spread around—probably by a bunch of hysterical women—about the various bakers in the rue des Terrasses.

The Palace

(followed by Si Mohammed)

I was born at La Goulette, a little Berber port near the capital, only a few hundred paces from the Walls and the Fort of Charles V, which are still standing. From the time I was born until I was four years old, so that I still remember it—like remembering a shadow that has been wrapped around all the houses I have lived in since—my parents, along with two other families, lived in a kind of small palace full of cupolas and terraces, verandas and corners that jutted out onto the beach and that were periodically linked and ringed by the sea. This meant that although the house was delightful in the summer, the humidity had made much of it unfit for habitation. In one of the bedrooms which, oddly enough, had not a single window and was constantly battered by waves during the severest part of the winter, the humidity was so dense that the room was filled with a heavy mist. Although we were frightened by the almost total darkness of the place, we had chosen it as our *hamman* and, in the light of little oiled paper torches, we played at taking the ritual bath.

It was said that the first owners of Dar el-Kouloub, literally the House of Hearts, had hardly lived in it. Either they had not succeeded in feeling at ease in that vast edifice, where the architect had tried to reconcile too many and too varied dreams—Arabian palace, Italian villa, holiday house open to the wind and light, winter refuge with corridors and nooks everywhere, not to mention some astonishing exercises, or errors, in building, like the complicated stairways leading to tiny useless terraces, or a succession of windowless rooms; or else there was a more tragic reason which I shall tell about some other time; or else they simply gave in to the ceaseless pounding of the sea, eroding the foundations (we could see the ravages it wrought right beneath our windows), slowly and implacably infiltrating through the walls and even the ceilings. Abruptly, almost noiselessly, large patches of plaster would fall from the ceiling and give off a clinging odor

of charcoal. "One day," my mother would say, furiously, "the water will tear the anchor away from our boat and when we wake up, we'll be out at sea."

We did not feel our parents' anxiety. Quite the contrary. We explored the labyrinth of rooms, nooks, stairways, and garrets constantly without ever exhausting its resources, and of course we went to all the forbidden places, despite the grown-ups' scolding and their warnings that cave-ins were always possible and scorpions must be hidden in the stones. Our parents thought that they had protected us once and for all by "sealing off" the doors with wires that had rusted so long ago they turned into dust in our fingers. And finally it was the same enjoyment of roominess, even when the roominess was in danger, that carried the day with our parents as well, for we stayed on in the Palace until we were forced to leave it, when it became unavoidably clear that my father had acute and chronic asthma and it was absolutely out of the question for him to live a few yards away from the water, and he decided to carry out his plan of having a store in the city itself, where he was convinced he would finally make money.

So we exchanged that open life, which constantly carried us far out of ourselves, for the one room in the Oukala des Oiseaux and the withdrawn and silent atmosphere of Impasse Tarfoune. At Dar el-Kouloub, although we had lived virtually alone on the beach, deserted nine months in every twelve, and facing a horizon that was barely marked by the purple shadow of Bou-Kornine, while the other two families lived on the northern side and faced landward, we had had a satisfactory social life. The grown-ups greeted each other with pleasure and went to see one another, and my mother did the big Friday cooking with the other mothers, of the same religion as ourselves. As for us children, we played games together and met regularly in this part or that of the Palace which only we could reach, and often we went on an expedition to the Sicilian village, abandoned now but still intact, to meet the fishermen's boys. . . . Because of this need we had of one another amidst the solitude of nature, we looked for one another earnestly and did not conceal our joy when we found one another, just as we had to shout in order to be heard over the unrestrained air and the wind that shouted louder than we did.

The Impasse and the Oukala were full to bursting, and a perfect separateness was maintained by the strictest politeness, broken by violence from time to time. People pretended not to see one another; no one ever greeted anyone else except to apologize, demand something, or warn of some happening that a life so tightly collective made inevitable. It was in the Impasse, in fact, that I learned loneliness, and that's the way it will always be. I have always felt more threatened in a crowd or in a ceremony of some sort than in the forest or even in battle, whereas—or because —I need other people so much at those times. Or am I imagining this now, as I look back? Perhaps, because we'd been isolated for so long, it was impossible for us right from the beginning to live with our fellow men?

My father, in any case, never got over it and all in all would never, I think, have left the Palace if he hadn't been expelled by the sickness that led to more and more frequent fits of choking so frightening that he let my mother talk him into leaving. My mother had never been resigned to the separation from her family and softly but ceaselessly she had plotted to leave Dar el-Kouloub. She even pretended to get the name wrong, calling it Dar el-Kharab, House of Desolation, and claiming that that was its real name, because of the sand and remoteness.

(She always distorted names that way, and since her own clumsiness seemed to amuse her, we couldn't really tell whether she wasn't doing it purposely, especially since—either through mischievousness or a sort of contagion of sound—her so-called mistakes often had a surprisingly suggestive meaning. For instance, one day our youngest brother announced he was going away to fight and, a little too solemnly, he cited the famous example of Bar Kokhba, who killed himself along with his entire garrison. Instead of crying, as we had expected her to, she began to make fun of his heroic model, pretending to get his beautiful name—Bar Kokhba means "son of the star"—wrong and turning it into Ben Kahba, "son of a whore," and even Ben Kalba, "son of a bitch," which was decidedly overdoing the clumsiness, even if you allow for her feeling upset at seeing her son leave.)

My father brought to the Oukala that silent disdain and bitter irony that made other people fear, admire, and avoid him. In a vague way, he seemed somehow to be of another blood, another caste, and at first I used to think I was too, even though I made every effort to bridge that unbearable gap that separated us from the other residents of the Impasse. My father didn't even try to narrow the gap and in a way he really behaved as if he came from somewhere else.

. . . And here I am in the Impasse again. I certainly keep coming back to it. What can I find to say about it now, that I haven't already told many times, openly or disguised in different ways? What can I find out now that I don't already know? Let's stop here; my intention was not to tell about myself all over again but to go back much further, to THE HISTORY OF OUR FAMILY.

But first, I feel that I ought to say a word about Si Mohammed, who owned the Palace.

Si Mohammed

When the nationalists managed—despite the occupying power, and despite tradition, both of which would have found it to their advantage to see an old man continue to sit on the throne—to establish that henceforth the eldest male member of the reigning family would no longer succeed the sovereign, as had been customary, the first victim of that victory was Si Mohammed, the Prince. Having waited almost all his life for his turn to reign, having prepared for the role with flawless dignity, moderate words, a distant manner toward others, including his own family, and even a careful attention to dress, in short, with a solitude befitting a prince, and having indeed become a prince, no matter what he had been in the beginning, Sidi Mohammed never became king.

For us, too, the consequences were important. Since Sidi Mohammed did not become king, my grandfather, who collected the rents from his houses, had repairs made, and in fact played the role of administrator, never became Administrator to His Majesty, as the family had counted on his becoming for such a long time. All that we retained, and handed down from father to son, was the privilege of living in Dar el-Kouloub, even after Si Mohammed left to live in his former residence which, truth to tell, was only half a mile inland. A privilege which, as I have said, we also had to give up when we emigrated to the city.

Nonetheless, my father was born there, like all his brothers and sisters, and in his own eyes, and in the neighbors' eyes too, of course, something special clung to him because he had been the son of the princely administrator. Above all, my father settled in the Palace with his young wife, whereas his brothers and sisters all left it as soon as they attained their majority. When political disappointments and tighter financial straits obliged Si Mohammed to rent two or three of the rooms in the Palace, the Prince himself asked my embarrassed father for permission to do so and required the new tenants to live on the north side of Dar el-Kouloub, so as not to destroy my father's impression of being its only guest.

I must have glimpsed the grand old man three or four times in all. He hardly ever went out, and when he did leave his house among the reeds, where he continued to sequester his wives, his sons, and his few servants, all of whom respected him religiously, it was to take a short walk along the edge of the water—always wearing a silver-fringed mahogany-colored jebba, his massive neck emphasized by an ample necklace of blue beads, his fingers covered with rings, his face itself ringed with a red beard, his head wrapped in a turban which was an extraordinary mingling of all the reds and greens possible and took on a fascinating intensity in the wet winter light. From our windows we could see the red and green turban relaying the sun long after it had set, receiving and condensing every scrap of hesitant light, bobbing slowly along the horizon and reminding even the most unbelieving that Sidi Mohammed had almost been king.

Today a comparison occurs to me which I can dare to make without being disrespectful only because, with the passage of time, my memory places the different characters in this story on much the same level: in a certain way, my father and the Prince resembled one another. It is possible, of course, that my father supposed, like every one else, that once Sidi Mohammed was seated on the throne, "great good would come of it for us," as my mother used to say, loudly and greedily. But I think that my father admired Sidi Mohammed most sincerely and that, when they met on the beach, and my father went up to him and reverently kissed his hand, the quality of his submission as he did so, acknowledging a just order, was paired with the utmost dignity.

The Medal

(followed by the History of Our Family)

This morning Mr. Rousset, the excellent curator of the library in the El-Attarine bazaar, sent me a small medal he had found himself. Nothing very extraordinary about that; everyone here is an archaeologist, for everything is brimful with remains of antiquity. All you have to do is scuff the earth with the tip of your shoe as you walk, and you turn up coins and bits of pottery. No, the extraordinary, the miraculous thing is that I have my proof at last. I can hold it in my hands. (Did I ever really doubt that I would end up having it?) A very handsome medal, with a name engraved on it, very legibly, and that name, beyond the shadow of a doubt, is MEMMI. Each side of the coin sheds light on the other. On one, the head of a Numidian horseman *wearing a crown,* therefore a hero or a prince, some important man in any case, probably the man whose name is engraved on the other side. On that other side, two horsemen on foot, each one standing next to his horse, all of it very finely engraved and ending with the inscription that takes up the lower third of the medal: L. MEMMI, Lucius Memmi, probably.

Now that I have the missing link, I can trace back the entire chain.

History of Our Family

For very good reasons, which I shall be coming back to, I have always been convinced that we are originally from the heart of this region, at least as far back into the past as one can go, up to those imprecise limits where collective memory hesitates between myth and fact. It pleases me to imagine that some of my ancestors were there to welcome Queen Dido's companions, when they took refuge on our shores, or the men who founded Phoenician trading posts. There is more to it than mere imagination, and soon the variety and concordance of the assumptions I have been patiently accumulating should turn them into proof. But, in all events, the first certain indication of our presence here (before Mr. Rousset found the medal) is found in the Arabian historian El-Milli. In his Arabian-Berber Chronicles, he lists one El-Mammi among the companions of the famous Judeo-Berber Queen Cahena. Given the uncertainty of the intermediate sounds between the *a* and the *e* in this language, it does not seem overbold to say that this is a barely deformed pronunciation of the Berber name, El-Memmi, meaning: small man; which would seem to indicate that my ancestor was not exactly tall. Even today, when a Kabyle mother speaks to her son, she says to him, Emmi (my son), and if she wants to add a touch of tenderness, she will say Meummi, which means, my-very-little-one. This is also what Ejsenbeth thinks; he has done the best onomastic and toponymic work on our area.

After fierce fighting, history says, Queen Cahena was finally beaten by the Arabian invader and killed herself. This was the first and possibly the most decisive of our historical catastrophes, since in that moment we lost the occasion we might have had of founding a State, of which we should have been the masters. The Queen's companions had to choose between death or conversion to Mohammedanism, the victor's religion. What did El-Mammi do? Did he become a Moslem or did he succeed in remaining faithful to the religion of his birth? We do not know. The simplest thing is to infer that not all of the family suffered an identical fate, since a Moslem branch and a Jewish branch issued from what proved to be a not very fruitful tree: in the whole country today, at least at the time of the last general census, only seven families in all, four Moslem and three Jewish.

The Moslem descendants did not earn very much fame over the centuries, as if the fact of belonging to the majority had sapped them of all their vigor. Not until the recent "events" was there what may be the beginning of a renewal; we were all surprised and amused to find out that most of the *fellahs* of the Sahel were receiving asylum, money, and advice from a local contractor named Ali El-Mammi. For this moderate, prudent, influential person, very well thought of by the colonial authorities, it was relatively easy to swell the number of his workmen with fighting men who had to disappear for a while. His own son, Abdel Kabir, had helped to organize the insurgents militarily; in recognition of his talent, he was first sent to a war college in Europe,

L·MEMMI

and has just now been awarded the job of building up the foundations of the new nation's future army. But we shall see, in time, whether on that side of the family the fruit will live up to the promise of the flowers.

In the obscurity of collective misfortune, the Jewish line shone far more brightly: a rabbi of the Kairouan school, both miracle-maker and scholar, who was not content to have people believe that he could cure simply by the laying on of hands but, in fact, wrote a treatise on medicine that is still authoritative. I suppose he also used all the remedies known in his day, as he writes accurately about them, but he was resigned to the naïve and credulous cooperation of his patients.

A series of high servants to the reigning beys, all of them but one adroit enough to avoid being executed on the death of their masters and even, frequently, to be richly rewarded, insofar as their inferior station as Dhimi enabled them to be: thus, there were three sheiks in the same family. There was even the beginning of a Palace but it was soon abandoned when its owner was hanged (the one execution I have just mentioned); it must be admitted that there he had made too glaring a mistake. Our family was one of the very few in the Community, starting from the end of the Berber cavalcade, whose members were given the right to wear a dagger in their belts. Lastly my grandfather, as I have already said, could, in turn, have attained to the highest function allowed us if the unheard-of hadn't happened, if the laws of succession had been left undisturbed. But, in any case, those days were over. For half a century, we had been passing the turning point, moving toward the modern way of being noble: we already have three renowned doctors, two important lawyers, and three big merchants dealing in oils, dates, and cloth. In short, it seemed to me that both branches of the family tree, with the gaps filled in by reasonable hypotheses, had just about been traced.

Now, when my uneasiness led me to look into the matter and to talk about it to various people I knew, I discovered, through some Italian friends, that the name Memmi is found in Italy, although it is also uncommon there: there are a few Memmi families listed in the Rome telephone directory. So there was Italian stock too in our family, Roman and Latin stock, possibly even older than the other! So there was an end to the careful edifice I had built up around my first theory! I was already slightly upset, but I felt really dismayed (despite a tinge of joy) when this important reference was brought to my attention: the Latin poet Lucretius dedicated his great *De Rerum Natura* to a certain Memmius Gemellus, likewise a man of letters, which aroused my curiosity further. Beyond the shadow of a doubt, Memmi is the vocative of Memmius, and Lucretius uses it in his invocations, "O Memmi! . . ."

Once my attention had been drawn in this new direction, the references began to pile up. I discovered that a whole plebeian family had existed in Rome, the gens Memmia, and that the famous Regulus family was one of its branches, which included several tribunes, one of them being Caius Memmius (toward the second century B.C.), who brought Jugurtha to Rome, entrusted the conduct of the war in Africa first to Metellus and then to Marius, and perished in a riot as he was intriguing to become consul. There was even an empress, Sulpicia Memmia, wife of Alexander Severus, renowned for her haughty manner as much as for her beauty. I obtained some additional information about Gemellus, my writer ancestor, and found that writing was only a sideline for him. Tribune of the people above all, like the other members of the family, which does not displease me, he vigorously opposed Clodius, Vatinius, and even Caesar, who played a foul trick on him, promising him the consulship, then accusing him of intrigue and collusion, and so succeeding in having him exiled to Mytilene.

I will skip over the centuries and the less important figures, although I must mention Memmie, first bishop and patron saint of Chalons-sur-Marne in France. His life was surrounded with legends; it was said that he was sent to Gaul by Saint Peter himself, an argument which weighed heavily in favor of his canonization. And since I believe that there is always some lesson to be gleaned from every legend, I deduced from this one that he was not a native of Gaul but of Italy, a valuable element in my investigation, which was already difficult enough.

But for a long time I did not grasp the most astonishing part of all. It had to do with a family of celebrated painters during the Renaissance, a period I admire so much and know so well. How is it that I didn't think of Lippo Memmi earlier? His name and his works are to be found in any dictionary of any size at all. At least one of his works, the *Annunciation,* is in the Uffizi in Florence. My mind had been so completely taken up with our African connections that I had not even made the connection with this

Siennese artist; yet he appears in a museum I have visited many many times and signed the *Madonna del Popolo* in the Church of Santa Maria dei Servi in Siena and the *Madonna dei Raccomandati* in the cathedral at Orvieto. How can I have forgotten the disagreement among art historians as to which works should be attributed to Lippo Memmi and which to Simone Martini, his brother-in-law, with whom he is sometimes even confused? And the other Memmis, less important of course but each of whom helped to give the family a collective place for all time in the universal history of art?

In short, confronted with such a concordance and such a wealth of new material, I began to despair of seeing my first theory confirmed and, always quick to change my mind, I began to wonder if we weren't from Italy instead. For a time I tried to convince myself that there was no real basis for this new difficulty. Perhaps it was just an historical oddity, a whimsy of fate that made the word which means *small man* in Kabyle have exactly the same sound as the vocative of the Latin word Memmius. Perhaps the purely external and fortuitous resemblance between the two families stopped there. But this was an illusory hope, I realized it perfectly well. As I advanced further into the chronicle of the Italian painters, I had to admit once and for all *that there was an undeniable link between the Italian family and the African family*. So that although I could not yet make any final pronouncement about where the original family source was located, my mind could no longer be set at rest by something vague. Fate was warning me that I had to choose: there was undeniably just one source, even if I did not yet know where to locate it.

I hope the reader will pardon me for all these details and all the exactness, which require him to pay very close attention. But exactness in this case is the only way of defending truth against flights of imagination. I wouldn't have bothered him with this if it weren't that the history and the problem of my family dissolve into the ups and downs of this unhappy country and that this complexity is the complexity of our common history itself.

At least I will spare the reader all the picturesque adventures of Silvio Memmi, nephew of Lippo. How he was invited by the Dey of Algiers to come and decorate the ceilings in the Palace, and his pride and enthusiasm on accepting. How, when his boat was attacked and captured by pirates, he protested in vain that he was going to the Maghreb of his own free will. How—irony of fate—instead of being welcomed as a great artist in Algiers, he was sold as a slave in Tunis. From that point on, there is no more trace of him. Did he go on painting? Was he recognized in spite of everything and employed where his talents could be put to use? Very probably, considering the number of artists and craftsmen constantly used by the Maghrebin sovereigns. Did he abjure Christianity? That's probable too, since there is no trace in our country of Christian Memmis.

But here again, alas, no sooner has the central fact been discovered which shores up the theory for good than a multitude of other references and parallels, overlooked until then, fall into order and take on meaning in relation to that center. For instance, I had sometimes been surprised, but in an absentminded way, to hear the Memmis who were bakers claim that they were from Leghorn (with us, people from Leghorn are considered, somewhat stupidly, as a superior caste). How could they be from Leghorn when all the Memmis without exception were from Africa? Well, they were right, they were descended from the painter. Like everyone else, I had been amused to find that one or another of my nieces or nephews, in the midst of a family gathering where all the others had very black eyes and hair, had Titian hair and blue or green eyes. But this was not grounds for making jokes about the mother's virtue—simply the Italian ancestor showing up. The two branches had joined and mingled again. The problem was merely pushed back.

And now the insoluble problem has been solved by Mr. Rousset's discovery, and order has been re-established. The origin of the family is here in this crowned Numidian horseman. Rome allowed him, as it allowed many little local princes, a certain amount of autonomy in internal affairs, including the right to strike coins and raise a few troops. A clever method, this, as practiced by the protectorate, freeing the mother country of the care of overseeing its new province. All the more clever because Rome did not practice the silly abject racial discrimination we do today and, as a result, the colonized peoples thankfully and eagerly sought to become assimilated, went to the capital, and sent their children there to make careers for themselves, the way French people in Algeria recently sent theirs to France. That is why there were people named Memmius in Rome some time afterward, that is, Romanized Meummis. One of them was integrated to the point of being a man of (Latin) letters, whom Lucretius held in such esteem that he dedicated his book to him. Several centuries later, a scion gave rise to the Siennese painters, one of whom returned to Africa, etc.

Now everything else fits neatly into the puzzle. The Turkish descendant, pointed out to me by Yachar Kemal, the poet-novelist whose major work, *Memed Hawk,* was published by UNESCO. A young boy kidnapped by the Janissaries (their customary recruiting method) during the Turkish occupation and who later became captain in the same corps and (he too) poet on the side.

Yer Demir, Gok Bakir—Memmi Si

The fact that the French writer Balzac mentions a family named Memmi from Venice (Massimilia Doni). The presence of a Memmi in New York, a Moslem this time, Mohammed el-Memmi (Manhattan telephone directory, page 1111). That of an Emile Memmi in Canada. And if I wanted to go back to the period before written history, as I have refrained from doing so far, I would even mention the extraordinary Sahara odyssey, in the valley of the Dra, which A. Gaudio, the ethnologist, tells about, on the authority of Jacques Meunier, the French Africanist. But one cannot be too prudent in things like this, and I'll stop here.*

Anyhow, from now on, if I begin to hesitate again, all I will have to do is look at the medal, front and back. I have had an enlarged photograph made and I am going to have the two designs framed side by side so that I can take them both in at a glance, just as I can now, at last, consider our entire history at once.

I should hope so! Why not go all the way back to the creation of the world!

Where should I begin? I'll have to write a book myself! Let's take it in order:

1) It's not Imilio who was born at La Goulette, it's me! Is La

* In Virgil's view, the Memmis are the descendants of the gens Memmia, which in turn had issued from Venus. But of course I am leaving these mythical ramifications aside.

Goulette a "Berber" port? Are the Fort and the Walls really Spanish? I ought to ask Rousset myself. . . .

2) Our parents never lived in that huge sinister ramshackle building Imilio calls "The Palace"—except perhaps when I was born, for a summer holiday? We were not far away, that's true, as our father always ended up renting something in the same place, two rooms in an old Arabian-Maltese fondouk whose artful owner reserved them for summer vacationers. We sometimes went to the Palace to play, but Imilio didn't go so often, it seems to me; I don't really know why.

3) The Prince. All right, he existed. A tall fellow, uncle of a bey, they said, who used to go walking alone on the beach, a bit proud, a bit silly. We were a little afraid of him, a little sorry for him. I'm not sure he was the one who owned the big house, and I don't see what other tie there could be with our family. Was one of our great-grandfathers or uncles steward to a bey? Perhaps; I'd have to get Uncle Makhlouf to talk, although I have the impression that he too mixes up a lot of things. In all events, it wasn't our grandfather; he never received such honors and never expected them.

4) This is the first time I've ever heard of this companion of Cahena. Why were the Memmiuses—assuming they really existed—necessarily Romanized Numidians, and not the other way around: Romans sent out by the mother country?

The Roman proconsuls also had the right to strike coins with their own effigy. And as for the Renaissance painters, I'll look them up in the dictionary, since Emile says they're in there.

I have nothing against the idea of a Berber line or an Italian line but it seems to me that a choice has to be made. Why such an effort to make a synthesis—which I suspect is largely false—of the two? Why insist so on finding one origin common to Moslems, Jews, Christians, and even pagans?

5) In any event, Emile seems to be hypnotized, to the point of delirium (?), exclusively by the adventures and misadventures of the paternal stock. What about our mother? What are we by our mother? Sarfati, if I'm not mistaken, means the Frenchman; in other words, the westerner. Although our mother has Berber features, quite pure in fact; and you yourself, Imilio, and me, just look at us. Maybe Sarfati simply means, resembling a Frenchman? Don't people say, "beautiful as a Frenchwoman"? That's a compliment but a very self-satisfied kind of etymology.

6) But, above all, what is the reason for this genealogical research? To build up a prouder, more ancient past for us than other people have? That's an affectation; and what good would it do us? We come from here; we were here before the Arabs, before the

Turks. So what? What matters today is that the Turks have disappeared and the Arabs have survived, and they form the majority, and now we have to live with them. . . .

Enough. I don't want to get caught up in Emile's game. What's the point of it all? Is it a reconstruction using real elements, or merely daydreaming? Anyhow, he certainly doesn't mean to use our name, just as it is, in a novel! Not that that shocks me (well, it does a little), but it would make the book less fictional, and that would be a mistake, wouldn't it? I suppose he meant to transpose afterward. Then what would have been the good of all this erudition, so many details, so many careful references? Unless they are partly imaginary, like the Palace? What was Emile getting at, exactly?

There remains the little medal. I have it here in front of me just as Imilio stuck it onto a sheet of paper by means of two thin strips of Scotch tape. Like coins generally at that time, it is not perfectly round. It is shiny, from having been cleaned by Rousset, I suppose, and there are the two horsemen, very fine, very handsome indeed. I must admit that I too am moved by this little medal, this fragile signal that has come down through so many centuries.

Bina

"Doctor, maybe you're thinking that I didn't love my father? Ah, nobody knows how my heart cherished him and my head admired him. The last week, the last Friday, when I kissed his hand, the same respect bowed my head, the same warmth flooded my temples, my eyes grew wet, but it had to be done, Doctor, it had to be done. Why did I do it? How I came to do it, you can't understand. I'd have to tell you everything. You'd have to manage to understand me, me first of all."

"Look here, Bina, nobody knows you as well as I do. I saw you before your own mother did."

"You shouldn't have let me live! Between my mother and me, you chose wrong, Doctor, but you were doing your job, you couldn't know, of course you couldn't. I didn't know myself either. Nobody knows what he's got in him. It wasn't until I'd done it that I knew what I was and what I wanted. I'd have to tell you everything at once including the details, and why this detail and not that one?

"And where should I begin? Ask your ears to be patient and may they forgive me if I don't put things exactly in order."

Story of Bina

I had to talk to him, I'd promised Ghozala I would. All three of us were pulling on our threads in silence. The poor quality leather of the rue des Tanneurs resisted, broke, and tore the string at every pull; unpleasant for the ears and for the nerves too.

"Do you know the story about the bone?" Baïsa asked me with sudden and considerable interest.

He certainly chose the wrong time. How can I talk to my father if Baïsa arouses his anger? My father looks at us over the metal-rimmed glasses he wears when he's working.

"Phonograph," he grumbles, "profitless words again."

"What have I done? What have I said? I can't tell this young man a story? I work with my mouth? I'm in prison?"

My father does not answer and Baïsa doesn't say anything else. He looks at me, taking me to witness, but I lower my head over the piece I'm working on.

Now, it's best to wait. Baïsa heaves a mighty sigh. I don't have to look at him, I know the technique. You fill your chest up with all the air it can hold, you hold your breath as long as you can until you're nearly bursting, then you let it all out through the nose and the mouth, and it makes a noise like a bellows being suddenly squeezed. This way, you give the impression of suffering some intolerable injustice. Best to wait until Baïsa stops and my father's mood changes.

My father has finished his seam before the rest of us, as usual, and he begins to put his piece together. His big fingers, calloused and split, yet astonishingly accurate, search in the box of nails.

"Baïsa, go get us a pound of number-2 tacks. Hurry, there aren't even enough left to last out the day."

Baïsa gets up heavily, as if unfolding himself, and becomes very tall, miraculously distributing over a huge skeleton enormous masses of flesh that are crushed together, glued together when he is seated. He stretches, taps hard on his knees to dust off his trousers, takes off the beret he wears at work, looks for his cap. "Where's my cap? I must have my cap." He finds it, puts it on. "There! Me, I always get my colds through the top of my head."

"Bag of sand," mutters my father.

Baïsa smiles because of his completely naked head, "a watermelon polished with oil, a loaf of bread shiny with egg white and browned in the oven, an egg . . ." I don't know how he manages to keep on finding more.

"I'm gone, gone and back already."

In the doorway he looks at the sky again. "No, it won't rain. The sky has a yellow complexion—it's constipated," and finally he is off to the tacks and nails man.

That's lucky. No matter how used I am to Baïsa, who's known me since I was born, it's better if I'm alone with my father, after all, to have such an important talk with him. Standing by the work-bench way at the back of the shop, he has lighted the small lamp wrapped around with newspaper and he's thinking. He has to get a cutting ready and, without moving, he is imagining all the things he can make out of the one piece of leather that is spread in front of him. Or maybe he's thinking about some problem from the Saturday meetings to which he wants to bring a solution. His face is concentrating, the eyebrows close together above the steel-rimmed glasses. What to begin with? Like at billiards, let's talk just for the sake of talking, at first:

"Georgeo came by yesterday. He still hasn't found a job.

"I ran into Attilio this morning on his bicycle.

"Selloum has a daughter. . . ."

My father doesn't even turn his head. He goes on thinking. He's placed his hands flat on the work-bench; that means he's almost decided how he's going to cut and he's checking it with his eyes and his hands. He's right. It doesn't really matter what Georgeo told me, since we haven't got any work to give him, or what Attilio told me either, since we won't be needing hooks for six months. I won't tell him what Georgeo and Attilio said to me.

Outside, the first fruit vendors are setting up their wagons. One of them undoes his carbide lamp and goes to get water at the fountain. The sickening smell begins to spread and since I know that it bothers my father intensely, I shout,

"Hey, old man, move that stinking thing away!"

"Where should I go? The street belongs to everybody and you're not the king."

"No, I'm not the king; I'm his son, but you—you're the son of a slave and a whore. Shove off!"

My father lifts his head because of the word "whore," and I'm not very pleased with myself.

My father leaves the work-bench, puts on his hat instead of his skull cap, takes his overcoat and his book.

"Tell Baïsa I waited for him and he should finish the tacking without me, before nightfall. As for you, forget the tacks and get some thread ready."

And he leaves the shop. There, I knew it; I knew he'd go and pray at dusk, and I haven't said anything to him. It's never good to be in too much of a hurry, and it was better to wait than risk a refusal. But what will I tell Ghozala tonight? The mere thought makes me numb and miserable.

I throw the halter I'm working on against the wall as hard as I can; then I pick it up and dust it off.

I hate to get the thread ready. Despite the wax, the raw string rubs against the fingers, making them hard and less sensitive. Bad for the lute and also for love, which is the same thing, as Qatoussa explained to me. But thread we must have. Four times the length of the work-bench and I cut, four times the length of the work-bench and I cut, just the right amount. Then I attach one end to the hook on the door and slide the wax along it; that's when my fingers begin to get warm. I could protect them with a bit of leather. "So, why not gloves?" says my father disdainfully. "Are we hairdressers?"

All right now, who is this doctor? Who is this Bina? And his father, and Baïsa, and Ghozala? But, in a way, I prefer this because this time, no doubt about it, we're dealing with fiction. But, what's the connection with *The Scorpion?* Ah Imilio, whatever made you throw everything you wrote into the same drawer pell-mell! I know it's easiest on your muscles that way; nothing tiring about it—this right-hand drawer, always open, in the line of the movement of your hand as it writes, where you slip in sheet after sheet, like letters into a mailbox. But afterward, how would you have sorted it out? (An idea, a horrible idea that I push out of my mind—maybe he was already thinking that he wouldn't have to do the sorting himself? Ridiculous. Does a person write so much in that case?) Anyhow, I'm lost now, what with the fragments from his Journal, the chapters from the story (I only hope there aren't two stories), the notes, the newspaper clippings that are carefully cut out and dated. . . .

Every aspect of his behavior, every part of his work can be explained by one thing: he was a foreigner. Protestant, he became Catholic in order to fit in better. He became a Protestant again when he thought he could do without retracting; he wished to be a Parisian writer but never ceased to plead with the one fatherland he had lost; his entire social philosophy rests on that famous contract, which is a reflection on the foundations of citizenship; his educational system insists on starting with the individual, alone and unadorned; his private life itself bore the stamp of this distance from the society around him, to which he yearned to belong and to which, in the end, he never belonged; pampered by women of the highest rank, he lived with a vulgar slut as if, at heart, he could not believe that any but the poorest and most outcast could adopt him; even that mysterious illness that made him rush out every two minutes to urinate and made any normal relationship with people impossible; finally, even the madness which turned him into what he had never ceased to be, at bottom: a foreigner.

I suppose that's all about Jean-Jacques Rousseau, I know he fascinated Emile. O.K. Nothing to do with *The Scorpion,* obviously. The Journal? Not for certain. A reading note then? a meditation?

Make a third pile? Unless—crazy idea—unless all these different pieces are not really independent. By that I mean that no sooner were they put on paper than they were meant to be part of one overall plan. Otherwise, then what would this note be doing here? Just chance? And the clippings? Just for the pleasure of collecting them? Fine; but there's a point to every collection. Why these clippings and not others?

It's a crazy idea, and an awkward one too, because in that case, there'd be neither fiction nor Journal nor document but instead, one complex intention. That would be worse. How can I put these pages in order? I'd have to know what his intention was, so as to move right inside what he's written. In other words, I have to have a key, and the key is lost.

The Father

Our father's last demonstration of authority was the terrible beating he gave Kalla. His last victory. After that, he sank incredibly fast but without losing his footing—he never did. He simply never had anything to do with our affairs again until he died; he listened gloomily as always, but without giving his opinion any more, without deciding, as he used to, with a word, a single sentence. Right up to his death, he remained Sidi Chaket, the Silent Lord.

Our mother: How did she manage to live with him for forty years? She must have been in exceptionally good health, luckily for us. She defended herself by clowning around. She would put a pan upside down on her head and skip around the room chanting

ADDA BLED	THIS IS THE COUNTRY
ES SINIGAL	OF SENEGAL,
Ô TAROUGA!	OH TUAREGS!

Exaggerated buffoonery that made us laugh and embarrassed us a little. We weren't very happy about seeing her destroy the respect we should have felt for her. She told him the most barefaced lies without even trying to make them plausible. She lied to us too, as we grew up and became men and she took the same attitude to us as she had taken toward her husband.

I'm convinced she robbed him. He used to hide money in a number of places around the house—under a tile in the floor, above the toilet tank, or in between two boards—because you should never run the risk of having everything taken away at once; because you always had to have some money "so as never, never to be dependent on anyone, not even on your children!" From time to time he would inspect his treasures, so absurdly small today, and when he found out, or thought he found out, that something was missing, he would be absolutely sick over it and stay in bed for days with an attack of asthma or wordless depression. He suspected the neighbors, he accused my mother. She would defend herself briefly, tight-lipped, but not overly indignant. She must certainly have sent money to Raïssa in the camp, and I myself received quite an astonishing sum in Algiers one day—at the time of the Americans, that's true. From time to time she would slip a banknote to Marcel, who was a young man then and always short of funds. Opposing our father, she would restore the balance in favor of life.

At the end she suddenly lost interest in him, in a way that surprised us all. She who had never left the house except to go to the hammam or to see her mother—she began to go out to the café! For whole afternoons she would leave him alone, sitting in his armchair with his pills within reach and a small radio he rarely listened to, and she would come home later and later, cheating about the time as brazenly as a child, claiming that her watch was slow or his was fast. Actually, I think that she was trying to escape from him. He did seem to need her less and less. He hardly had asthma attacks any more; his eyes were unhappiness enough from then on. And he had just discovered the new miracle drugs. He who had been used to drinking so much black coffee all day long, as strong and concentrated as alcohol, now replaced it by taking those tablets of living death in regular, methodical doses. We weren't awfully surprised by this. He had never been much of a talker, but our mother, who knew him better, had probably guessed something more. This silence was of another sort; it was already the silence of death.

A. M. Benillouche: Poor Alexandre Mordecai Benillouche! What with Kalla's madness (Kalla, *my-share-of-night;* come back to this), and our father's collapse, and everyone fascinated by the tragedy of it, he inherited the job of being responsible for our family.

A. M. Benillouche, who imagined himself a university professor at twenty-five, like Nietzsche, then giving up teaching but doing it out of pride, having achieved everything, become a great writer, accursed and hallowed both, of course, at thirty; who aspired to be a prince—of what he didn't really know—of a big family that expanded, as it were, to the point of becoming a people . . . Perhaps that's what his secret ambition was? The only model he ever knew? But, after all, he was just little Sidi Chaket, head of a large family. Not even that, simply an eldest son whose father was still alive, so that he had the burden without the position, like all the rest, like everything after that.

Marcel's studies to be paid for; Raïssa still stuck in that camp in Rhodes, needing everything, especially after her miscarriage; Kalla still interned; the maintenance of the other children; all this to be paid for out of a student teacher's salary, and the harness-maker's shop, turned over to Peppino, where our father hardly ever went any more because of his fits of asthma and his eyes that caused him more and more suffering. They stung and watered; he had complained of that all his life and we scarcely took it seriously, but in fact those symptoms were steps on the way to catastrophe. Suddenly the oculist said there was glaucoma and that sooner or later—the sooner the better—an operation would be needed. Immediately my father refused to go to see him again.

"Be a doctor, my son! You will cure me and you will have your father's blessing." At that point he wasn't thinking of his eyes but of his asthma. That's why I arranged things so as not to be a doctor, whereas they were all for it: my father, and Mr. Louzon, the grade school principal, and Mr. Bismuth, my benefactor. And in fact, in my heart of hearts, I wanted to be a doctor. Did I really want to or had he managed to convince me? In the end, I didn't become anything at all.

Any profession is a piece of clowning. Writing is not a profession. Writing is the opposite and the negation of any profession, perhaps of all life.

Sometimes I wake up suddenly and look for some source of light, in the total darkness, anywhere, anything, and for a few seconds, my eyes are still gazing inward and unable to gather that reassuring little scrap of light. I panic, I sit bolt upright on my bed: I'm blind! But already a vague glow begins to come from behind the curtains, under the door, and I fall back, and for a long time my heart pounds heavily in my chest. Even there I've hit on a trick: I place my watch so that the luminous dial faces the bed, and this is my landmark, my shield against further anguish. But that is only a compromise, I know it perfectly well. How can I bring myself to stop this game once and for all?

Kalla: Who had told him that Kalla went to meet a lover in the ruins of the Messica house? A neighbor who had just happened to see them? Not likely, because especially at nightfall, people went out of their way to avoid going by the charred remains of the unfortunate dancer's house. Anyhow, he went there alone, without talking to anyone about it, and came upon them as they were kissing. He appeared in front of them and said nothing to his daughter but "Come," ignoring the boy, who was petrified at first. Then the boy tried to talk but my father pushed him away with his arm, held out as stiff as an oar. He led Kalla away to the house, locked himself in with her, undid his belt and began to beat her, savagely, methodically, as if he couldn't hear her terrible screams or the cries of the women who came running, or the pounding on the door, then the pleading of our mother, whom someone had hurried to get.

Kalla was bed-ridden for three weeks, disfigured, dazed. Then came her wedding, hastily arranged through a marriage broker, to a vulgar man much older than herself, and the frightful scene in the hammam, and her madness. Meanwhile she had learned that the boy was dead; he had enlisted in the mine detection corps and was blown up the very day he arrived at Pont-du-Fahs. Of course, they all disapproved of my father, and although nobody dared to tell him so, he could feel their reproaches all about him. "He still goes by the customs of Am Kakah, in the dark ages." But it wasn't just that. There was Kalla, Kalla who would remain standing—white, paralyzed, mute—at the head of his bed while he coughed and gasped, whereas the other children went on sleeping and our mother herself sometimes dozed off, when his fit lasted too long. Kalla, who would not go back to her own bed until he had calmed down and finally begun to do no more than moan and then, exhausted, had sunk into a fearfully silent sleep. So, even Kalla! "It wouldn't have happened at Dar el-Kouloub. . . ."

In the end, months later, we took her away in the car. My father and I brought her down the two flights of stairs, he holding onto one arm and I to the other. But when she saw the car, she understood and she began to scream, "I don't want to die!" A young man who was standing on the sidewalk began to shout too, in a strangled voice. He thought we were kidnapping her. He grabbed my father's arm hard; annoyed, my father hit him on the hand, which made him let go. Panicking, the man ran as fast as he could to the police station on the corner; in the doorway was a policeman who remained impassive before the young man's explanations and frantic gestures: luckily we had thought of warning the police. Kalla continued to struggle and refused to get into the car; yet we had a hold of her by the waist and the two of us, two men, tried for a long time to force her in without any appreciable result. Finally we succeeded, or nearly did, as there was still one foot sticking out desperately to prevent the car door from closing. And since our arms and legs were all mixed up and fighting one another, for a moment I didn't know which were mine and which were Kalla's or whether I wasn't going to crush my own foot by closing the door. At last the car drove away. Kalla calmed down immediately and there was no one left on the sidewalk but that poor young man who stood motionless, with his arms dangling and his back to the police station, his face upset and still incredulous.

The others: In short, each one made his way as best he could. Raïssa, who runs away at sixteen with fake papers, a faked permit to get married and go to Algiers, then the secret embarkment on the freighter that turns into a floating concentration camp before the bewildered eyes of all aboard, then the English hailing the ship, the barbed wire in Rhodes, the miscarriage, blood-poisoning that nearly kills her, finally victory, a strange victory that makes her carry a rifle on her shoulder all the time. Jacquot, more or less delinquent at first, who brings home a machine-gun "borrowed" from a drunken American, opens an ice cream stand, then another, and another, sets up a stand in virtually every main doorway in the city and suddenly, just as he is beginning to win the respect our fellow citizens feel for money, even if it's the money of an ice cream vendor, drops everything and leaves, like Raïssa, but without the ideological pretext, and turns into a professional soldier in a country that will never stop fighting; in other words, he chooses perpetual combat. The two youngest ones, twins, brother and sister, the only ones who seem to have come out of it normally; the odd normalness of a world that is sufficient unto itself and escapes everything, because it no longer needs to communicate with anyone; a possible solution, at that.

Finally, Marcel, the only one in the family who seems to have succeeded, even in my father's eyes: it was Marcel who became a doctor, Marcel who was never asked to do it, never urged. Marcel became a doctor and even an ophthalmologist; but too late for our father.

Marcel is Sunday's child, primarily because he is handsome (except that his nose is a bit long, but that's not very noticeable); he realized it very quickly, and took advantage of it. At a very early stage each of us had chosen his or her weapon; we had to. I remember those long sessions after our nap, when he would carefully iron his white shorts, make his hair shiny with lotion and then, before going to meet the bourgeois girls with whom he was beginning to go out and from among whom he took a wife, he would hang around under the windows of our Aunt Fortunée—the youngest and most understanding aunt—and borrow money from her that he rarely returned. And on top of that he had the grace, the free and easy manner, the jauntiness I never had. Because of which no one ever took him seriously. Our father didn't, in any case; he never asked anything of him.

Result? He doesn't owe anyone anything, doesn't feel indebted to anyone, knows how to live effortlessly, a thing I've never known how to do. As a bonus, his self-confidence, strengthened by the confidence that comes with that magnificent profession. Magnificent, provided you don't take yourself altogether seriously. Provided you remain anxious and humble deep down inside. Provided the impassiveness, the detachment, the irony and the "scientific" objectivity are never more than an antiseptic mask or gloves. Despite the tenderness and indulgence I feel for him, the way everyone does for that matter, I don't like him when he talks solemnly about "our profession" or when he says calmly, as he did yesterday, "Do you want an example? You know the lancet, that little instrument we operate with? That tiny lancet is a perfect blade. You have to aim just right, without trembling." How can he do that? And in an eye, a man's eye! "Otherwise, it's nighttime forever." That's just the point. How can he dare?

It's not true, I don't dare! I do tremble! But before, and after, not while I operate. Would he really want me to tremble during the operation? Or to give up operating? . . . Did I talk about a "perfect blade"? It's too well put, it's a writer's phrase. Maybe I did after all. Anyhow, that's exactly the case; a lancet can't be used

more than three or four times. But, "calmly," coolly? No, even today I'm always afraid before I operate. When I was an interne, my supervisor used to say that the ones who don't tremble have killers' hands. Mine are always about to tremble, but they mustn't tremble, I have no right to let them. The eye is an isolated zone, the blood is hardly reabsorbed again. One minor error, one second-rate gesture and the eye's done for. Other surgeons are like blacksmiths, compared to us; but we are goldsmiths. We're the only kind of surgeon that doesn't mutilate; we restore a function instead. . . . I am proud of my profession, that's perfectly true.

And how contradictory it all is! First he accuses me of taking myself seriously, then he says I'm frivolous. Well, I am frivolous sometimes, when I'm not working. I can play marbles if I want to, I've got a right to, and it's true that I won a prize in a tango contest. I was even selected for the national rugby team. Odd that Emile doesn't make the distinction between amusement and professional acts.

But why am I defending myself like this? An unpleasant feeling of struggling with Emile the farther I read. Sunday's child. So that's how he thinks of me. All right. What's so much more worthy about seeming to carry the weight of the world on your shoulders all the time? What's the point of global responsibility and continual feelings of guilt? Disagreeable allusion to my "bourgeois" marriage; all right, Marie-Suzanne is the daughter of a bourgeois; does that make her any less intelligent or pleasing? As for being a doctor, it was Imilio who pushed me into doing medicine. Now I'm very happy in my profession but I must admit that I might have gone into another one.

I've just had an incredible thought: would he be envying me by any chance? Why does he say so strangely that he didn't become anything at all? Can it be that he regretted being a writer? My father would have liked him to be a doctor. Their controversy was part of the family legends. He finally agreed to be a teacher but right from the beginning he said he would write and not make a career of teaching. My parents were resigned to it; besides, they confused teacher with schoolmaster. Is it possible he wishes now he'd led a more ordinary life where success can be officially recognized—a life like mine? And I owe it to him! After all, he's the one who paid for my studies, and I am overwhelmingly grateful for his determination. I'm not the only person who owes him something. For several years he carried the burden of the whole family. He helped Raïssa to leave, against our parents' will and against his own will too, but because he had realized that it was necessary for her to leave. When the third boy made some stupid mistakes, Emile quietly made them good. Our father, who had been so strict at first with the two eldest children, began to pay us only an absent-minded kind of attention. So Emile became our real educator, our model in many ways, and although I put up some resistance (but it was barely noticeable), I'm sure I've not yet finished realizing his importance within myself.

That's what I should have explained to Emile if only it had been possible for us to talk together, if he had only dropped that ironic, solemn manner of his—affectionate enough but it chilled me, and if only I had been able to overcome my distrust, always on the verge of resentment. I would have told him how well we all knew what we owed him, how much we all admired him, how proud of him we were with other people. When someone who hears our name for the first time asks me whether I'm related to the writer, I am moved and I answer proudly, a bit obviously, "Yes, he's my brother." Maybe we didn't tell him these things enough because we were paralyzed by the family inhibition that keeps us from kissing one another, for instance, and prevents any other show of affection such as I envy so much in Marie-Suzanne's "bourgeois" family. Only our mother, of course, would let him know what other people were saying and tell him about her encounters at the market, where her maternal pride competed with that of some other glorious mother. Naturally, the result was almost always funny. One day, she was telling us ecstatically about the volleys of congratulations she had exchanged with some housewife she met at market:

"A coincidence that was willed by heaven: her son also is a writer!"

Whereupon, our father said: "Yes, I know them; and do you know exactly what their son does? He's a scribe, with a board on his knees. In fact he's just bought the board; before that he used a big piece of cardboard."

It was so rare to hear our father joke that we all laughed indulgently. But to our astonishment, Emile went pale with anger, biting his lips to keep from answering, so that I wondered whether our father was really joking and whether, after all those years and despite Emile's successful career, our father had ever forgiven his eldest son.

Their relationship was always ambiguous, though they never brought their dissension out into the open and always treated each other with the most circumspect politeness. "Your brother always honored your father," our mother said unctuously. "Never did he raise his voice in your father's presence, except once; I'll tell you about it." Which she forgot to do, of course, and anyhow she was lying; I know her tricks. She knew, as I did, that they did not love each other and she took advantage of this, almost overtly, to ask her son for help. Our father treated his son with respect, the same respect he demanded for himself, but they were too much alike and neither of them cared for this too-faithful reflection. The day I announced that Nino had the beginnings of asthma, Emile asked me whether it was hereditary—an allusion to our father's illness—and although I assured him it wasn't, he made me indignant by saying darkly, "Anyhow, it would have been better if he'd killed himself, the way he threatened us he would for such a long time."

Kalla.

What is this "scene in the hammam"? For that matter, who is Kalla? I didn't notice it until now because I thought he was talking about Marguerite. But that's as far as it must go. We don't have any sister who's insane. The scene about the beating is true, they told me about it; I was a student at the time. But the scene about the car is completely made up, or else copied. It may not please the romantics, but the fact is that Kalla (whose name is not Kalla, just as A. M. Benillouche is not Imilio; and I'm glad to see he's finally given up the Memmis)—Kalla-Marguerite that is, quite obediently agreed to be married, very well, to a perfectly acceptable, industrious, amiable man whom she gets on with perfectly well, in every way too, since they've got four children and laughingly say they "have a great time" and don't like to go against the laws of God. Sorry to disagree with the madly-in-love school, but she would not have been as happy if she had married her ex-boyfriend, an idle good-for-nothing who sneered at the match for a long time before getting killed—that at least is accurate—in a mine-detecting operation. So, no tragedy or madness there. Can't literature be a healthy undertaking, instead of wallowing in tragedy, including imaginary ones? In this case as well, scientific objectivity (without quotes around it!) is the only reasonable attitude; the only effective one too, I think.

Ghozala

I didn't have to broach it to my father. He already knew, and it was he who mentioned it first.

"About Ghozala: I know."

My heart was beating hard out of shame and fear for what he was going to say next. I had never referred to these things in front of my father, and his answer was going to determine all the rest of my life. But he didn't add anything, he didn't say no. He went to the back of the shop and perched on the high padded stool to work at the work-bench. Only then did he say:

"Wait until your sister is married."

So it was yes! I got up and went to kiss his hand.

"Bless you, beloved father, may your life be long and your riches increase."

Then we went back to work in silence. That I should wait for Noucha to be married before marrying Ghozala myself, this was only just and right. My sister would get married quickly (and my father didn't know everything . . .). She was pretty, a good housekeeper, a good seamstress, spent little, and was reserved like our father, but her silence did not have the frightening gravity and bitterness of his; since our mother died, they said. Ah, Noucha!—discreet, gentle, reserved; our mother's qualities, they said. I loved my sister so much! And my father didn't know everything: Noucha already had a sweetheart. Doctor, you can just imagine how I got through the day until it was time to be with Ghozala!

So from noon until evening I waited, with this great news bursting inside me. Now, how should I announce it to Ghozala? I want to surprise her, tenderly, and first of all I take her in my arms and I say softly in her ear, "He's willing! I spoke to him!" She pushes me away abruptly and I see her, brunette, turn adorably pale; her nostrils are quivering and her eyes shining with such happiness that my own eyes have tears in them. Then, nat-

urally, I mention the slight condition added by my father. "A week after Noucha, we will be husband and wife, I swear to you . . ." What have I done! What have I said! Why didn't I hold my tongue! Ah Doctor, Doctor, three times over you must know that you should never tell the family everything, even if the patient is already dead. Ghozala began to talk in a rush and scream in a shrill voice that made me shiver. She reminded me of everything, everything they say in the district about my father and about us, about me, and everything I had confided to her myself and that she had gathered together in her head as if she had become my whole memory, more faithful and more pitiless than myself.

She reminded me of the story about our mother. "He killed her! He killed her with jealousy and wickedness!"

It wasn't true. Our father had adored our mother. He never remarried, never looked at another woman. No other woman, he would say over and over, somberly, no other woman could compare with the extraordinary beauty of our mother.

(If I close my eyes, I can recapture one of the rare images of her that remain to me: behind the closed bedroom door, in the tangle of shadows and clothing hung up on nails, an enormous woman, so beautiful with her black hair and her eyes dazzling with kohl, lifting her skirts, holding them up with her elbows, taking down her pants with her free hands, then squatting over the chamber pot that I couldn't see but that I knew was there from the triumphal laugh of the gushing stream ringing on the porcelain.)

Ghozala reminded me of the story of my schooling. "He kept you from studying, and you obeyed him!"

That wasn't fair. My father would have liked me to study in the religious school, I preferred to go on at the ordinary public school. At that time I belonged to a youth movement called the Red Eagles, where they strongly encouraged us to study non-religious subjects. And, above all, there was Mr. Tartour at the religious school. He put dunce caps on us and made us take off our shoes so as to beat us on the soles of our feet. I was horribly ashamed—more perhaps for the dunce caps, that burned my forehead, and for the holes in my socks, than for the beating itself. But I didn't have any mother, and the aunt who took care of us went out and worked as a cleaning woman. To show that I was sorry and to avoid being humiliated, I cried in advance, as hard as I could. But I didn't have any tears, and Mr. Tartour found it out immediately. Then, with his finger pointing at me in front of the whole class, he would say loudly, with a sadistic laugh:

"Crocodile tears, crocodile tears! He thinks he can fool us! Take off your socks too!"

With disgusting complicity, the others laughed a sickly laugh, in the hope that this scene would go on so long that they would be forgotten.

But with my father adamant, I had no choice. I could only go on being a dunce and accepting these tortures. In the end, luckily, the Principal summoned my father and asked him to take me back: "He is too thick-headed." As a result, I went to neither the religious school nor the other one, and I was destined for the shop. At the same time I quit the youth movement because my father already looked on it distrustfully and because they took us out on Sundays, whereas Sunday was not a holiday for craftsmen.

Ghozala also reminded me of the many times when I had promised I would speak to my father and I had come back in the evening, hanging my head. "You tremble before your father."

I was afraid of my father but, after all, what did we really want to do: convince him? or turn him against us once and for all? After what had happened about school, I was quite determined not to go work with him in the shop. I already knew Qatoussa the hunchback and he was beginning to teach me to play the lute. Right away he told me that leather was not good for the fingers. Anyhow, I didn't want to become a craftsman. My father had said to me generously, and maybe he even believed it, "From now on, no more beating on the hands. You want to be a man. All right; tomorrow you will start to work in the shop."

I had told my troop leader about it; he advised me to refuse and to insist on going back to the non-religious school. This made my father furious, and with one of his violent gestures, very rare but with such force behind it that for an instant he seemed to have gone mad, he threw his hard straw hat at me. It whirled around like a record and cut my cheek. I was bleeding but he did not pay the slightest attention and decreed, through clenched teeth:

"That is the end. You are no longer my son. Leave the house."

It was very serious, but I was not so afraid of him in those days because I didn't quite realize how much I cared about him. Instead of apologizing and asking him to forgive me, I went to Aunt Maïssa's. It wasn't very far away, since Maïssa lived in the same Oukala, on the other side of the courtyard. I decided to sleep at her place. But it was as if I had crossed over oceans and at nightfall I found I was filled with a dreadful anguish: how can one sleep without one's father's blessing? The thought of it gave me horrible nightmares. The next day, my aunt said to me:

"Go kiss your father's hand and ask him to forgive you."

"I won't go," I said. "You go first."

She got his basket ready for lunch, the way she had been doing every day since the death of my mother, her sister, and then she took it to my father. I waited with a heart heavy as stone.

"What did he say?" I asked her when she came back.

"That you can go to the ordinary school, it's none of his business any more."

I was beside myself. I kept watching the door; it was still closed. Then my father came out, thin and straight, his chest thrown out, his Adam's apple prominent, his eyes enlarged behind his glasses, the tassel from his hat swinging against his back. I rushed to him and stammered,

"Father, my father . . ."

He didn't answer, didn't turn his head. I followed him down the steps, then into the street, staying a little way behind, and we covered the entire distance from the Oukala to the shop in that fashion, he absent-minded and sad, I filled with anguish and shame, and yet something held me back from doing what I knew I had to do. Unfortunately, once we arrived at the shop, Baïsa was already there, so there was no possibility of my displaying my chagrin and submissiveness any more. My father changed jackets, put on his beret and settled down to work. I remained standing in the doorway, at a loss, miserable. At last Baïsa got up to urinate against the tree on the square. I threw myself on my father, kissed his hand, and then sat down on a stool.

Ghozala said a lot of other things too. What could I answer? She felt a little calmer now for all the words she had hurled at me, and she began reminding me that her life at home, between her father and her jealous and impatient sisters, was hardly bearable; that her mother was urging her, that she was the eldest and was blocking the way for her three sisters and even for her brothers;

that everybody in the entire district, even in the laundry, knew about our relationship and she was ashamed.

To appease her altogether, I called her my little she-lion, my hot pepper, my ogress, my prancing, kicking mare. A good thing; she always liked that and she was softening, I could tell. But why wasn't I wise enough to hold my tongue after that? Because she reported to me her father's threats that he would prevent us from seeing each other, I answered her laughingly that Hmaï'nou, her father, was too fat to be really frightening and that I knew perfectly well that the poor man—he sold lemons, and all he possessed were his wheelbarrow and his three daughters—would never force us to break up; he wasn't about to forget that my father had a shop, and tools, and customers, that I would inherit. Ghozala's anger blazed up instantly; she let loose even more violently than before. Since I liked to joke, she would give me something to laugh about: she too had had enough, and that was the truth. She was beginning to dry up, her girl friends had warned her; she wasn't even sure by now that I was a man. I was stunned, and ashamed for her sake; those are things a girl doesn't talk about before she's married. How could I have imagined that that displeased her, since she held herself firm and straight, while I rejoiced against her?

What could I say to Ghozala in reply? What could I do right then and there to prove to her that I was a man? I swore that I would talk to my father again. Of course there was no question of betraying Noucha by revealing that she had secret rendezvous in the ruins of the Messica house; my father would kill her. But I could suggest to the matchmaker that she intervene, that she go to see the young man's parents to find out what their intentions were and then pay my father a visit.

I tickled Ghozala, I called her Ghzizla, Ghazlouna, Sittana. I repeated that no one would ever be able to keep us apart, that if I lost her, the only thing left for me to do would be to kill myself. She answered that she didn't want to see me die but just become completely a man. She would agree to anything, anything it pleased me to do. She would agree to my becoming a musician, giving up the shop, even leaving the country if I wanted to, provided that first of all I talked to my father as I should, at last. Actually, Doctor, women are better than we are. They're stronger, surer, simpler than we are. Because just as she was saying this and I should have been rejoicing over it, I felt afraid all over again: I no longer knew whether I really wanted to devote myself to music, leave the shop, and leave the country.

But why is Emile giving our father—if not a rank, then a role, or dimensions, that, frankly, he never had? As far as I'm concerned, I stopped taking him seriously when I was twelve. I didn't become a doctor in order to please him, as Emile seems to suggest. I did become a doctor, that's true, an ophthalmologist in fact. Isn't my choice more than amply explained by the frequency, the variety, and the gravity of eye ailments in this country—the result of too much light, heat, faulty hygiene? It was old Cuénot who talked me into it. Besides, what use would my decision have been to our father? He'd already had two glaucoma operations, and I was still in my fifth year of medical school. Why place such a mysterious aura around our father's power—around his failure after all! Since failure there certainly was, a complete failure, and I'm just saying out loud what each one of us thinks. Why didn't he ever earn a decent living? He was certainly more intelligent than most of his fellow craftsmen. By what miracle has the little harness maker been turned into this lofty Lord of Silence inside Emile's head? Our mother invented that phrase, but we had long since realized that it was mostly ironic. "Little Lord of Silence," she would add, when he wasn't there.

For a long time we were impressed by his contained violence, a sort of magnetism; too late, I understood that it was merely the reflection of a constant internal agitation. Moreover, he passed on to us that sudden fury that I have too, Sunday's child that I am; sometimes I have it with my patients, when they don't listen or don't follow my prescriptions, and it terrifies them and I'm ashamed. His fury was still and silent ("a frozen torrent," Emile), almost wholly concentrated in the movement of the eyebrows, the black eyes suddenly darting at the customer, or at my mother, while the heavy lines on his forehead went pale, completely empty of their blood. Of course when we were young, that made us go icy cold even before he laid a hand on us. But, since then, why not put our father in his rightful place, and everything else along with him? It's as if, for Emile, nothing is ever resolved once and for all; everything is always there at the same time, the past, the present, and the future, what has been and what might have been.

I almost forgot: our father is not dead! He might as well be, that's true, as he's three-quarters blind and stuffed with tranquilizers. But he is alive, and in relative peace, such as he had never known.

Uncle Makhlouf—1

(Notes for a Portrait)

We made a good deal of progress; that is, I listened to Uncle talk, and he talked and talked in his broken, often inaudible voice that shush-shushed softly and would have been unbearably distressing if it had been anyone else's, on and on all afternoon until the room became completely dark and for some time already I hadn't been able to make anything out, whereas he continued to follow his silken threads, coming and going from one wall to the other and talking all the while, mingling fables, meditations, quotations from the Cabala, from the Mishna, from the Sages, but always linking everything together perfectly, questioning one author to find the answer in another, confirming, consolidating his advancing thoughts with a certainty that never failed. And above all (what I admire most and try to understand), without any trace of the anxiety, the voluptuous uneasiness that gripped me each time we moved on to another level. How does he manage to rise that way, effortlessly, fearlessly? How does he manage to go ahead always with no other feeling but that peaceful joy? To contemplate our discoveries in that bold but unbragging way?

If a writer tried to say *everything,* in a single book, would it heal him, reconcile him to himself and to others, to life, or would the effort be fatal to him? Intolerable for others and for himself? Or would he find peace at last? And if so, what would that peace be worth?

If now and then we encounter pages that explode, pages that wound and sear, that wring groans and tears and curses, know that they come from a man with his back up, a man whose only defenses left are his words. If there were a man who dared to say all that he thought of this world, there would not be left him a square foot of ground to stand on.

Uncle Makhlouf:

"What am I? What are we? Nothing! A bug, a mosquito! Fine, and yet: if you have a little dog, a little bird, you can talk to it; sometimes, in the dark reaches of unhappiness, if you haven't got a little dog, a little bird, you go mad.

"So then, take God, all alone—can you see him all alone, in the vast vastness of the seven heavens? What would become of him in the long run, in the vast duration of eternity? May God forgive me, he's not in danger of going mad, no, of course not; but he needs to talk to someone just for the sake of checking up on his power and exercising it.

"So, he made man, you and me. I am his little dog, his bird, I am nothing but he can talk to me, he's not alone any more.

"So, although we exist only through God, you see that God who is everything needed not to be everything, not to be alone."

Or this:

"The Hara district is just the area between the place where Sidi Mahrez was standing and the place where his cudgel fell when he threw it so as to assign us a place. So, the Hara is not very big and yet it's the entire world. In it you will find goodness and wickedness, intelligence and stupidity, greediness and prodigality, unhappiness and every possible joy and, in any case, twenty-one places for prayer, that is, twenty-one of the most direct paths by which to reach God."

Countless Saturday evenings I slept in this common room because of my four cousins, Uncle's sons.

The little window above the fold-away bed where I slept, that looked onto the alley—so narrow that you could touch the opposite wall if it weren't for the grating—whose name I never knew—I didn't know it and then forget it, no; I *never* knew it; because the communal house is so enormous and odd-shaped and gives on to so many different streets and alleys that it is impossible to imagine it in its entirety.

The day I tied a handful of yellow and red silk threads to the bars of the window and went racing down the stairs and ran through all the alleys around to try to find that little window. When I came back upstairs, the silk was gone: one of Jacquot's tricks? Another time, I threw out a handful of threads but this time I didn't stir, so that I could ask the first passerby to wait for me just long enough for me to come down and get the silk. The skein of thread stayed there most of the afternoon, nobody came —or perhaps, because the alley is so narrow that it is impossible to see the ground, perhaps I didn't hear anything?

We never heard anything there as a matter of fact, except for sounds that came from the right, in the same wall as ours, a window probably identical to my own, the children of an Arab family. I was sure of that because of the special accent, but that was all I knew about them. There again, we were never able to see one another, talk with one another, and knew each other only by an occasional burst of voices, muffled and stripped of meaning.

I ask him questions about his work, to give us a rest and because he is always pleased when I do that. Besides, we won't stay on this first level for long. He is poor, half blind, his children have all gone away, married, settled down, but he won't ask anything of them or accept anything from them. Tirelessly, using the huge wheel that fills the whole room, he puts the threads of silk together, yellow, red, green, white, making large, gorgeous, twisted coils.

"If you don't want people to treat you like a beggar, begin by treating yourself like a nobleman."

"But what if you're poor, helpless, overlooked by others, Uncle Makhlouf?"

"All the more reason to do so, my son, all the more reason! . . . But whom are you talking about? Me, I'm not poor and I'm not powerless. Are you trying to say that sometimes you don't show yourself enough respect? That's always a mistake. It's always more important than other people's insults. Are you trying to say that you are angry with yourself? Hurry to make peace, my son, or else you'll remain poor and divided indeed."

I talk to him about other things and he does not insist. I ask how his health is, how his eyes are. How does he adapt to his gradual loss of sight?

(The slight haze that occurs more and more frequently and filled me with anxiety in the beginning—in the end I find it reassuring. It softens everything, takes away the unevenness and bitterness, makes everything less interesting, as if nothing could reach me anymore. Of Wisdom as near-sightedness of the soul—well, why not? And death = return to equilibrium.)

"Because of that, now I have to concentrate only on the texts I know by heart. A step in the right direction, certainly."

Yes, that may in fact be the other solution.

The perfect man is as dead. Does he move? It is as if he were fettered. He knows not why he is on earth nor why he should not be on earth. Before the gaze of others, he does not alter his outward behavior. Nor does he alter that behavior when he is sheltered from the gaze of others. Alone, he goes away and he comes. Alone, he goes out and he comes back.

Colors. He came back to the subject himself, as if by chance, without any apparent link with what went before:

"What is more, colors talk; each of them speaks to me in its own language, each with its own timbre and degree of strength. Perhaps this is because I need to hear them."

(He even added, "Do they speak to you?," which made my heart beat faster, but already he had shifted gears, moving on into quotations.)

"Is not death called 'the red'? Is not caraway called 'the black'?"

I preferred not to interrupt him; I'll let him go ahead, giving me the maximum number of suggestions, and that way they will have come from him. Then we'll see.

What Uncle says is never false, never ridiculous. A way of speaking which is surprising at first and may seem childish but always proves to be astonishingly coherent because—how shall I put it?—fortified from within. In the last analysis, it expresses all the other possible ways, in its own way.

To sum up:

1) The various types of wisdom may not all be equally valid (but, after all, I don't really know), but they all talk about the same thing. About what?

2) If that is so, then how shall we distinguish the degrees of truth in each of them (and in all of them) amongst the childishness, the daydreams, the picturesque, even in the words of a hum-

ble craftsman or in a naïve folk tale as well as in the pronouncements of a learned man?

3) How can these degrees and these differences be expressed in a common language? How can we go from one wisdom to another?

Always: the need to have a key.

Coincidence: this morning, weekly visit with Uncle. Fridays from now on because there aren't many patients at the Dispensary, or even at the Center. I take advantage of it to go and see relatives, friends, and the few chronic illness cases that don't get around very easily. I must admit that until now, I had avoided that day, convenient though it is, because it was the day Emile chose to go and chat with Uncle. I did not like the idea of a possible three-way meeting, where I would seem something of an intruder, or even the idea of seeing Uncle after Emile had been there.

What's this business about colors? Another one of their little secrets. How can Emile take pleasure in chatting so seriously about problems that are outworn and—worse still—gratuitous?

No way of convincing Uncle; he refuses to let anyone treat him. No way of convincing our father either, until it was too late; no one could do anything for him by then and nothing mattered to him any more.

"I can see well enough."

That's not true, he bumps into his big wheel and he checks on his threads with his fingers or brings them up close to his nose.

"Excuse me, Uncle Makhlouf, soon you won't be seeing anything at all."

"What is there to see? Answer."

"It seems to me that sight is the most important sense."

"No, your ears are all you need if your eyes don't work, or your eyes if your ears don't work. Above all, a man must know. And anyhow, you haven't answered my question. . . . How can you expect to move ahead if you leave unanswered questions behind you?"

"What questions? Ah yes, well, let's not get into a *pilpul.* Don't you want to see better? How will you live?"

"I am too old now to live any other way. I know all the prayers by heart. My children are grown up. Who's going to refuse me a bit of bread and some water, in exchange for a coil of silk? And I'm always ready for a group prayer."

No way of getting the slightest help from his children either: "He doesn't want to." I can't tell whether they say that because they respect their father's decision or because they're indifferent. I remember Emile took the same attitude toward our father—"He doesn't want to"—and I was very shocked.

I decided it would be smart to play along with him a little. How can a man lose interest in his eyes, even in the strange phenomenon of sight itself? Why shouldn't Uncle Makhlouf, who handles so many "important" problems, be excited by sight? I don't mind admitting that it is the only thing that makes me enthusiastic enough to feel like using the word "miracle." Such a tiny area of the body and it localizes one of the most complex, delicate, and extraordinarily efficient systems. The crystalline lens, transparent flesh, long before glass was thought of; the allotted number of cells used for sight, that doesn't change from the day we're born till the day we die, as if the noble tissue were meted out to us for all time—and what a tragic situation that is; the astonishing distribution of retinal cones and rods in color perception and peripheral vision; and even now, even after all the progress we've made, all the ground we've covered, the veritable continents we have already explored in what is an almost magical universe because, minute though it is, it turns out to be inexhaustible, always capable of new revelations and unsuspected landscapes—suddenly new instruments allow us to enrich our store of knowledge so much that those landscapes take on a totally new aspect. We may have to postpone the explanation once again—a really inexhaustible, dizzying prospect!

This endless postponement of the explanation is as disturbing as it is thrilling. In spite of all the progress we have made, our powers of investigation remain limited, whereas the world is unfathomable. Now, how much of all that do we manage to take in? Hardly anything—between four thousand and seven thousand angstrom units. Ah, our perception of the world is terribly limited! And yet all of that acts on us, transforms us. . . . Just think of the X-rays in the atmosphere. . . . Why couldn't there be creatures that we cannot perceive but that do exist, that perceive us, on the contrary, that go through us, invade us?

In my enthusiasm, I nearly said to Uncle Makhlouf: and even a sort of God, why not? In all events, a mystery of some sort envelops us, no doubt about it, even if that's a word I don't like to use. Let's say I hesitate between two ways of putting it: "I don't know, but I know there's an explanation," and "There's an explanation, but we'll never know what it is."

Was Uncle Makhlouf looking at me ironically? I don't know why it is, but that devil of a man always wins. Let's put a halt to all

these speeches; that isn't what I came for. I came to practice my profession as a doctor, to reassure and to cure.

"And yet," I hastened to add, "we act, we decide, we get results. . . . Uncle Makhlouf, do you know the most marvelous, most reassuring thing of all? People find these things so natural—all that complexity, ingenuity, and wealth, the whole incredible machinery of sight that works for us, it's such an obvious thing—that our patients aren't terribly grateful to us, the way they are after undergoing some ordinary kind of surgery; especially (oddly enough) those who recover their eyesight completely. It's as if, once the difficulty was removed, they forgot it had ever been there."

Uncle's conclusion, once I had treated him and had spent half an hour slyly (or so I thought) trying to convince him:

"Do you know," he said, "I had exactly the same conversation with Imilio—may God bless him wherever he is. He also was worried about my eyes but he—he doesn't try to be right. He asks only the questions which should be asked because they alone have answers. That's very important, believe me."

This kind of scholasticism always leaves me nonplused. I have the feeling that anything I might say to him would slide off without touching him, like water off a duck's back.

Same impression when I talk with the new politicians. Now that the initial euphoria has worn off, I discover that they're not much better than the old ones. There's not one problem that can be looked at or solved directly, on its own merits. Everything seems to be judged on the basis of something else, I don't know what. Yet the Minister is a doctor, or was at least; he wants to cut back the budget for the Center by almost half, whereas even up until now we haven't had very much, and he knows it. "There are other matters needing urgent attention." More urgently than the country's eyes! Or else was I supposed to understand that those urgent matters were really others, indeed? When I said that to him, his grand ceremonious politeness surfaced again: could it be that I doubted his esteem and confidence? He annoys me.

Emile, what's this business about a "slight haze"? Does it really mean just that or is it symbolic? Why didn't he ever come and see me about it?

Qatoussa

Every two weeks, Qatoussa went to see the women. He washed and shaved for the occasion, sprayed his hair, his armpits, and his groin with eau de Cologne, powdered his skin to make it softer, using barber's powder that he continued to get directly from the suppliers, who knew him from the days when he had been a hairdresser's assistant, placed a bouquet of jasmine over each ear—a ridiculous thing to do, you don't wear flowers at both ears; but he wore them just long enough to reach the District, the second bouquet being for the woman—and, as the last touch, bought an entire pack of cigarettes. The whole works.

Every two weeks, he would say to me:

"Come with me."

"No, I've got Ghozala."

"You haven't got anything at all. Kisses don't make a hole, and what you need is a hole. And even if you did have Ghozala, so what? How can you renounce all the riches in the world? Even once you're married."

Personally, Qatoussa didn't intend renouncing anything. He systematically changed women every time he went to the District: a redhead, a brunette, a blonde, a black-haired woman; a little Spanish girl draped in a bright-colored shawl and perched on the highest heels possible, with an enormous comb to make her seem taller; or a Negress tricked out as a nine-year-old schoolgirl with sandals and baby blue rompers, and her smooth hair adorned with a red ribbon; an enormous Flemish woman in a pink silk bedspread turned into a poncho; a Jewess playing whore—the eyes extraordinarily sooty, the mouth rouged up to the nose, a white mask of powder, the eyebrows gone and replaced by a heavily pencilled crescent moon. They all knew him, teased him about his hump and his pretty mouth (and it was true, he had fine full lips), called to him gaily: "You don't love me anymore! You're deserting me! It's my turn! Next time I'll bite you!" Qa-

toussa was the discriminating client, choosing thoughtfully, determined not to let anything distract him while he made an important bargain.

Afterwards, he would tell me about it and explain calmly:

"A pretty brunette with a moustache—a miracle. Those long, almond-shaped black eyes, that dark forest of hair—isn't that a miracle?"

He wasn't joking, not even about the moustache.

"When a brunette has excess hair—it's like a fire spreading, the heat that is in her and makes her perspire as soon as you embrace her and she begins to get excited in your arms."

One day he argued hotly with Georgeo, who called women trashcans, sperm-boxes. He spluttered with rage.

"There's pleasure, and there's paradise; there's both of them in every woman, especially paradise. You want proof? A woman's like music, see; when you go in, you know what happens?"

"What happens?"

"You'd like to go in even more, even farther. How do you explain that? It's tiny, it's limited, and yet it's bottomless, endless, you're gratified, overflowing, and still you're not satisfied, you want paradise, it's like music. Take music, now . . ."

Then we shifted to music, which is what all of Qatoussa's speeches ended with. I told you already, Doctor, it was Qatoussa who taught me to play the lute. The idea was that later on we would team up and play in public. Meanwhile, I was content with the group's evening performances at the café. Later on we would play together at betrothals, weddings, births, first communions until we could go on stage and, one day, play at the Sovereign's Court, and at last would come the theaters of Europe and even of America. Hadn't Ninou the Kanoundji already gone on a tour that had taken him as far as Paris? And remember Ouarda, the dancer—hadn't she danced in an American movie? Qatoussa no longer even reminded me of this program in full, he merely alluded to it as to a triumphal march, already arranged down to the least little detail, an unquestionable part of our destiny. "When we sing at the Palace, outdoors, you're going to have to sing louder, you know."

Qatoussa, who lost his mother very young and was abandoned by his father, was put to work with a hairdresser because he had a thick mop of hair and a slight build. He sang to the customers as he shaved them and earned a little popularity that way. Though people joked about it at first, they began to respect it when he was encouraged by Bichi, who took to him and taught him to play the lute. Soon families began to invite him to their homes, where he drank and played and dined abundantly on all the good things that are served with the aperitif. When they began to think of giving him a little money, he left the hairdresser. From then on, he didn't need anything.

Because from then on, music gave him everything. His feast-day audiences were his family, his warmth, and his permanent joy; fig brandy gave his pale face color, the rich food every evening filled the hollows of his face with fat, his neck grew broad and his hump mighty. He had been slight, he became stocky. Above all, he had been restless, he became calm. To everyone's surprise the little black devil who could not control his hands, his head, or his eyes turned into a sort of wise man, indulgent and sententious, with faith in himself and concerned only with hoarding his strength until nighttime. Then, gravely, happily, he would give of himself until he was exhausted. When he said, "Music makes me live, in every way," he was not joking.

"I'll explain it to you. Music should be everything. That's why you take people who're born blind and that's why even, not so long ago, before children were taught music, their eyes were gouged out. They must give everything they have to music, and music will give them everything; that way the entire world will be given back to them, only more beautiful and more perfect. It's like women; if they are everything for you, then you can ask anything of them."

Deep down inside, I wasn't so sure. First of all, maybe, because I was never supposed to sing alone. That's what Qatoussa had decided, and he was right. Though I was making satisfactory progress in lute-playing, I had only a small voice without the right proportion of low notes and high notes, so that, according to Qatoussa, I would never get very far. I had to make do with responding and also with repeating along with him, to warm up the audience, once he had sung the first verses in his strong and somber voice. On top of which, neither my father nor Ghozala approved of what I was doing. My father believed that the only real truth and the only real self-respect lay in daily work, work done with the hands, at the shop, and you couldn't expect to do both—stay up late every night and get up at dawn every morning. Ghozala let me live as I liked but she did agree with my father: music was not a profession, and you couldn't dine on toasted almonds, salty boiled beans, and cakes every night. And to tell the truth, I wondered whether they were so very wrong, the two of them. After all, what did Qatoussa keep telling me? Exactly that. That music was not a profession. A profession was something you practiced in the daytime, at regular hours, for a regular salary. Whereas Qatoussa slept every morning and never knew ahead of time where he would be that evening and what would happen to him later. This Qatoussa thought was marvelous and it convinced him he was superior to anyone in the whole universe, but I don't mind saying it worried me, instead. Although I didn't tell my hunchback friend, who would have disowned me instantly, I wondered whether I wasn't playing some peculiar game along with him; he played it to the hilt but I kept holding myself back to avoid having my mind wander like his. I've known only one other man who thought the way Qatoussa did, and that was Lablabi the poet, who got everything mixed up in the end and killed himself more or less accidentally.

Qatoussa's Classification

When he talks about women, Qatoussa grows animated and looks more than ever like someone out of the Arabian Nights—the big head with long black hair on a small, stocky horseman's body; the blackness of the eyes and eyebrows; he must have some Turk in him. Who knows what's in each one of us? And then of course that enormous hump, that trembles when he gets excited.

"There are:

"Edible women, and women you breathe.

"The edible women include:

"Candy-women, quail-women, and nursing-women.

"The women you breathe include:

"Flower-women, perfume-women, and spice-women.

"Obviously this classification is too clear-cut. In real life, you can find every kind of mixture and every variety, the way you do with coffee, melons, and olives, but it's not a bad idea to have a few guideposts.

"There are women to suit every taste, every nature, that you

know already; but there is also a woman for each one of your tastes. Which means that women give you everything, everything you need to live, and not just to live—all that you need for your joy, for your mouth and your heart, for your intelligence and your eyes."

I tried to kid him a little, saying, "Like music!" He answered gravely:

"Like music.

"If it wasn't so expensive—because you have to dress up, and put on perfume, and then there's the jasmine, and, on top of it all, you have to pay—I'd go see the women every day. . . . Yes, it's just the same. . . ."

He resumed his speech:

"That's not all. Conversely, you can come to like anything, you can get to like them all. Here's an example. Take the mouse-women, you know, the ones with all their features squeezed into a tiny little face, a small nose and a small mouth and all of it pointing forward, and then the body that's slender and frail, all bones, flexible, invisible—well, that can be pretty. Personally, I don't like it an awful lot because you haven't got much to hold on to, but even that type you can like for that very reason, because you can hold on to everything at once and you feel like protecting it and swallowing it.

"They're endless, endless, and not just when I touch them. They're the joy of my eyes and my dreams. When I see a woman in the street, I kiss her in my imagination. I look at her lips and in my imagination I kiss her the way that suits the shape of her lips. There's a whole classification for that too. Fruity lips, that are enough in themselves, and lips where all the work and pleasure are left to your tongue. . . . Just seeing them and smelling them fills me with joy! Boxes! Trash cans! If it's boxes he wants, all right, then let's call them spice boxes, holding cloves and black and white peppercorns brought by boat from every corner of the world, just for you. Even if you don't eat them, even if you just breathe them, that's enough to make you happy and start you dreaming."

Qatoussa and Music

I have a feeling that by stressing the material advantages of music, I haven't been altogether fair to Qatoussa.

The day he told me how they gouged out the eyes of the children who were supposed to become musicians, I felt cold shivers down my back. The hell with music!

"Look, Qatoussa, would you have let them gouge out your own eyes if that had been necessary in order to be a musician?"

He hardly hesitated:

"Yes, I think so. In fact I think it would have made me better."

But I'm also afraid the portrait I've made of Qatoussa is too serious. He's not a symbol or a mythical figure. I really knew him. I could tell hundreds of stories about him; I'll just mention two others. As everyone knows, one well-chosen anecdote is enough to suggest everything.

Qatoussa in Love

From time to time, Qatoussa would make himself fall in love. He chose the girl and then applied himself to a certain number of methods which, he said, had been proven successful and were to be found in all the great books on love. Before going to sleep, for instance, he would repeat his beloved's name over and over, discovering its musical qualities. ("Women's names all have hidden musical syllables and rhythms.") When he met her in the street, he avoided looking at her, modestly lowering his eyes and watching her through his long lashes until she was out of sight. Every night, as he lay in bed, he thought of her and imagined himself courting her, respectfully at first, then more and more boldly while she, yielding more and more, was soon altogether willing and they reached the supreme happiness together. Then began a period of felicity in which he did with her what and as he wanted.

In the beginning he had worried and even annoyed husbands, fathers, and brothers with his play-acting in the street and because he could not keep from spilling out his stories. Then, people began to guess, however vaguely, what was really involved—at any rate, that this all went on only in his imagination. Wasn't it a matter of public knowledge that every two weeks he went to the District? He stopped worrying anyone, and from then on he was jibed at and pitied. With the mock serious manner in which people speak to the insane, the men asked him how his love affairs were prospering. Even the women, who were the objects of his platonic passion, forgot their modesty and had fun exciting him, looking for him in the street, gazing into his eyes until he reacted, and then they laughed outright when he ran away (for he did grow excited, reddened, and fled). So, in the end, everyone played along with this strange game he had made up.

"You know, Doctor, I'll tell you something else. People made fun of Qatoussa, they pitied him for being so silly and soft in the head but I can't help wondering whether they didn't envy him now and again for conquering all women, even if only in his dreams."

The Sea Voyage

Finally, here is the story of his crossing, as he told it to me several times.

"When I sailed to France, you know?"

I knew. It was a unique and possibly an imaginary voyage; I never asked Qatoussa any questions. He smiled, grateful for my indulgent complicity:

"Oh, it was wonderful! I was on deck, and the sea was getting rough. Personally, that didn't have any effect on me; no matter how bad the sea gets it never does anything to me, but then I see this woman, see, beautiful and white, must have been a Dutch woman or a Swedish or a . . . a . . . well, from very far away anyhow, and the dress she was wearing had marvelous colors that I couldn't take my eyes off of. She was leaning against the wall and moaning, ay ay ay ay . . . I came closer and asked her if there was anything she wanted.

" 'Help me, help me! Ay ay ay!' "

Qatoussa moaned, felt unbearably sick, his head hanging down to one side, his eyes half closed, his arms dangling limply.

" 'To do what, madame?'

" 'To pee, I want to pee and I can't. Help me!'

"I was touched by so much beauty and goodness," Qatoussa added. *"Would one of our women do that? No! and yet . . .*

" 'Come, madam, I will accompany you,' I told her."

And Qatoussa was compassionate and serious in his role as rescuer, nurse.

Then he drew himself up straight, triumphant:

"Then do you know what she said to me? Can you guess what she said?"

I pretended to wait.

"She said to me (once again he was plaintive and gasping), *she said, 'Ay, ay! No, I can't walk. Just lift up my dress.' "*

Qatoussa's eyes had become glazed, fascinated, his face froze; there was only the imperceptible movement of his lips saying,

"I lifted up her dress. She didn't have any pants on."

He was silent after that. He had nothing else to add. The moral was so stunningly plain. Never would one of our women have done that, so simply, so confidently. Never had such a thing happened to anyone, ever.

Once, when Qatoussa tried to tell the same thing in front of the group, someone interrupted him:

"Hey, cut it out. You're a liar! You've never been to France. And anyhow, even if it was nearly true, nothing happened after that. What's there to make such a fuss about just because a woman —and even if she was a Frenchwoman, so what?—peed all over your hands!"

Qatoussa rose from his chair like a devil enraged, tried to talk, choked, turned his back on us, and stalked out of the café. We all shouted:

"Qatoussa, Qatoussa! Don't be mad! Tell us the rest! What happened afterward?"

Already the scoffer was feeling remorseful and was running after him. He caught him by the shoulder but with one movement the mighty hump twisted away. Qatoussa deigned to look around, shouting haughtily,

"Who are you, Terma Flatta, with your behind as soft as breadcrumbs! I don't know you! I don't want to know people who don't know what a woman is like, people who don't know what happens afterwards, when she's peed on your hands."

What game are you playing now, Imilio? Are you going to step into *The Scorpion?* "I really knew Qatoussa." Who is I? Which reality is this?

Apart from that, I like it. I've always wondered why writers turned a blind eye to one whole part of life, possibly the most important part at that. Take saliva, for instance: it does exist! Or a kiss—after all, what is a kiss? And why not describe blood? Physiologically, I mean—the tepid, red, sticky liquid—and not just through allusions to its "mystery," "the source of life," and nonsense of that sort. Never in any novel have I found an accurate description of an eye except as "the window of the soul," "the mirror of thought," etc., which is not so very wrong, at that. Imagination is all very well and good but why not also explore all of the real world, first? Why do they never talk about certain gestures even though they are so familiar, so common to almost every couple in the world? What a huge area literature has overlooked! Take smells, now. I've never dared tell that I like smells—yes, all of them, even the ones that are called bad; they don't bother me; on the contrary, they interest me. Yes, that's it, they arouse my curiosity. The bitter, acid, irritating smell of hot pepper on the grill takes me by surprise; the sharp bitter cloves smell of carnations. . . . But those aren't exactly bad smells, I was really thinking of . . . Hey, am I hesitating too? Maybe it's more difficult than I thought it was? My little boy who says, and is already surprised at it, "You know something? I like *my* smells. . . ."

O.K., let's mind our own affairs. I'm not a writer and our own affairs are not so good. The least little bit of gossip, generally wrong, or the least little rumor, unjust though it is, and that's enough to create a new wave of departures. You hear the names of storekeepers arrested without justification, or people kidnapped: "They shaved his head and put him in with the thieves and criminals." "What did he do?" "Nothing."

Colleagues are leaving discreetly, one after the other. A talk with Bellicha at the Doctors' Club; he's closing his office in August and going to set up in Marseille in September.

"I don't see why I should leave. They need me," I said to him again.

"That's just it. Once they don't need you any more, they'll manage to make you leave."

"But, meanwhile, let's be frank: all these people who are leaving are not doing the right thing."

"Are they doing the wrong thing? What about you? Do you think you'll be able to be right all by yourself for very long? Will you be able to stand it much longer? "

My Travels

The truth is that all of my attempts to leave for good have failed miserably. And yet I'm considered a great traveler! A hundred times I've gone away, and I continue, in a ritual way, to go on trips that are so long and so improbable for the people about me, and without ever promising to return or taking any of the customary precautions, that they've come to look on me as a sort of nomad, an iconoclast. If they only knew! If they only knew why I've cut out the practice of strewing sugar and beans over the threshold. It's not just a whim or an effort to show off or to provoke anybody: on the contrary. Every time I did that I was trying to stretch the thread, hoping and dreading that it would snap. Each time I went away for good, or almost, vowing that this time I would really find it, I would settle down—until the day I realized, admitted what I already knew, it was so obvious: I couldn't live anywhere else but here.

Algiers, first of all. It was on our doorstep, despite the distance in miles, and, as a student, I had a first pretext—my degree to get. But it was just too near. I realized that the very first evening. I was in a little alley just like our own; the walls almost touched. Behind a piece of perforated cardboard that covered their window, a family of some uncertain tongue, French-Italian-Spanish, all screeching at the same time,

"But where's that saucepan gone to?"

"Inside your ass! Hey, there it is, sitting on your nose!"

Tired though I was, that put me in a good mood, and I felt like chiming in through the silly cardboard, telling them that the pan couldn't be in two such different places at once.

Moving in, if it can be called that, into that bare place with nothing but sacks of chickpeas and beans inside, where Jacquot and I slept on two doors we'd taken off their hinges. The only trouble was, there was no toilet, so we had to wait until six in the morning when the public toilet in the Place du Gouvernement opened; you had to stand on a line that was often twenty feet long before you could relieve yourself. It reminded me of the camp, the waiting in front of the urinals, seven of them for two thousand men. We figured they must have functioned thirty-seven hours out of every twenty-four. Then the Casbah, the voluptuous uneasiness I feel in all Arab cities. The blood of the butcher's stalls—all those severed heads—the cobblers' broad sharp knives—the light held captive under the arches—the shops like long windowless tunnels—the spices, the candles, the acid-colored sweets, the close smell of fabric—one song common to them all, sung over and over a hundred times, always in tune, always grips me by the guts. . . .

Only perhaps an Arab city of which I would be the prince

In short, I could have stayed in Algiers, if only I hadn't come there for another reason. It was Jacquot who gave the signal that it was time to leave again. Barely three months after we'd arrived, he told me that he absolutely had to go back to be operated on for a cryptorchid condition. This, he explained to me, meant that one of his testicles had never descended and was still up inside the abdomen. In the long run, staying on in a place that was too comfortable, and a climate that was too warm was likely to stifle all his love-making capacities. He was leaving me in the lurch and I was furious. I would gladly have left Algiers, but not to go back home.

"Maybe it's too late by now anyhow," I suggested slyly. "Maybe your balls have had it."

"They have not! My mother's been to see a lot of doctors."

"Your mother! She's the one who's cutting them off, by making you come back!"

We separated on bad terms, and it was somebody else who told me that when he got out of the hospital, he let himself be married to a cousin who was rich and homely. I shuddered. I too had a rich cousin; she was even pretty, and people kept trying to bring us together, all eager to see us get married. Even today she's the prettiest heifer you've ever seen, fat, dumb, and covered with frills, but after all, her husband seems happy enough.

Then came Argentina and the fooling around with Henri that I've told about elsewhere; prairies and horses. Only to discover that I hated nature, especially the too-green kind you find in countries that are too well-watered. Ah, for the red clay that crumbles silently in sun-blazing fingers! Besides, what could be sillier than a tree? And as for horses, what stupid, cowardly animals! The myth that's been built up around horses—of course, idealizing the steadfast and faithful servant. An animal-servant, that's what a horse is. Ah men! men my brothers! how I need you! How lonely I would be without you! Anyway, Henri hadn't come looking for his uncle's ranch any more than I had; we never found it, by the way, since there'd never been any ranch, just a small bar and a sort of a country house—which explains the ranch. After only a few months, Henri went back to Italy on a freighter and I, after making a roundabout detour by way of Mexico, New York, and Canada, went back to France, each of us to attempt a personal showdown. Henri had studied at the Italian high school and the Dante Alighieri, then in Bologna; I had been to the French lycée, then the Alliance Française and the University in Algiers.

France. Would I ever come to terms with that country once and for all? All that it stood for from a distance, the great disappointment it was when seen close up—so disappointing I could have died, literally, since it meant the collapse of all that part of myself which I thought was given over to it and held up by it. When I remember how hopefully, how feverishly I arrived in Marseille for the first time after sleeping night after night on the decks of freighters or on waiting-room floors with travelers stepping over me, and waking up with sticky cinders in my mouth and down my neck; anything, to get to Paris at last—Paris! And then, the dream came to an end, dully, in a way that was not even violent or painful, just ordinary, bland. The Eiffel Tower didn't even seem ridiculous or touching. The Arch of Triumph wasn't even a piece of jingoism or a provocation. It was worse. I had seen them so many times in films, in my books and, best of all, in my daydreams, that they produced the same effect as Algiers: old hat.

It wasn't really true, just a trick my eyes and my memory were playing on me. After some time I discovered that this false familiarity was part of the French *politesse:* you can be on good terms with someone for twenty years but if, one day, you take a slightly more cordial tone, you find you're guilty of bad taste, you've made the error of forgetting that you're not "one of them." But I'm getting ahead of myself. A few days later I went to see Marrou.

"So you too have come to ferret out the secret of the West," said he, solemn, always the same.

"As a matter of fact, the West hasn't got any more secrets," I replied sharply.

He went on to make every possible mistake that day. I had brought back five or six pounds of coffee and I gave him a little. To avoid showing that he was pleased, he said, "You trying to bribe me?"

I nearly snatched it out of his hands.

He asked me why I hadn't shaved. I hated having people take any notice of how I looked. I snapped at him so fiercely that he finally forgot to be haughty and looked at me and smiled. It was through Marrou that I had the chance to earn my first money—and in the field of letters, I kept exulting to myself at first—until I realized that this fine literary work boiled down to reviewing dull books. Then I felt an overwhelming, definitive disgust for any and all literary tasks. Never would I accept that kind of literature. A book, any piece of writing should be a piece of your own skin that you rip off. At this time I read *L'Homme à la cervelle d'or,* and it moved me to tears.

But the real disillusion as far as I was concerned, the one that finally made me leave, was the Sorbonne. A complete misunderstanding. My fellow students came to immerse themselves in discussion sessions, polish their store of knowledge, and acquire a professional diploma. I could not have said exactly what I was looking for. In all events, I suffered a decisive defeat; the idea I had had of philosophy fell in ruins. Eagerly I had entered this temple of meditation, after waiting all through the war and all my life long, after crossing two continents and half the oceans of the world. There I expected to reflect on the most grave and cruel problems affecting the fate of man, under the guidance of the most outstanding thinkers and in the company of students selected from among the best in the country. Instead, what did I find? Whole courses spent on detailed exegeses, exercises, formal lessons in which the way of saying something was far more important than the truth and the real weight of the problems that were taken up. Cautious professors systematically screening themselves behind other people's thought until they had become mere historians and had expended all their energy on securing their posts; from there they were supposed to send forth rays of enlightenment but the effort of getting there had made their own light dim and go out.

Pale and desperate students, waiting in dread of the final examination that would either open up life to them at last—or else relegate them once and for all to the murky ranks of University failures. What I found most revolting was their resignation, the total lack of any inclination to rebellion. It can never be emphasized enough how many generations of what were, to begin with, the richest, most intelligent young men this system has destroyed! The work team I belonged to included five people in all, and here's what became of them: one died of tuberculosis, brought on by privation and overwork; one was a genuine neurotic whose face twitched with tics and who kept saying that once he had passed his exams he would earn money and then be able to afford to have himself psychoanalyzed; one dropped out, and one succeeded—but what a success!

My first paper was disastrous. We had been told to discuss the finite and the infinite. So I described and analyzed the bewilderment I felt before our inadequacies, our fragility, the poorness of our consciousness, the narrowness of our senses when the world was so threatening, varied, complex and . . . infinite. I added that philosophy was essentially just that—a vigilant astonishment, a painful becoming aware of our limits and the constant effort to take them into account in the way we behaved. In short, I conceptualized one of my own sources of distress as best I could. Judgment was immediate and final: "Irrelevant; you have not quoted Leibniz, although he is on the reading list."

This was the comment written in red ink on my paper and read aloud to a full lecture hall by the historian of philosophy, Jules Barrier. It was true, I hadn't exactly quoted Leibniz or any of the other philosophers on that fancy reading list, but it seemed to me I had followed their thought processes, or at least explained my own thought process—still shaky, no doubt, but deeply felt and lived, and I thought that that was what philosophy was. Even today I can't reproach that awkward paper with anything more than making banal and obvious statements, not with being irrelevant. What could be more relevant, more worthy of meditation? A few days later, the first-year students played a horrible trick on Barrier, who had only one arm: they pinned back the other sleeve of his overcoat. He called me into his office and, using what he must have thought was a tried and true police interrogating method, accused me point-blank of having committed the crime in order to get revenge. His theatrics struck me as grotesque and laughable. Most of all, I was outraged that he could have suspected me, me! who had admired him so—from a distance. I don't know whether my indignation convinced him, but from then on, I found everything that had to do with the Sorbonne quite nauseating. I must admit that I had also come looking for a way of living and would have been glad to take one of those highly respected men as my model. I quickly decided that there wasn't one of them whose existence or reactions or even whose success I would have liked to call my own, not if the price to be paid was that cautious conformism they displayed in their way of thinking and living. Besides, something odd was happening: soon the reading of certain texts became unbearable—actually, physically unbearable—to me. I remember I was reading Spinoza one day, when I had an intuition that these cold and seemingly transparent phrases were the precarious outcome of his desperate effort to overcome his own anguish and the chaos of the world. Abruptly, it seemed to me that these abstractions were materializing, taking on palpable shape, and they began to weigh upon me to such an extent that I had to let go of the book. I was panting and my hands were trembling.

I was off again, around the Mediterranean this time, to check up on a few places—Italy, Greece, Turkey, the Palestine of that period. But great God, what (I'm still wondering today) do you really look for when you travel? Scenery? It's all alike; except for maybe two or three times when it came as a total surprise, a genuine novelty—the desert, for example—a picturesque landscape soon bores me. My eyes grow swollen with fatigue, bringing on severe headache. People—that's what interests me most, in the long run. But the few people who form my familiar circle are inexhaustible as it is—Uncle Makhlouf, Qatoussa, Bina. Do I really have to go thousands of miles away looking for other people who will still be inaccessible to me because of the tedious obstacles of language and picturesqueness itself? Actually, the only thing I like and understand is the genuine process of settling down in a city and slowly taming it until it almost becomes mine; immediately I become intimate with certain people, I am their brother, and from then on I feel them and recognize them as if I'd never left them. But then can anyone tell me why I have to go off and leave my own people?

When I returned to Paris from this swing around the Mediterranean, I became engaged to Marie and decided to go back home. We got married almost right away at the *mairie* of the XIVth arrondissement, with no one else present at the ceremony. I wrote to the Board of Education to ask for a job, any kind of job. Nothing available in the high schools, they told me, but something in a normal school. I assented A few days later, a cable: nothing left in the normal school; something in a technical school and I would be teaching only a little philosophy, at least for a while. I agreed again. I'd have taken nursery school! A far cry from the time when A. M. Benillouche meant to be a university professor at twenty-five and a philosopher by profession and sole inclination.

Of course I kept finding all sorts of excuses for myself. The main thing was to go home, find a suitable setting again, find people you know and who understand you, harness yourself to daily, meaningful work. That was real life, that was equilibrium and health. I had countless plans, and I actually began to carry some of them out. I wanted to found certain institutions and overthrow others, and I did it, more or less. I had ideas on housing, on nutrition for grown-ups and children, on race relations. The local psychiatrist and I founded an anthropological society that is still active, and opened combined psychology-sociology consultations—the only kind, I think, that are suited to this country, where the most disturbing problems are those of cohabitation. Before long I even found an opening in philosophy and had pupils whom I liked, including Y. M. With the help of an architect friend, we built a little house on the hill that people came to admire and copy. But all of this went on in a sort of dream, as if it wasn't quite I any longer who was taking part. Moving closer every day to a bland indulgence, that I dared to call my "wisdom," I didn't even recognize that austere rage that had driven me for so many years.

Yet I had returned to my native country and I had brought my wife with me from that wondrous West that I had traveled over in every direction, devouring it. Hadn't I achieved the main thing? My wife was admired, handled with care; we were made much of and treated with such grateful emotion that it wasn't clear whether the rejoicings marked the start of a long festival of homecoming or were really a taunting sign that the group had won the final victory and was parading its hapless prisoners. Personally, I didn't even need to ask myself; I knew the answer to that question even before I set foot on the boat.

A week before going on board, I suddenly decided to write a long narrative. This had been a project of mine for a long time and I'd kept putting it off until I could find the necessary peace and quiet. Feverishly I set to work as I never had before, as if I had to pile up as many pages as possible before going back, as if I already knew that soon that would be the only thing left to me. I don't mean this as an expression of regret, exactly, or as an attack on literature: what would I have done without literature? It allowed me to survive. It was thanks only to my books that I was able to straighten up some of the clutter inside myself and devote myself a little to philosophy as I understood it. It's just that this activity was soon going to supplant all the others, and it's never a good idea to have only one way out.

I must admit I never realized that he looked on his Paris period as such a failure. He never mentioned anything but minor difficulties, food or lodging, and joked at the same time about the morals of the French in metropolitan France . . . until the day Marie appeared on the scene, which supposedly changed everything. The classic love story, infusing all with its glow and embracing all mankind in its tenderness. From what he says now, it was disastrous, he never became resigned to those people or that atmosphere.

All right then, but why does he seem to feel that his return here was another disaster? Apparently his ties to this country are visceral, like mine, and he can't live elsewhere for any length of time. Yet he never stops knocking it and making almost vicious swipes at it. He's not usually the talkative type, but once he gets going, he goes on and on, taking off everybody's accent and being sarcastic about every one of our customs—for instance, saying our beans make an ideal poultice to soothe the burning effects of boukha and our meatball couscous is a potent factor in the general lethargy. You'd think it was Marie talking, if only she'd opened her mouth, and in fact we did at least suspect her because we found it so unbelievable that one of our own people could be so continually corrosive. Especially since it's such a contrast with his books, where he talks about those same dishes and the same people with lyrical enthusiasm.

Maybe I'm not being fair to Imilio; maybe I still don't understand anything about writing and writers. I recall the anecdote about André Gide that Emile told me himself. Delighted to welcome his illustrious fellow author at his dinner table, Emile had gone to an enormous amount of trouble to find him grapes in the middle of winter. To his dismay, Gide refused even to taste them: he didn't like grapes. "I thought you adored grapes, you've described them so magnificently." "Oh, I like them very much—in literature," answered Gide.

So Niel has been "placed at the disposition of the French government." Dubuisson has written a petition and passed it around. I'll sign it, despite advice from some people to act prudently. I won't tell Marie-Suzanne about it. I find it a ridiculous and revolting measure to have taken, though. Legally, it's foolproof. Niel's contract was renewable every year by tacit agreement; since the new administration has decided not to renew it, he must terminate his functions and leave the psychiatric hospital. Now he's a foreigner. That's also part of the end of colonization, and I wanted it too. But the contract had been running for twenty-six years! Do you kick a doctor out overnight from the department he's been in charge of and that's been his whole life? Especially when he's been running it with unchallenged devotion and capability. It's madness to get rid of valuable technicians that way just so as to follow independence strictly to the letter. Who's to replace him right now? Amar, his assistant, I suppose, who's never worked in any other hospital and received all his training from Niel himself? Europeans have become foreigners, they have to leave. But what if the country suffers from their going? What if the patients still need Niel?

I'll sign that petition even if it puts me on bad terms with Amar, who will probably succeed him, and even if the Minister doesn't like it.

Noucha

I was finishing a game of dominoes at the Mazouz Café with Qatoussa, Chibani, and the others when Maïssa appeared. Her hair had come undone and was flying all about her, she was flapping her short fat arms and pounding her chest as she howled,

"Run, Bina, run and rescue your sister! Rescue your father! He's killing her! Run, Bina!"

Usually I think Maïssa's funny and I make fun of her; we call her "the squash," because she's round all over like a barrel. But this time, I sensed that she was borne by misfortune. A shock went all through my body and my blood froze. Instead of running, I was so weak my legs could hardly hold me up. In an instant, without the slightest hesitation, I had guessed what had happened.

Even today, Doctor, I still don't know who it was who sent our father to the ruins to catch Noucha with Moumou. It's a good thing I don't, because otherwise there'd have been two people dead instead of one. Hopping on those little feet of hers that had to carry so much weight, panting, her enormous behind and breasts jiggling from side to side, Maïssa told me what she knew about the incident.

"When I saw them coming along, and it was so early, with the sun still hot, my heart understood. Noucha was walking ahead of your father and they were heading toward the bedroom. As soon as the door was closed, the most horrible shrieking and howling began. I rushed in, and there was your father beating Noucha with his belt, his big leather belt. I thought he'd strike her just a few times and then let me take it away. I grabbed his arm. 'Go away or I'll kill you.' I stepped in between them. You know what he did? Look at my back, look at my arms: he began to hit me exactly the same way he was hitting Noucha. His eyes were red! He was Satan! I ran out of the room. Somehow I got down the stairs, somehow my poor legs dragged me all the way here! Do some-

thing, Bina, rescue her! Rescue him! He'll kill her, and they'll hang him!"

By the time we got there people had gathered in front of our door, which was closed, but it was all over, they couldn't hear anything anymore. They came up to me and muttered,

"He's your father, Bina, don't forget, he's your father. What are you going to do?"

But they were mistaken. I had no idea what I was going to do. That was my father in there, behind that door, locked in with my sister, and maybe she was dead; my father and my sister; Noucha, my little sister, my heart torn away; my father, my shame, before all the assembled neighbors and their pity for our misfortune. What could I have done?

"He's your father," the neighbors keep repeating, making a living wall with their bodies to prevent me from adding to our misfortune and gently pushing me along toward the door of the Oukala, where they turn me over to Qatoussa, who has just arrived.

Suddenly they stop talking and stop pushing me; the door to the room opens and my father appears in the doorway. Stricken, he looks at the crowd, sees me, and says to me over their heads,

"Come, let's go."

The crowd stands aside as if the order had been meant for them and I obey, I follow him into the street, where we walk for a minute in silence. Then he says to me, painfully,

"I nearly went mad when I saw them, for I saw them, with my own eyes. Pray God that nothing has been done as yet. Now she must be married, quickly. Once a girl has started to know about men, you must act very quickly."

"Yes, you must, Father."

Then, since he didn't say any more, I went on softly, as naturally as I could:

"We could send Menana, the matchmaker, to Moumou's father. That way we would know what his intentions are."

He jerked up his head and looked at me with dilated eyes and his jaws set so tight that the lines stood out white,

"Have you got blood in your veins? Are you my son? Noucha's brother? . . . Moumou is dead."

I wasn't thinking just of myself, Doctor, I swear I wasn't. Noucha is my little sister, my protegée, my other self. One day Noucha and I were playing apricot pits with Bohla, that big goat of a girl, who began to cheat. We came to blows. Bohla was older than I was and she was stronger than the two of us put together. What are you supposed to do when you're fighting with a girl who has more strength than you do? I grabbed her hair and pulled. So she grabbed Noucha's hair and began to pull too. "If you pull, I pull!" she yelled. I pulled, she pulled and Noucha screamed; I pulled again, she pulled, and Noucha screamed. Will you believe it, Doctor? Every time she yanked at Noucha's hair like that, I could feel it in my own body as if it was my own hair that was being pulled out and my own eyes that were crying. My head hurt from it and perspiration stood out on my forehead, and I was shivering. We hadn't had a mother, Noucha and I, so we'd always had to stand together until we'd become a single person and a single soul.

When my father had grown a little calmer, he explained to me:

"Noucha didn't have a mother, Bina, and a girl without a mother . . . You're young, you don't understand everything. How—forgive your father for speaking to you bluntly—how do you suppose the brothels get filled? Do you want your sister . . ."

I was filled with horror.

"Keep quiet," I said to him for the first time in my life.

But he was so drowned in horror himself that he let the insolence go by without a word. I wasn't even so angry any more with my father for having beaten Noucha. What should I do, my God, what should I do?

After I'd left my father, I went by the laundry where Ghozala worked. She saw me immediately. I raised my hand to my collar, which was the prearranged signal for asking if we could meet. She touched a lock of her hair: yes. But her face did not light up and she did not smile: she already knew. The whole district must have known what had happened. Half an hour later she came to the ruins and before I could touch her she said, in a neutral voice that hurt me more than all her displays of temper,

"We will never get married. It's all over."

I protested. On the contrary, my father was going to get in touch with Menana right away, tomorrow. He had promised he would marry Noucha as quickly as possible.

"Your father is your father and you are his son. We will never get married."

She wanted to go home right away. She was cold. Then I got angry. I can't bear to be repulsed and when people open a gap that way between themselves and me, I panic. I began to shout. I told her all women were whores.

"When a girl has begun to know about men, then you have to take steps very very quickly, isn't that true? Otherwise she's on her way to the brothel! My father is quite right."

Ghozala, who is sometimes so quick to anger, didn't answer. She didn't say anything. She just stood there waiting, rigid, with her eyes turned inward as if she weren't there anymore or were having a cataleptic fit. Yet she knows how uneasy that makes me. I shook her, I yelled at her.

(How can she stick those awful balls of wax into her ears? How can she possibly not realize just how uneasy that makes me, how it cuts me off from her and even from the whole world, at the same time? "I need a woman! All of her—heart, breasts, wide open arms, always, even when I've been unfair, even when I've been mean and awkward! I don't want just a housekeeper, or a schoolmate or even a nurse!" And there she was smiling pleasantly and pointing to the ear-plugs already in place, and fortunately not hearing the insults I was shouting at her. She had already taken leave for the night.)

I shook her and yelled at her,

"Go on, leave, if you want to leave. I don't ever want to see you again, ever!"

She began to run—because she was afraid, I think—and ran out of the ruins by the garden door.

As I watched her that way from behind and saw how well shaped she was, how perfectly proportioned, and watched her black braids swing, so thick and full, against her shoulders, I knew that no one in the world could ever take Ghozala away from me, not even my father. Qatoussa had his music but I—I could not live without Ghozala.

My Women

Two things will have saved me, perhaps: women and literature. I'll talk about literature some other time. As for women, it's not fair for me to deal with them in just a few pages, a single chapter; I ought to have used a whole book for that. I haven't done it because actually everything I've written is full of them, more or less implicitly. I could rewrite it all from that standpoint—not just this book but all the books I've ever written. The novels of course, and the little treatises on metaphysics, especially the *Treatise on Relationship,* that's obvious, but also the political and sociological things and naturally the poetry, even the least little verse—everything, everything can be understood in terms of women because my relationship with women symbolizes all the rest.

I could never bring myself to share my comrades' joking about sex—I've already told about that; not that I was unduly shy or just not interested. On the contrary; it was a thing that overwhelmed me and fascinated me too much for me to treat it so lightly. How could they dare to talk about a woman's body—a marvel!—in such preposterous terms, comparing it to various fruits and utensils or even horrid vegetables? How could they laugh their loud laughs and wisecrack, "My gun with the whiskers went off all by itself last night," or "My little cat starts to bristle as soon as I touch it and goes hiss, hiss, hiss!" Spontaneously I became the absent-minded puritan, unbothered, or so it seemed, by their jokes and even their suspicions and their insults. Later on, the Youth Movements did a lot to reinforce my protective armor—because of or despite the fact that they included girls. We looked on girls as "comrades" and treated them "casually"—which was just as artificial an attitude. How can you treat a woman any other way than as a woman? As if you could overlook everything that comes radiating out from them to light up the entire universe! But at least I was able to keep so many questions and vital emotions intact and was deeply aware of it. I have also told about the loneliness of love in a brothel—rapid, abstract, reduced to the fleeting and voluptuous experience in itself, so that I came away each time with an aching sense of impossibility, a failure to establish communication.

It was not until Algiers that I discovered what a real exchange with a woman could be, and it was a woman—may her praises be sung!—who took the initiative and brought me this revelation. For the first few weeks, I despaired. In my native city, the women's district had had a clearly marked out geographical location. I headed straight for it and once I had entered the first magic circle that surrounded it, I had only to make the exquisite effort of choosing in a realm that had been created and organized entirely for love. In Algiers I didn't know where to go at first or where to turn (afterwards I discovered the Casbah, of course, where everything was almost as well regulated as in my own town). The entire city was possible and entirely impossible. I watched all the women on all the streets, waiting for a look or a signal. Nothing ever happened and I came home worn out and exasperated from those long searches. Until the day that astonishing thing happened—an incredible thing for me, who had to make such an effort just to go up to a woman, who didn't know where to find words to say that wouldn't sound ridiculous to my own ears, who didn't dare to make the slightest gesture without wondering instantly whether it wasn't going to get me a slap in the face (an unknown danger) or maybe even set off a chain reaction of disasters—the police, a court trial, jail, heaven knows what. How are you supposed to know, in this boundless area, at what point the greatest joy may turn itself into a scandal of the worst kind? So it came to pass that a woman took the first steps and even touched me—yes, that's exactly what I mean, she touched me.

We were driving in her car. She was the president of the foundation and director of the students' center that had welcomed us. She had asked me if I knew how to drive, I said yes and slid into the driver's seat with her next to me, and away we went. She had to do some shopping for the center. For a moment she waited and then, since nothing was forthcoming from me, she began to talk. She told me she had noticed the way I looked at her. What way? I looked at all women with just as much interest and greed and almost obvious tenderness. As she talked, she placed her hand on my leg and gradually moved her fingers upward while I was driving and was supposed to keep the steering wheel straight. I had to stop the car.

That was many years ago and she is dead now, but oh! how I still thank that woman, twenty years older than myself, for having opened the triumphal way to freedom for me with a single gesture! For having taught me that everything is possible because the game is played by two willing partners and because women are far from being merely awesome sphinxes whom the slightest thing offends; women too are waiting, waiting for me to play that marvelous and inexhaustible game. And ever since, women have been a permanent festival for me.

Two weeks after being emancipated, thanks to my lady president, I met a young woman in the train going from Algiers to Constantine where my mistress had sent me to bring back provisions for the center. Half an hour after the customary preliminaries—would she like a newspaper? a cigarette? Where was she going?—I was kissing her full on the mouth. Freedom is total grace; I now found it as simple to dare anything whatever as I had been completely paralyzed before. Our mouths clung together until the end of the trip, which at that time lasted all night long, without being the least bit bothered by the other passengers, who either dozed or pretended to sleep, and we were prepared to talk back to anyone who might express his disapproval. But nothing else happened but that long caress we exchanged uninterruptedly in the sleeping train, and I was hardly surprised by this extraordinary freedom, and enjoyed it all the more, whereas two weeks earlier I would have thought it an unattainable summit. I saw my unknown partner a few days later in Algiers, where she had returned too. I realized that I had hardly looked at her: she squinted a little and, as she had a grocery shop, she smelled strongly of spicy food. But I was not the least bit disappointed; she was a woman, and I tucked her away alongside the lady president, but already I was looking differently at all other women and was getting ready to replace my grocery woman as soon as something better turned up. Which happened very soon, so true is it that only the inner attitude counts. And so began the marvelous, enchanted round that has never stopped since.

How can I express the splendor, the variety, the complexity of it? I have said so often already that a woman is more than a woman, love is more than love. Otherwise, so much effort and ingenuity, such a dance and such roundabout maneuvers—for what? For the sake of finally putting that little bit of flesh into that little hole of flesh! That can't be all. Instead, isn't that climax the symbol of everything, the preliminary to everything, betrothal and fusion, promise and fulfillment, the espousal of all that exists, life and the mind?

I shall look out from my flesh and contemplate divinity.

Take hygiene, for instance. Fears of germs, disgust—how flimsy they are, how quickly we forget them when it comes to kissing; not to mention the rest. What man does not mate with any woman, or almost any, encountered anywhere in the world? I do anyhow, and I don't mind admitting it; I can make love with any woman at all, and I can go from one to another. It has happened I don't know how often that I have been unable to be satisfied at the time because circumstances did not lend themselves to that, or because I have not wanted to, wanting to save up for another time or wanting just to enjoy, and so I have gone and spilled out my excitement with another woman and was every bit as ardent and sincere. I said the same words to her as I had just said to the first woman, I completed the gestures I had only begun a little while earlier, and when I left her I was sated at last and in every way as happy as if I had not changed partners. This even became a necessary technique for me whenever I had reached the end of one affair and was beginning another; I did not want to break too suddenly with the old partner and hurt her and at the same time I had to be as devoted and effective as possible with the new one.

The fact is, I love them all. Although, of course, as I have grown older and now that my extraordinary craving for them has tapered off, I have learned to choose. I know I have preferences.

A friend of mine who's a caravan driver has told me how finding a fig tree in the desert seems to be a remarkable present from heaven.

At first the men throw themselves on the figs indiscriminately, gulping them down, skin, dust and all, without even chewing. Then, once their thirst has been quenched and their hunger satisfied, then only do they begin to choose the finest, the most luscious, the juiciest. They stop when they are replete and on the verge of feeling sick.

But before going on their way, they clean the fig tree, carefully picking off the parasites and hoeing up the ground around it a little. For they do not forget that the fig is a miracle deserving gratitude and care.

Doubtless, I began to know how to judge with a more and more practiced eye, setting aside so as better to consider—the knee joint, for instance, and whether it separated calf and thigh distinctly enough, the slenderness of the ankle, the ever amazing curve of the hip. Doubtless, I don't care too much for women who are too thin, since I can't believe there'd be room in them for such a desire of them as I have; I don't care for the ones who are soft as gelatine either; I have a feeling I would bury myself inside and not encounter any of that exquisite resistance which strengthens pleasure. Perhaps I am less fond of faces that are too fine, with contours that are too discreet; it seems to me that each feature has to be somewhat emphatic if the whole is to be well proportioned. I am not very keen on lips that are so thin as to be nonexistent, and elude kissing and biting, nor on lips that are overly full, edible to an extreme, choking and nauseating my own lips like food that is too heavy. Doubtless I lean to harmonious faces and assertive rumps; figures that are slim and even frail and which at the same time have quite a distinct and even obvious femininity; a slender neck, elegant bone structure and narrow waist, but the hips round and right, the bust promising and even a little astonishing, just short of too full, round and curving lines all over, the mouth greedy, the eye open and delectably elongated—everywhere, in short, successful and appealing features, discreet but clear, there for sure—that's what I would choose if I had to choose, and I do have the choice when I have time to choose amidst all that vast and fascinating display.

But, once again, I love them all. Joyfully, happily, gratefully I can taste all these marvelous fruits, each in its proper season, each for its own particular sweetness and perfume. My love and my tenderness for all of them does not point to stupidity, anarchy or hypocrisy on my part. On the contrary, because of this avid diversity, I have learned to organize and discipline my forces so as to make them yield the maximum of pleasure for them and for myself. In my first encounters with the lady president, I was dazzled by my discovery, wild with the fresh conquest of my freedom, so that I didn't stop until I was overcome by weariness and genuinely drunk; my happy stupor sometimes lasted until evening of the next day. My work began to suffer. I discovered that a normally constituted woman whose appetite has been aroused seeks satisfaction a limitless number of times. My only choice was to give way or to pretend. Since I cared too much about my first mistress to take the risk of dissatisfying her, I had to pretend. Instinctively, I found the way to parry her. I did not let myself go completely more than two or three times, and then only as late as possible. The rest of the time I used a few tricks to keep up the illusion—an obliging swoon, expressions of gratitude, even sighs, so that she imagined that I was accompanying her to the summit each time. Now don't go thinking that this discipline, this play-acting if you like, was disagreeable for me. I picked up all the small change of pleasure and although I may not have reached the same paroxysm as my mistress every time, I did go along with her right up to the last platform and the way there was always exquisite. Besides, this sort of sport gave me another kind of pleasure: the triumph of mastering myself.

In fact the only disadvantage was that in the long run, since I always gave her what she wanted without ever protesting or asking for mercy, she thought I was inexhaustible. She took all restraint off her greed, and I saw that it was infinitely greater in women than it is in men. We sometimes spent four and five hours in bed, whole afternoons; pauses were few and brief, just long enough to doze and relax before resuming, a respite as quick as a wink, and they brought on a state of exhaustion anyhow where I seemed to float outside my own body, whereas she was forever able to draw some new harmony from her body and mine. She was in a hurry because of her age, of course, and where I was ardent and delighted with this discovery of a love other than the impersonal and furtive kind I had known in the District, she, being greedy, anxious, and grateful as well, was at least as ardent and violent as I. In all events it was she who revealed to me for the first time all that a man and a woman can attain together when both are moved by the same eagerness and the same impulse. Even today, now that I have known so many other women—younger, more beautiful of face and body, with more appealing minds—far from making the slightest reservation, as I look back, on her age or on the fact that, as an aging woman, she dared to approach the very young man that I was at that time and obtained from me all that I was capable of giving, I would like to build a monument in her honor.

I said that I could write an entire book about women—and so I'll stop here. Some other time I'll describe how I came to feel that the love relationship should be the essence of the social relationship and should not only dispense tenderness and voluptuousness but also be the model for all friendship and solidarity and even the intuition of all metaphysics. Meanwhile I told myself over and over again, As long as there's one woman left, I'll never be completely desperate! Neither drugs nor death will I ever need since Woman is there—sweet refuge, exaltation of myself, life itself always possible and always renewed. That was my outlook later on when I thought it sufficient, before returning to my native country, to bring one woman, one wife back with me. My marriage with Marie made me safe, I imagined, against all anguish and ruin. By marrying Marie, precisely because she was so different from myself, I was marrying the world and I was including myself, all of myself, in my wedding gifts to her. I was forging my own unity.

But several months later I used the possibility of going to the Sorbonne as a pretext for leaving my lady president, despite her tears and despite the fact that for the first time in my life, I did not have to worry about earning a living since, in exchange for a few small services I did the students' center and for my personal service to my mistress, I was practically kept by her. But for one thing, I couldn't stay put any longer. For another, my liberation was only one of the preliminaries that were to open up the whole world to me. No matter how pleasant this stage of my journey was, I mustn't linger there or I wouldn't get very far. And finally, no matter how grateful I was to my mistress, I told myself that since all women were wonderful, I would find some everywhere and one would be as good as another.

Was this before, during, or after Marie? Hell of a chronology! Let's just hope it was before or after and not during. But, even so, who would have believed it? He seemed so puritanical he made us laugh, since that sort of thing was pretty rare here; in a colonial society, morals aren't overly strict. All the ladies admired and coveted Emile and kept inviting him everywhere—writers are so decorative—and paying him compliments that were almost embarrassing (doing it openly, in front of Marie, who can't have liked that very much although she always smiled sociably; probably despised the old hags too much to be afraid of them). "I'm envious," they would say about his hair, so black and wavy; "if you'd let it grow, you'd be just the prettiest brunette, I'm sure." Or his very dark eyes: "Isn't it a pity you wear glasses. Take them off and let's see?" "I knew it, they're almond-shaped. And aren't they big!" But so far as I know he never gave in to any of these solicitations, and so far as anyone knows, he's never had an affair since Marie left (not even . . .).

Unless all this is just pure imagination once again! Once a writer gets going, watch out! They're worse than soldiers in their barracks; we at least didn't try to turn stories about a nice piece of tail into metaphysics! He wants all he's ever written to be considered from that standpoint! The strange thing is that I don't see where sex plays such an important role in his books, though it does crop up pretty often. By the way, what treatises on metaphysics is he referring to?

Marie-Suzanne's reaction, the common-sense reaction:

"You know what your brother's doing? He's pretending to have a dirty mind. He's not even a real—a real sensualist. I'm sure that all these women he's describing one after the other are only one woman—maybe only just Marie, and he just imagines her differently, blonde one time and brunette the next. Real sensualists don't do so much talking."

Perhaps. Then what is it that Imilio's interested in? Words? What do women really mean to him?

Marie-Suzanne says:

"Maybe it's not even Marie! . . . The 'lady president,' why not? Haven't you noticed how there's a character that keeps recurring all the time, even in the Essays—the older woman, older than the hero. That's who it is, it's the lady president. She was the only woman, then there was Marie and then that was all. There were just those two women, believe me. And Marie went back. Do you want me to tell you something? Your brother's a virgin. No, he's a . . ."

"Stop it, Marie-Suzanne! You're beginning to talk nonsense, you're getting carried away with yourself. He does have two children, after all."

"That doesn't prove anything. Well, never mind. Let's say there were two women: the lady president, and Marie. And, even so, the lady president was the only one who . . . succeeded.

Nothing before and nothing since. He never managed to break out of himself."

I can't deny that this conversation bothered and upset me, because of that solitary life he led at Sidi Bou after Marie left and because of the awful things that have already been whispered. The one time he appeared in public—the one time he went to the effort of having people in—was when he had that preposterous idea of celebrating Mahmoud's birthday. The birthday of a servant! Naturally nobody came, not even the Moslems, and everybody decided that they must be sleeping together. What got Emile angry was not the stupid calumnies about him but the fact that for all the talk about acceptance of decolonization and social justice and new brotherhood, no one was willing to do honor to Mahmoud.

And the only result was that Mahmoud was humiliated and resented it. So he left him—to come work for me at the Dispensary, discreetly and urgently recommended by my brother. After that Emile lived more alone than ever in the old two-story Arab house that's damp and moldy because the ground floor is narrow and the sea is so near, almost never going out any more, doing all his own cooking and, when he wasn't writing, daydreaming on the terrace or in a corner of his study and listening to the same music over and over again, folklore stuff from all countries and all peoples, series like the Songs of the World and Treasures from all Nations, which are all right, but also sometimes things in the most glaring bad taste, on the pretext that he was a "barbarian" and that at heart he'd never really liked western music. It was too clever. It tired him.

Another unexpected conclusion: you start off with "all the riches in the world" and you end up making do with a single dish, the idea being, I suppose, that all dishes would be made from the same ingredients. He wants all women and in the end he confines himself to Marie alone, and even does without her. Is he defending Don Juan or marital fidelity? Or is he raving like a shipwrecked man maddened by thirst?

I signed Dubuisson's petition in support of Niel. It won't do any good. Niel will go. Especially since rumor has it that the European colony itself, which never liked Niel very well, is just as glad to see him disappear through the trap door. Paradox: Niel brought down by a coalition between the ex-colonized he defended, took care of and loved, and the ex-colonizers, who've never forgiven him for that betrayal.

All in all, I begin to wonder whether the main reason Niel's been fired isn't his very effectiveness. A particular sort of effectiveness that got in too many people's way. He took care of every kind of family in every class of society and every community in this country. He knows too many secrets and he knows about too many tragic situations, too much poverty. "I could draw an emotional map of the country," he told me one day, sardonically. It's not—or not just—economic competition nor even his political activity that defeated Niel, but simply his knowledge. Niel knows, and he looked at things in a way that no one could stand.

Kakoucha

The Anniversary of Mbirakh's Death

My father had told me that the anniversary of the death of Mbirakh, the husband of Kakoucha, was the following Wednesday; Maïssa had reminded him of it that morning. One of us had to go to the ceremony, but not both of us. As far as possible, my father avoided leaving Baïsa alone in the shop.

"You can go," he added.

"No, Father," I said. "I'd rather stay here."

He thought it was a trick. Usually, as he well knows, I prefer anything at all to staying and working in the shop. Nor does he try to stop me from going to see Kakoucha.

"I know. I know what you'd rather do. Go ahead. At the same time you'll take a nose-bag for Si Hammadi."

But this time it wasn't a trick. I didn't want to see Kakoucha even though, on an occasion of that sort and in public, there wouldn't be any danger.

"No," I said, "if you don't mind, I'd rather stay here."

He got impatient.

"Go, I'm telling you."

But I haven't told you about Kakoucha yet, Doctor.

Story of Kakoucha

Kakoucha was my first fiancée. In fact I wanted to marry her very early: I was five years old when I asked her and she accepted and we had the general consent of both our families. On the very next New Year's Day, they arranged a little party. By that I mean that I went into my fiancée's room, which wasn't far away, since Kakoucha is the daughter of my Aunt Maïssa, who lived in the same Oukala as we did, and there, amid the clapping and joking of all the assembled relatives and the women going RI-RI-RI, *I took a big banni-banni firecracker out of my pocket and threw it on the ground as hard as I could. But it didn't go off. Luckily I had another one ready and I threw it even harder. It didn't go off either and rolled under the wardrobe. I went face down on the floor to look for it and when I touched it I found that it was wet and already limp. My aunt had washed the tiled floor of the bedroom and hadn't mopped up enough under the furniture. I got up, very chagrined that the first part of my plan hadn't worked, especially since I could hear them joking on all sides—"He's limp!" "He hasn't got any juice!" Luckily I still had the ring. In those days my father was still willing to join in the fun at times, and he had helped me for this part of my plan by giving me money to buy a ring for Kakoucha. I'd been to choose it at Uzan's; he sold a mixture of toys and needles and thread and tricks. I took the ring out of my pocket and proudly held it up for all to see. I must have been impressive, for there was an awed silence. I don't think they were expecting to see me offer such a jewel. Before these suddenly silent people, I said to Kakoucha solemnly, "Give me your finger." She held out all her fingers, spread out. Only, the ring wouldn't fit on her ring finger; I had based the size on my own finger, which was too thin. The jokes were beginning again and the racket was even louder than before. I didn't know what to do, when Kakoucha came to my rescue: she took the ring from me and put it on her little finger herself. At last the people were clapping and shouting, "She's won, she's defeated him!" Which wasn't meant to be mean, as I well knew, because that's what they shout, you know, at the fish ceremony when the new bride manages to cut the fish after the groom has pretended to try for a long time, without succeeding.*

We were finally engaged. As far as I was concerned, anyhow. For them of course it was just a make-believe betrothal. I had to acknowledge it one day, when I suddenly discovered that Kakoucha was old. I was twelve and she had just turned twenty. Our marriage had been for fun; now she was to get married for real, whereas I was still just a little kid, and she made this very clear to me.

This is how it happened.

I can still see her now. She was standing chatting with a neighbor girl at the foot of the stairway that leads to the gallery of the Oukala. It was summertime. I was swinging on the railing and looking at her from up above. A little bit plump, she was wearing a tight cotton dress that emphasized the moving curve of her hips and showed the dip of her fine full breasts and her dimpled arms.

I felt a great surge of affection for her. I leaped down four steps at a time and threw myself on her, caressing the softest part of her arm.

"Kakouch', you're beautiful!"

Then the most unexpected thing happened. She jerked away from me, red as a tomato, and said in a sharp hard way I'd never heard her use with anyone:

"You crazy or something?"

Then, seeing how alarmed and upset I was, how bewildered, and maybe ashamed of her own overly startled reaction, she smiled at the other girl, who smiled back in an odd way, and Kakoucha said to me more gently,

"You're a man now, Bina."

I couldn't see why being a man should prevent me from caressing Kakoucha and showing her my affection. What crime had I committed? Maybe it was that incident with the chickpeas; I had to apologize to her for that. One thing I was sure of was that I had lost my little fiancée once and for all.

The Story of the Chickpeas

Oh, it's not a true story, Doctor. Maybe it's not even a story at all. At noontime on the Friday before, I was playing with a bunch of boys when Kakouch' appeared at the end of the street. My heart beat the way it did every time I saw her. But there were the other boys, and I did not run to her. It was she who came toward me to go home to the Oukala. When she saw me, she smiled and was about to go home when she changed her mind, rummaged inside her basket and brought out a handful of chickpeas. It was Friday and the chickpeas were warm for the evening. Joyfully, I was about to take them, when the boys behind me began to yell, "Boo! Boo! He's accepting a present from a girl!"

Hesitantly, my hand reached toward hers, that was held out, palm up and expectant. She was looking at me affectionately, as usual.

The boys went on shouting even louder, "Sissy! Weakling! Miscarriage! Girly!"

So, what did I do then? I'm going to tell you something, Doctor, something awful. I don't remember what I did. Did I or didn't I take those chickpeas from that hand that was waiting for me so tenderly? Did I hit that hand furiously? I guess I must have, because I remember that the chickpeas went flying everywhere and rolling on the ground. That's it. Suddenly, instead of taking them, I gave her hand a hard slap from underneath and sent those nice warm chickpeas flying into the air. It had rained for several days and the ground was muddy and the little yellow chickpeas stuck in the black mud all around. . . .

Kakoucha stared at me incredulously, angered and mostly sad. She did not say a word and anyhow, before she could open her mouth, I'd already turned my back on her and was running away while the kids clapped.

Only, I still can't remember even now whether that really happened or not. Afterwards I told Kakoucha this story and she told me I'd made up the whole thing. If that had happened to us just before the incident on the stairway, she would have remembered it. But maybe I did that to some other girl? Did I hit that hand that was held out to me, or did I take those chickpeas? Did I or didn't I knock those chickpeas that girl was offering me into the mud? And supposing I did make up this story, why would I do that? Doctor, can you explain that to me?

Story of Kakoucha (continued)

In any case, this incident didn't completely spoil things between me and Kakoucha. In fact, we became closer friends than before, even more intimate. Before, I'd admired her from afar. Now, she would listen to me, advise me, cheer me up when I was feeling sad. I had lost my little fiancée but I had gained a big sister. When my father drove me out of the house because of that school business I told you about, I went and took refuge at Aunt Maïssa's house. Kakoucha hugged me to her chest and it was soft and warm. I often had headaches in those days and she would take them away with a secret massage, a Japanese method, pressing on the eyes, the temples, and the neck, which made me shiver and really took away the pain. She didn't like Ghozala very much. She called her "your little she-goat," because Ghozala was small, nervous, and dark, whereas Kakoucha was tall and quite strong and calm—a very big she-goat compared with Ghozala. But she wasn't jealous and later on, when she got married and went to live in l'Ariana, she allowed me to go to see her each time I came to bring halters to the small farmers in the area.

She married a boy who was very good, very thoughtful, a

truckdriver named Mbirakh, but I wouldn't have liked him anyhow, except that everyone kept telling me there was just one thing wrong with him. He had only one good eye, which wasn't his fault, after all. Since she didn't have any children and her husband's wages weren't enough, she opened a small grocery store. Once a week she came into town to see her mother and came to see us at the same time. She always brought me something from her store—halva or sesame seeds or some resin to chew.

Of course it was Qatoussa who gave me the idea but, actually, it was my own fault. We were talking once again about the nature of love. I was all out of arguments to make him understand what love was, so I said to him:

"Look, take me. Why Ghozala and not . . . well, Kakoucha, for example?"

"Yes, why?" he said, asking me my own question. "That's just what I've been wanting to ask you for a long time."

I looked at him as if he was going out of his mind, shrugged my shoulders and explained that there were two reasons:

"1) Because Kakoucha is older than I am.

"2) Because she's married."

Twice he answered the same way:

"So what?"

"What do you mean, so what?"

"So, this is what I mean:

"1) The best fruits are the ones that aren't bitter and aren't rotten but are just right. Kakoucha is just right.

"2) A married woman is the most convenient: she knows how to make love, and she knows how to avoid having babies."

He concluded:

"Love is when it works, and with Kakoucha, it works."

I got angry. I told him indignantly that I didn't make love with Kakoucha because she was like a sister to me, a big sister. . . . He didn't say any more, just muttered a little, but I think I made out that he was saying once more:

"So what?"

I decided it would be better not to see Kakoucha so often any-

more. But a little while afterwards, her husband died in that horrible accident: the tipping bin of the truck hit him on the head, on the side where he couldn't see. He was smiling while everyone watched his death coming toward him from the left, where darkness veiled his eye. The people were yelling but he didn't understand and went on smiling until his head had been crushed, and still he was smiling. Could I abandon Kakoucha under the circumstances? On the contrary, I went to see her more often, to console her and keep her company. When it happened to be a Friday and we shut up our store early, I came earlier than usual and helped her a little in her store; then we would withdraw into the apartment and she would serve me a couple of meatballs with a glass of boukha. Until the day I asked my aunt why Kakoucha stayed in l'Ariana alone and why she wouldn't come back to the Oukala—and my aunt answered that she was really looking for a man so as to stay in l'Ariana. Then I determined not to accept these little parties at Kakoucha's any more and little by little I stopped seeing her altogether. She never protested.

The Anniversary of Mbirakh's Death (continued)

So I left for l'Ariana and arranged it so as to arrive after the ceremony had begun. At the end, when the people began to get up to leave, I was one of the first to go and greet Kakoucha so that I wouldn't be alone with her. But just as I was kissing her cheek, she murmured in my ear, "Come back in a little while." I didn't answer. I kissed her on the other cheek and left, determined not to come back. Then I went to drop off the nose-bag at Si Hammadi's before taking my train.

But when I reached the station, I could see her far away, waiting for me with her head leaning to one side, anxiously watching the entrance to the platform. I stopped and hesitated for a long minute. The weather was cold, so she had taken a shawl that she held in her left hand and that dragged on the ground; she stood there unmindful of the people who bumped into her as they went by. I was still trying to decide whether I shouldn't go out for a walk and wait till she gave up and went away, so that I could take my train, when she saw me. So I walked toward her and we went back together. Once we had reached the house, she shut the store and while she took care of a number of little things, I sat on a stool with my arms dangling and waited quietly. When she had finished, she pulled me into the bedroom and began to undress me. It was astonishingly easy. I realized that with Ghozala, maybe I was afraid, even just to kiss her; my mouth was dry and my hands trembled. Whereas with Kakoucha, I was like a child, she could do with me what she liked.

Then she made me coffee and put Nestlé's condensed milk in it because she remembered that I didn't like ordinary milk, and made toast with honey, not butter, because she also knew that I hated butter.

"Next time," she said, "arrange to spend the night."

Then she explained to me that it was out of the question to give up my father's shop later on. Lots of people had two stores. Baïsa would take care of it all by himself mornings. He was an able and honest man and my father was wrong not to trust him more. All I would have to do would be to spend the afternoons there with him. I had never seen Kakoucha so happy, and I was grateful to her in my body. Going back in the train, it became very clear to me that as long as my father lived, and if he lived long enough, I would never have the strength to win Ghozala. And yet—I don't know whether you've really got the idea, Doctor, but I absolutely had to have Ghozala, or else I would never become a man.

Uncle Makhlouf—2

I managed to bring the conversation back to the advantages of my System. I didn't have to maneuver; Uncle listened to me patiently. But when I had finished listing my arguments, he answered, "No," almost in the same words as before. All the commentaries are true at the same time, and so there was no reason to use colors to differentiate them.

So, he hasn't given it any thought since our last meeting. As usual, he's the one who's right. Last time, I hadn't been able to answer his objections, so it was still my turn.

But as a matter of fact I had gathered my ammunition together meanwhile. This was only a preamble. I pulled out my little piece of paper and read aloud, triumphantly:

> It is said:
> When this flame grew and spread
> It brought resplendent colors to life
> Deep in the heart of that flame
> There gushed a spring
> Overflowing with colors
> Concealed in the most secret mystery of the infinite.

Without the slightest hesitation, Uncle left his great wheel and went to the book cupboard. He brought back a huge, faded, tattered in-quarto volume, patched up with wallpaper; drawing near the window and running his middle finger along under the lines he read in turn:

> It is also said:
> In the beginning
> When the king began to exert his will
> He traced signs in the celestial aura
> A dark flame flashed

In the remotest realm
Of the mystery of the infinite
Like a formless cloud inside the ring
Neither white
Nor black
Nor red
Nor green
Nor any color.

"And that," he added mischievously, "is only what happened in the beginning. Because you have not given me either the beginning or the end. Now, this is how the end goes:

But the spring did not penetrate the surrounding ether and remained altogether unknown. . . .

Unbeatable! I was put out but I couldn't help admiring the old man sincerely. He went on reading that extraordinary passage —I had mutilated it, I must admit—but I couldn't hear him any more.

Although his lips continue to move, his voice fades away at times and becomes almost inaudible. I don't dare ask him to repeat because I don't know if he's aware of it himself and I'm afraid of offending him. There is nothing to indicate that he is aware of it—or else, if he does know it, he accepts that it is so, the way he accepts the idea that his eyes don't see everything. . . . No, that's a bad comparison. Uncle knows everything his voice does not express; it's just that I don't hear certain passages. He doesn't bother about it, that's all. This means that I often find big blanks in one of his speeches, and yet all I know for certain is that it is flawlessly complete and coherent.

I can see there is no point in trying any more for today. I had prepared an outline with examples and even passages colored with colored pencils, just in case. But that's useless with Uncle Makhlouf as long as I haven't won on grounds of principle.

He finishes reading and goes to put the large bound book, decorated with purple flowers, carefully back in its place in the cupboard. Then he comes back to make the wheel revolve again. It's my turn once more.

I don't know why I'm so anxious to convince him. I'm not

even sure we're always talking about the same thing. And yet I've got to convince him!

"But, even so, Uncle Makhlouf, authors do contradict each other sometimes, one commentary can contradict what another one says!"

"The contradiction is within yourself. It comes from your not having a view of the whole."

"All right. Let's say there isn't any fundamental contradiction. Even so, a commentary hasn't the same value as the original text! A commentary on a commentary hasn't the same value as the commentary itself!"

"Yes it has; everything is right once it has been said; and in fact everything was already right before it was said, before it was known to us."

I get impatient:

"But look here, Uncle Makhlouf, that's impossible."

"Impossible—if you don't know how to reconcile the whole. Impossible indeed, if you forget that there is unity first of all. The Word already includes everything you develop. It is in the process of development that the details seem stranger to one another. You ask yourself: from commentary to commentary, from commentary on a commentary to commentary on a commentary—which is the essential, which is the embroidery? A bad way of looking at things, a dangerous way even: you end up wondering which is the text and which are the commentaries. You end up doubting the text. Bad. Pernicious. Remember: everything is a development of a single text. And shall I tell you something? Even that text is a commentary."

"Ah, now that won't do! If the principal text itself is only a commentary, then how can you be sure of anything at all?"

Uncle's voice grows dim; it is reduced to a hissing, it almost disappears. His lips continue. These breakdowns in communications are the only time when Uncle's presence causes me some uneasiness. I feel as though I'm stifling.

The voice comes back, muffled at first, wrenching the words from Uncle's chest, bridging a void several seconds long.

"If you don't try, if you don't pray or if you pray badly, it's your own fault. You haven't been able to find what you need! Whereas you must find what suits you, because what suits you exists. I'm going to repeat it, because repetition is the safeguard of the heart and the mind: remember that you are under God's gaze and that you can always talk to Him and that He's always there, ready to hear you."

"Like on the telephone!"

The words just said themselves because I was annoyed at not being able to make Uncle budge even a fraction of an inch and I was furious over the way he was so sure and I so powerless. It was silly and insolent of me, though, and I bit my lips. But Uncle Makhlouf answered calmly,

"That's a good example: like on the telephone. I'll borrow that for the Meeting. In fact it's even better, because you're never cut off."

One day the inhabitants of a village in Poland were desperate because it had not rained for months and months. The grass was drying up and the herds were beginning to suffer. The people prayed harder than ever but it did no good. God seemed to be refusing to hear them.

A poor shepherd, a bit simple-minded and almost mute, saw the anguish of the whole community and would have liked to join in the collective prayers but he could not because his tongue was lame and he did not know the words.

He was thinking about it sadly, alone on the hillside in the midst of his animals, when he had an inspiration. Gathering all his strength together in his chest, and shouting as loudly as he could, he raised a tremendous cry toward heaven.

At that very moment, the people in the village saw the sky split wide open and the next instant the rain began to fall. The poor half-dumb shepherd had just found the right prayer.

"How can anyone despair? How can you lack dignity when you are always, at every instant, responsible for this Dialogue with God? Where you make your mistake is in thinking that the Dialogue has to deal with difficult problems, matters of utmost Wisdom. No, you can talk to God about anything you want, about the entire universe but also about the minutest detail. There is no detail that he cannot sanctify. . . ."

He liked to bend his thoughts in that direction, as I knew from experience, and he began to argue along those lines, backing up his statements with quotations; telling me an apologue he had already used, about the rather simple-minded wife whose husband made fun of her because she asked God to help her cook the holiday meals well. Until the day she accidentally dropped a piece of soap into the soup and it made her husband so sick he thought his last hour had come. As he thrashed about in agony, he had a vision. A Sage reproached him for the way he behaved to his wife and reminded him how important a little piece of soap in the soup could be, saying, "You haven't even had strength enough to pray today."

"Speak to God any way you can and He'll answer you in your own language. For God also speaks, through everything around you. Only on great occasions, of course, does He speak with His own voice. But ordinarily He speaks to you every day through the bread you eat and the wine you drink, and you should thank Him for them with every bite and every swallow. He speaks to you in everything you see and everything you touch, and the main thing is that you must keep on turning the Great Wheel, even if you don't see it clearly, or even if you don't see it at all any more. If you stop, it's all over with very quickly. Look at your father: is there still somebody sitting in his armchair?"

(I try to use a dictaphone, it would rest my eyes, but it's no good. I don't feel the words. Must refuse those instruments of the devil, keep in touch with paper.)

"When you need to hear God's voice itself, you have the Text. After all, what is the Text, if not the permanent presence of the word of God? It's up to you to understand it, as best you can, as you need to. That's why the commentaries may seem to differ."

"In short," I said:

To every man the book speaks, but the earthly destiny of man depends on his reply.

"Ah, that's it exactly!" answered Uncle enthusiastically. Suddenly curious, he added, "I never heard that one. It's very good. Where did you find it? You see, you can question the Bible and the Bible will always answer you. You've found the right answer."

I was ashamed. I hesitated but finally I said:

"Only it isn't in the Bible, little Uncle, it's in the Koran."

He is abashed and almost angry. I am sorry I took my little revenge. He's apparently thinking, then he says:

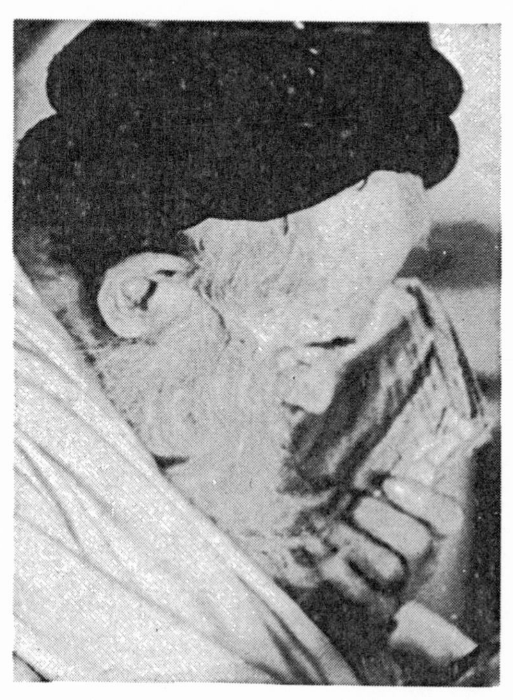

"I didn't pay close enough attention. 'The earthly destiny.' There's no such thing as an earthly destiny and a celestial destiny. They're the same thing. I should have realized, I should have listened more closely before I spoke. You see, Imilio, before answering, you have to listen. I didn't listen very well, so I was punished. I answered all wrong."

Amusing idea Emile's got there, coloring the different Commentaries different ways—according to their age, I suppose? Because, after all, how could you distinguish which was the most truthful? Obviously Uncle Makhlouf couldn't go along with him—the very idea of laying a hand on his texts!

In fact I'm going to have to see Uncle again pretty soon and talk with him firmly, doctor to patient. Have a family council with his sons, if necessary, and this time I'll tell them plainly what I think of them! But it's my fault. Every doctor has a special relationship with his patients, but I'm afraid I didn't find the right sort of relationship with Uncle. For one thing, he treats me as a nephew that he's known since I was a boy, and not as a doctor, and for another, I cannot take him seriously. There has to be a feeling of confidence, of course, if the doctor and the patient are going to build up an effective relationship between them, but confidence isn't enough.

Maybe this communication with the patient is the most important angle of my work (along with drops in the eyes daily—the alternative being disaster) for both patient and doctor. We tend to forget that the doctor himself needs it; every creature without exception needs it.

Uncle and I don't get along terribly well because I haven't managed to achieve that communication. Now and then that's the way it is—you fall flat on your face, you fail miserably, whereas until then you were doing everything right. Actually, all I had to offer him was eyedrops, and his speeches didn't appeal to me, so we were just about useless to each other. Between Emile and Uncle, there's something else, and I'm jealous of it.

Amar, Niel's assistant, doesn't resent the fact that I signed against him. I'm just as glad. He even invited me to an Oriental party he's planning on giving very soon, once he's moved into Niel's apartment and the garden around it, which he wants to occupy as soon as his boss has left. He's in such a hurry! The body will still be warm. I'd like to refuse, but how?

Menana

The rest of it, Doctor, the rest of it! Noucha, my tender bleeding heart, my lamb taken from its mother, Noucha my dark night, my blinding black coal, Noucha my broken arm that I carry with me, forever lame . . .

But my father kept his word. The very next day he went to see Menana the matchmaker. First of all, there was the spectacle of Menana herself. She came to the shop and insisted on sitting on my father's own stool. "My buttocks are broader than yours, and I've been walking since morning." She sat down and sure enough her buttocks stuck out beyond the stool on every side.

From out of her bosom Menana drew her tin box and methodically stuffed a large pinch of snuff into each of her huge tobacco-burned nostrils; then she waited for the sneeze and brought it on by grimacing oddly with all her great round face that was creased and chapped and bristling with purple warts and yet was firm and taut and wonderfully tanned, golden amber and French calfskin. "A feast-day plum pickled in cloves" (Qatoussa). "It's the sun that does it! Until I began matchmaking, I was white-skinned as a sultan's daughter." Baïsa winked at me and I turned my head away to keep from laughing. She sneezed once, and again, and again and, each time she said to herself, "God bless me! God protect me!"

But when it came to playing this subtle game of waiting and not saying anything, no one could get the better of my father. He sent Baïsa to bring back coffee from Funaro's and didn't open his mouth once after that. Menana took the time to drain her cup, slowly, and wipe her face quarter by quarter with an astonishing handkerchief—brown, studded with yellow suns—that she folded up carefully and put back in her unfathomable bosom. She sighed and finally said:

"So?"

"So? Where do we stand? He's a good catch, you know. You'll be sorry."

My father would either get angry or shrug his shoulders.

"He's a good catch, so. And my daughter? She's blind, maybe? or bow-legged? What does he think he is? His father was a street-porter and as for himself, he's a butcher, which means he sells rotten meat, go and see! My daughter is a new-born lamb."

He fell silent, embarrassed, remembering why he wanted to marry her off. Menana smiled slyly:

"Mbirakh, you are right, but it's wiser to marry girls young."

Menana wouldn't try any more that day. She would talk about something else—the weather, the difficulties of life, and two days later she would come back with a slightly different offer, or even a new offer, if our ideas were too far apart. She would sit down and say:

"This time I know it's agreed. You know the younger Uzan? That's right, the haberdasher's in the rue des Dattiers . . ."

Then came the difficult part.

"A complete bedroom suite, that's all he's asking. You're right, Mbirakh, it's shameful really to give your daughter and *money, both; you're giving twice. But a bedroom suite—that's only natural. These children are our heart and our blood, they have to have a bedroom at least. . . ."*

"Complete!" my father cut in. "Complete? Never! I know what that means. It means even the roller for cutting the noodles, and a pail in the toilet."

In the evening, I would tell Noucha how it was going, and her eyes would shine as she listened but she never said anything. Only once she asked me, blushing, if I'd ever met Moumou. And only once, Menana said to my father:

"Do you want me to go and see Moumou's father?"

He answered her the way he'd answered me:

"Why would you go see the father of a dead man? That's going to bring him back to life?"

Soon, Menana began coming only once a week, then only once every two weeks. Soon my father, who had pretended in the beginning not to need her very much, went to see her. One Saturday morning I went with him. She was playing cards, with only men, no other women present, and using the most obscene language and taking snuff and spitting (and doing worse than that, too!), so we couldn't talk to her. The next day, she came back to the shop.

"This time . . . look, you know Ganem, the wool merchant? May God bless him, he has enough to feed ten women, as you know, and he could even make life easier for the whole family."

"Ganem has a son?"

"No, it's for himself, may God refresh your memory. You know perfectly well he's a widower!"

There was a silence, then my father said:

"It's obvious that you're going out of your mind, Menana. Noucha is a little girl. You know why I'm marrying her so young. Ganem is an old man—sixty, at least."

"Fifty, Mbirakh, fifty; may God enlighten you!"

"Fifty? That's just the weight of the pods without the beans."

"All right, Mbirakh, fifty-one or fifty-two. But he's not asking anything. He'll take her in her nightgown."

"No," my father said. "I refuse to give my daughter to an old man, even in her nightgown."

That evening I told Noucha the whole thing. It was too funny. But Noucha didn't laugh with me; she didn't even say anything. Just as well, too, I thought afterward, because a week later, my father and Menana came to an agreement.

Then came the feasting and ceremonies that preceded the wedding. Did I sincerely believe that Noucha was going to grow accustomed to her new state? Ganem turned out to be quite a nice man and was happy to spoil his very young fiancée; "little pussy-cat," he always called her. Did I want to believe it because that meant that soon Ghozala and I would be married? Anyhow, I didn't dare look Noucha in the eyes any more; and although I did toss my egg, that was because I was supposed to do it. When I come home to the Oukala late at night, the mark of that broken egg still shines on the wall in the darkness. And as for the other thing I was supposed to do—I couldn't think about it yet.

One of those afternoons my father had gone out and left Baïsa and me alone. I don't know what got into me but I said to Baïsa:

"Wouldn't you like to be the boss some day, Baïsa?"

"Who doesn't like honey?" he answered.

"Why shouldn't you set up in business for yourself?"

"Why! Why! You making fun of me? What about the rent, and the tools and all that, and the stock?"

"And suppose someone offered you a business and you could pay on credit, would you accept? Would you promise to pay it back?"

"You know a madman?"

"Answer first."

"Whoever wants to do good doesn't have to ask permission first. . . . But you're dreaming, Bina."

"Well, dreams come true sometimes. We don't know what God has in store for us."

Which made Baïsa give me a queer look and say:

"Son of a whore! What are you thinking of? Your father's still alive, you know!"

Suddenly I was frightened myself by what I had said, but I protested:

"What have you understood? Who's talking about our shop? Baïsa, your tongue is rotten."

"My tongue knows what it says. Ah, children nowadays! Is your heart as black as that or is it just your mouth that's gone crazy?"

"Baïsa, you're as wicked as an old black scorpion."

In the courtyard of the Oukala, the women were bustling around Noucha, the silent heroine. She smiled now and then with a poor distant smile like the sun during an eclipse. At last, when her head had been rubbed with greasy, amber-colored henna, she looked like a bride. Her turban prevented her from hearing very well so I leaned close to her ear and said, forcing myself:

"Anyhow you're happy, aren't you? A husband's a husband."

She looked at me with her shining eyes and I felt myself blush. I threw an egg against the wall the way I was supposed to but I threw it so hard that the white of it splashed over me.

The Hammam

(Have I devoted enough space to the hammam? To my regions of half-darkness peopled with countless figures of flesh and still echoing with disquieting voices, pointed virgins, greedy opulence, withered old women? "Look how that little one's looking at me, you'd think he was a man!" "You know, his little fountain's going to wake up too early. It's not good for him." "At what age does sin begin, Souraya?" And Souraya saying perfidiously in my ear, "So much the better for you, my boy. Keep your eyes open. Eat them, gobble them up." For ten years after I was expelled from the hammam I refused to go back there, even to the men's part. Even today, even in a sauna, which is an antiseptic imitation, all that flesh in the half-light . . . Did I really look as hard as that!)

It was the Chebagh's little girl, Fartouna, who came and got me. When I reached the hammam, Noucha was wrapped up in a bathrobe and lying on a resting-mat. It was nothing, just a fit of hysterics. Maïssa scolded Fartouna; it wasn't worth going to disturb the men about a little thing like that.

The women had gone to the hammam in the usual way. Meanwhile we men paraded in the street, with the musicians in front and the baskets of presents coming behind, and more than ten candlesticks to light the way. Ganem had done it all up lavishly; it was he who had filled up almost all the baskets. Qatoussa had agreed to play and sing the whole way for nothing, because she was my sister. We sang, and we danced with the scarves. At the same time, what was to happen to Noucha, happened. Maïssa told me about it.

"We had gone into the hammam, into the big room first with the warm steam, and we cried RI-RI-RI *a lot of times in the candlelight and were very gay. 'You're as beautiful and white as jasmine,' I said to Noucha. 'Your husband will be lucky to have you in his bed.' She smiled and that fooled me. My heart didn't warn me. I'm ashamed. Then we went on into the second room, that's darker and hotter. Souraya the Negress held the two candlesticks —you know how you have to hold two candlesticks with lighted candles during the bath that precedes the wedding; otherwise, in the darkness, it might be easier for the* jinn *to harm the young virgin. Suddenly we were plunged into darkness and I heard Noucha scream and then the women were shouting, calling for Souraya and each other. Souraya must have slipped and dropped the candlesticks. . . . My heart told me I must find Noucha immediately and I called out her name several times. Noucha didn't answer and I thought of the* jinn *a little but I said to myself that all those stories weren't meant to be taken really seriously— though you never know. Just then someone bumped into me and I was knocked down onto my knees.*

"Luckily things didn't stay that way for very long. By the

time I got up again, which was hard, because the tiles were slippery, there was light in the corridor. Souraya had somehow brought back a lighted candle. That was when we realized Noucha wasn't there anymore. I began to be really very frightened and scolded myself for having doubted the existence of the jinn. *We all rushed to the big resting room and there, praise heaven!, was Noucha, stretched out on a resting-mat. The owner of the hammam was already with her and so was the other Negress, Mabrouka. She had had a fit of hysterics and then fainted, but thank God in heaven, she was there. She'd managed to find her way back in the dark and then collapsed in the main entrance. The owner and Mabrouka had picked her up and covered her."*

It was decided to postpone the wedding for a month. Besides, her fall was making her rib hurt again.

A week later, she tried to kill herself.

Story of Noucha's Suicide Attempt

"I took Uncle Fallous' revolver from his night table and I went out to the Belvedere. It was raining. First of all I walked around for a while, and held the revolver tight against my chest. No, I wasn't hesitating; I was quite determined, but I felt like walking around a little while longer. Then I went and stood under a tree to get out of the rain. I tried out my finger on the trigger, to make sure I'd know how to pull it and my finger wouldn't slip. Then I pointed the weapon against my chest and pulled. I didn't fall. I was surprised at not falling all in a heap, like in the movies, and I remained standing against the tree. It hurt, a burning pain, but not too bad. The rain kept on falling and it trickled down from my hair onto my neck, but I wasn't too wet because of the leaves. Finally a watchman found me, and I told him that I'd hurt myself. He made me sit on a bench and went to get a calash."

"Would you do it again?"

"Yes."

She repeated it all again to the doctor calmly, irrevocably.

"What do you think?" he asked me.

What could I say? I told him the story of Noucha's first job the way she had told it to me herself.

"I told our father that I wasn't refusing to work but that I didn't want to leave our district and, especially, I didn't want to sleep in the house of strangers. Our father got angry, of course,

and refused to discuss the matter. He took me to my employer himself. That was in the residential area, with private houses. She was a French lady, very young and very nice. She said to me, 'You'll see, you'll be very happy with me.' I answered, 'Yes, but I won't stay.' She laughed and told me I was a little savage. The next day she wanted to go out and she said to me, 'You'll wait for me, won't you?' I said, 'No, I won't wait.' So she frowned and told me I was bad, then she locked me in and left. I wandered around the apartment. Then I went to the toilet. I stuffed the hole up carefully with newspapers and then I began to pull the chain to flush the toilet. I pulled and pulled and pulled all afternoon long. I was still little at the time and I had to stand on tiptoe. Toward the end I was pulling like a robot. I just pulled and pulled and pulled without stopping. I wanted there to be as much water as possible on the floor and then on the rugs."

"Why didn't you just turn on the faucets?"

She shrugged her shoulders irritably.

"I don't know. I wanted to flush the toilet. We don't have a toilet that flushes in our house. . . . I pulled all afternoon."

Our father beat her furiously on the soles of the feet, with an old worn-out leather shoe. She was sick and had to stay at Maïssa's, but she did not go back to that employer. She was apprenticed to someone in our own district.

"And now, Noucha?"

"I'll kill myself."

"What for? You won't marry Ganem anymore."

"I'll kill myself."

She had to be put in the hospital under observation.

The Kidnapping in the Car

We brought her downstairs, my father holding onto one arm and I onto the other. When she saw the white car, and the male nurse sitting behind the wheel, she understood. She wanted to go back into the Oukala and began to scream, "I don't want to die any more!" A young man who happened to be going by in the street began to shout too in a strangled voice. He threw himself on my father and grabbed his shoulder. My father shook him off. Panic-stricken and obviously not knowing what to do, the young man ran toward the police station on the corner. It did look like a kidnapping, I must say. Noucha screamed and kicked at the open car door. The nurse-driver finally got out to help us; we were holding her at arm's length and trying to get into the car with her. I didn't know Noucha was so strong. My father nearly closed the door on her foot, which was sticking out in desperation. At last the car started up and as we turned the corner, we saw the young man, who had come out of the police station and was standing on the sidewalk.

On our way back, I was alone with my father. He sighed and said:

"Now it is you who will bring me the spraying bulb and the powder."

Noucha didn't stay in the hospital very long, just a month. Then they gave her back to us, saying she was perfectly docile and didn't talk about killing herself any more. But I knew that she wasn't the same Noucha—my heart torn away, my glowing coal, my Noucha!—and would never be the same again. And it was our father's fault. Once again I told myself our father was preventing us from living.

So that's where the story of the so-called madness of Kalla-Marguerite comes from.

The spraying bulb and the powder—I suppose this is an allusion to the "Poudre Legras" and the little insufflation bulb that our father uses (the way anyone with asthma does).

Nowhere until now had I noticed that Bina's father had asthma. Our father does.

Marie

Was my marriage the most important event of my life? Or was it just the symbol and the summing up? Did it ruin my life? Or was it the disastrous, ineluctable result of my life, that brought all the rest in its wake? Was it my greatest ambition, my boldest project, the hope of the highest freedom to which a man can attain? Or the thoughtless, imprudent, inexperienced act of an adolescent who had deceived himself as to his real strength and his secret ties; whereas he had buried them disdainfully deep inside himself, only to find them surprisingly resilient?

I have already written about my life with Marie so many times—how we met, as young students, then the many inevitable ups and downs in the daily life of such a strangely assorted couple—that it would be futile to go on about that picturesque side of things. I have tried to depict it as faithfully as possible in my books, chiefly in *The Foreign Woman,* even though I did mix reality and fiction, of course, so as to convey the truth better. I even tried to draw the philosophical conclusions of it in a long chapter in my *Treatise on Marriage, Misfortunes of the Married Couple, and Woes of the Single Man.* So all I will do now is dispel a few interpretative errors that crop up here and there in what the critics have written about me, even though they have been cautious on that score, not prying into what they seem to have guessed was one of the nerve centers of my work and my whole life.

I must admit that I probably haven't been able to explain who Marie was, but, when you come right down to it, have I ever really known for sure myself? My wife was not German, as rumor had it. She wasn't pretending to be from the Lorraine, she really was. If my readers only knew how incapable she was of feigning or passing herself off as anything—and yet how it would have suited me if only she had had that quality, or that weakness, or that resignation, which so many women have! Her accent was simply that of the border provinces where people do in fact speak

German, that's true, but where—perhaps for that very reason—they are virulently French and stubbornly Catholic in order to make the distinction clear between themselves and those Germanic, Protestant countries whose culture, language, cooking, and fashion make them the common fatherland of all the border peoples.

It is true that that civilization and its customs were just as foreign to me. When I went to her native country for the first time, everything surprised and delighted me, and made me uneasy. I don't mean just the pleasant excitement you feel in a picturesque situation that you adopt for a few days because you know you'll be leaving it soon and eventually you'll forget even the color and the smell of it. The cooking and the sausages, for instance—heavy and hard to digest, but altogether delicious. Or even all those religious pictures all over the walls, so many plaster Gods blessing everything, at least one on every bookshelf. I found them amusing and overwhelming at the same time—I who had rebelled so violently against the one God of my own people and now found dozens of them all around me! Instantly I felt an infinitely deeper, graver anxiety, anguish almost, the kind you feel when you see a movie about a completely unknown universe that seems to be built around dimensions different from our own. In any case it was when I came to her house that, for the first time in my life, I had that revelation I'll tell about later on and that has recurred so often since (though I strongly suspect that the groundwork for that sort of discovery is laid down a long time in advance).

But she didn't belong to that universe any more, she told me immediately without my even asking her. She had left her parents so long ago; because of the war she had traveled so much all over Europe; like most of the girls she had grown up with, she was so used to the idea of making an exotic marriage that she had not had to make any effort or feel any regret at not belonging to her parents or her native country any more.

She didn't feel Catholic either. I flattered myself that just at the time she met me she gave up her faith, and at the same time that worried me. But no, she had rejected Catholic rites at a very early point in her life and begun doubting the dogma long before she knew me. She hardly ever went to mass, just when she came home for vacation. She gave me a very amusing account of her run-ins with those teams of young Catholic students at the Sorbonne that were known as the "Rats" because their mission was to convert other students by gnawing away at them all the time, from all sides, with arguments of all sorts, and of how she found out that the best way of duelling with them was to give them artificial nourishment to chew upon or put them on the wrong track. One day, with a girl friend, she managed to steer them onto the secretary of a communist cell by claiming that he was racked by mystical doubts.

She wasn't . . . She didn't . . . She wasn't . . . All these negative statements I'm piling up. But, then, what *was* she then? Did I really try to understand her? Was it really she who was involved throughout? Didn't I always end up measuring her in terms of myself? in my effort, of course, to act as if she were myself. Anyway the result was that I was always testing her to the limit, putting such impossible pressure on her that one day she simply had to rebel, or disappear.

(Later I told Niel how I had wanted, without a single lapse and with utmost sincerity, inasmuch as one can be sincere—how I had wanted to make her happy.

"Such eagerness!" answered Niel, smiling his shark's smile.)

So we went back to my native country. As for what made me go back home with Marie, though everyone advised against it—I won't go into that any more either. I have also described that rather burlesque first reunion with the whole family waiting for us on the wharf. I realize now I haven't said anything about the other homecomings, and yet there's an astonishing number of memories connected with those instants where our feet touched land again. But they're a little blurry, as if a long series of sleepwalking stunts were being squeezed into one another, so that you no longer know which was the time you walked on the edge of the roof and when the other time was when you tried to defy gravity and fly out the window, when you took the ground for water that you could swim in and you took the air for a concrete stairway that you could climb up surefootedly.

Like the day we were left alone in the deserted harbor. In order to avoid a repetition of the scene at our first landing, I hadn't told the family we were coming, though I had written to a friend to ask him to come for us in his car. We had been held up in customs, I don't remember why, and there we were, prisoners of our luggage; no porter, no way of getting into town. The last passengers had gone long ago and when the lights in the customs building went out, we were plunged into the unusually dark night. My friend certainly did not seem to be coming; probably he hadn't received my letter.

Then out of the shadows emerged two young hoodlums who stopped in front of us, as silent, watchful, and threatening as wolves; then came two more, then another. We were literally surrounded. I said to myself that alone like this, anything could happen to us and I focused all my energy on not letting Marie know how worried I was; she was holding my arm tight. Just then I heard the little bells of a calash, beyond the gates, and though I don't mind saying I had a lump in my throat, I called out to the coachman. Oddly enough, the idea that we were going to have reinforcements brought our assailants to life. They began to taunt us and say all sorts of awful things, and they tightened their circle when the calash drew up. But then they climbed onto the running board and the wheels, still insulting us and grazing us with obscene gestures. I asked the coachman to help me put up the luggage but he didn't budge from his seat; I suppose he was frightened himself or just didn't want to get mixed up in it. Hurriedly but forcing myself to keep my movements calm, I got Marie seated inside; then, pretending not even to notice our assailants, I shouted to the coachman to start up. They jumped off at last when the horses went into a gallop, except for one who clung on for a long time and kept looking at us strangely while the others were still running behind the coach.

Except for holding on tight to my arm, Marie had not moved once throughout the whole episode and it was only when everything had become calm again and we had come in sight of the first city lights that she began to cry. Those tears were the only reaction she allowed herself at the time and the only one I could have stood, I think.

Another time, just as we were coming off the gangplank, we witnessed a brawl—two men punching each other on the nose, the eyes, all over the face, violently, coldly, without a word or a moan. Soon there was blood; it shone in the sun, on themselves first, then on the ground, like a celebration of death.

"What savages!" she said, astounded and fascinated.

I too had felt a sort of sacred horror at that gleaming, silently spilled blood and she had used exactly the right word; possibly she felt dismayed on aesthetic grounds. But the fact is that the word sickened me, because by choosing it, she forced me to see ourselves from the outside.

Not that she ever asked me to be indulgent in any way toward her own people either (but, then again, neither was she ashamed of her origin nor did she try to conceal it. "Yes, I'm French," she would say calmly, and I wouldn't have liked her to act any other way). Even when the conflict was at its worst, and men were being shot down in the street by one side or the other and sometimes, through one of these appalling mix-ups that are so common during revolutions, by their own comrades—even at those moments when we had to choose between the two or three opposing factions. And when I had reached the point where I could no longer bear the sight of the revolvers placed next to the mail on meeting-room tables or the sound of the snickers that accompanied the gesture; when at the lycée itself I could no longer bear to see the pupils lined up against the wall and the policemen's machine-guns trained on them; when I could no longer bear the steady killings of so many men I had known well, honest men of good will, as if neither side wanted things to work out even temporarily—for instance, when a certain moderate, or well-known union leader was executed, whereas only they might have been capable of restoring peace; when things reached that point, she thought it perfectly natural that I should finally choose as I did choose. She always understood everything, accepted everything, to such an extent that, curiously enough, I would have preferred to encounter some resistance on her part.

But what she didn't understand was why I took it upon myself, without anyone forcing me into it, to live things that I knew I couldn't bear. I had to make an effort to keep from shouting at her that if I was supposed to live only what I could bear, then it would be better for me to leave her too, since she represented one of the remotest poles of my own being and yet I had to hold onto it by force. Because otherwise the whole edifice would lose its balance and crumble into ruin.

She lived on the memory of the student she'd known in Paris. It was his casual manner that had appealed to her, and his irony, his apprentice philosopher's cleverness, his dogmatic self-assurance, born of his inexperience of life. At times he would deliberately play the Oriental—Turkish coffee, the demanding character of a pasha or a spoiled child—and at times the pure westerner (purer, of course, than the Europeans themselves, as they supposedly had not grasped the essence of their own civilization), but, either way, he was always playing. Contrast with herself—talking little, looking for just the right word and so usually preferring not to say anything; whereas I'm like a cartoonist making a great many strokes and hoping that eventually truth will emerge from the heap of pencil marks.

"That was the man I married."

"Have I changed that much? "

"No. You still have both of them in you, but they don't get on very well any more. . . . Before, you knew how to keep both of them at a distance."

She had put her finger on it, and that made me angry. I accused her of confusing things when it was all so clear really, it was becoming impossible not to take part, and there was only one side that could be chosen. I accused her of being politically and humanly unjust. Right away I avoided the issue by talking about universal ethics and philosophy—transparent proof that I didn't know how to answer when it came to my own life, whereas that was quite simply the only thing she wanted to talk about.

How can I have kept on pretending so pig-headedly that I didn't see what she was trying to get at! Acting in bad faith that way must have been necessary for me if I was to go on living.

"Or else," she would say, in a sort of extraordinary short-cut, "reconcile everything! Be strong enough to live both at once! "

Sure! Just like that! I exploded bitterly against people with the extraordinary privilege of having just one country, one language, a strong government, a culture that was universally admired, and who took the liberty of advising the people who lived in a state of historical fragmentation, doubt, and distress! I was forgetting that, by choosing me, Marie was almost giving up her lucky situation and making herself suspect in the eyes of her own people—I could already see that clearly in the French colony here in this country.

Again, another day, she laughingly told me what one of our acquaintances had said—a woman from Paris who had moved here not long ago and who was horribly affected and unbearably sharp. She had married a Moslem and suffered simultaneously from the unjust attitude of her own people and the violence of her husband's people. She had summed up the situation in these terms:

"The French are bastards and the others are brutes."

I nearly crowed. That was exactly what Marie thought too.

She stared at me, taken aback. For once she was almost angry.

It was too stupid. She didn't despise anybody, only, having sided with me and knowing that the people I upheld didn't like us and would force us out if they could ("How do you know?," I would ask her, just to bother her, whereas I knew full well that she was right and that she knew that I knew, etc.), she did not understand how I could side with them. You had to be masochistic or perverted to go against yourself.

Obviously I should have been grateful to her for simply taking my side. But at the time I didn't think of it, I didn't want to concede that taking your own side was the healthiest attitude possible. (Oh, I've conceded it since, all right! But has my behavior ever changed, for all that?) I still preferred to get angry and suspect her of not having really, deep down, approved my choice, and of not hoping sincerely to see justice done, the great historical justice of having peoples make themselves free, and of being unwilling to see things from the standpoint of mankind, universality, philosophy, etc. . . . —in other words, of not being disinterested. Whereas she was only interested in seeing me happy—and herself too, of course, along with me, but not herself without me. No matter what she did, she irritated me. I would have liked her to confirm all of my decisions—which were contradictory—at once, but then, what would have remained of her? And, also, I might even have resented her reflecting on all my impossibilities that way and not helping me to overcome my inner chaos.

So, does this mean I didn't care about her? If that's the conclusion you're going to draw, then I have really failed to make myself understood. I need only recall how great my need for her was (is!), for her and nobody else, a need so great that it became anguish and panic, so great that out of inhibition or pride or fear, I never let her know how much I missed her as soon as she went a few miles or a few hours away. So great in fact that I exerted myself to loosen the thread a little, for fear that she wouldn't be able to breathe, and then she would panic too and her own fear would fill her with an irresistible need to leave—and that, I thought at first, would kill me.

To put it another way, in more ordinary terms: she's the only woman I've ever really loved. I mean completely, therefore tragically, in the truest sense of the word: it was impossible for me to live without her and therefore impossible to live with her and to just let her live. Let's take an example. I was never unfaithful to her, as they say; I never slept with another woman, though there certainly wasn't any lack of chances to do it, especially toward the end of colonization. Aside from any question of human respect and loyalty, I couldn't have done it; the mere idea of it upset me; it seemed to me that if ever I did, I would literally explode. And yet at the same time there was the mute anxiety that spread through me, more and more, every time I came near her. All in all, the only woman who embodied simultaneously what I needed to live and what was needed to destroy me, so that I even asked myself earnestly (but could never find the answer) whether I had become that way on contact with her and had then reached the point where I could no longer see myself or even imagine myself without her, or whether I had sought her out—her, and not another woman—because I was already and irrevocably as I was.

Then why, why didn't I do everything in my power to hold onto her? Because, in a way, everything that's happened is the result of her departure. . . . Ah really, anyone who asks me that question hasn't understood anything! Besides, things don't need to be understood in that order, it's not true. Was that departure the result of what was to happen to me? or was it the other way around? In not holding her back, I was acting out of a feeling that it would be useless and also—no matter how pompous and ridiculous this may sound—out of love for her! Yes, for her, because I couldn't see how, far from saving me, she could avoid smashing herself in the process. Because I couldn't see what reason I could invoke for not leaving *her* a chance to come out of it whole, if she could, if there was still time. By letting her go, I was making my best, and, unfortunately, one of my very few great gestures of love toward her.

Moreover, I was beginning to get used to the idea of doing

without everything and the necessity of doing without her. Sometimes I would say to myself, why not leave this place and go live in the midst of industrious people in a big busy city, the way Descartes did; he felt much better for having got away from his own people. Every day I would write and that way, every day, I would be scrubbing my soul, just the way I wash my body—my health and equilibrium depend on it. I wouldn't have to pay so much attention to the bad mood of the people around me, with their quarrels and their grousing. And one day, if their temperature began to go too high, if they began to get ready to commit some act of folly—a war or a revolution—then I would go away to some other big city and live amidst some other, wiser people; you can still find them on this earth, thank God. There is no such thing as a final contract with one individual or one people. You have to be crazy to sign away your past and your present once and for all. But immediately the vanity of the undertaking was apparent. The disorder was within myself; Marie merely represented it. In order to save myself, I used to say (and I was barely joking), I'd have had to take along neither Marie nor myself.

No, no bridge and no rope could stand the strain of stretching over that gap, precisely because the gap was there and nothing could fill it or even distract me from the intolerable dizziness that my life grew to be. My one mistake was to have believed that Marie could possibly stand for Health and—briefly—that I could end the struggle by leaving her. But in fact she has never, whether with me or away from me, ceased to be at the heart of my particular battle, and I will have literally struggled against her all my life long.

Only, here's the thing, the final touch. By letting her go—out of pride, or dignity, or lassitude, or out of love—I stripped myself of any possibility of withdrawal. Like my mother who, in childbirth, refused to cry out; she bit her sheets instead and everyone admired her courage. The only trouble is, she lost almost all her teeth that way.

I reread these pages. God, how long-drawn-out and "psychological" they are! Everything I hate in literature! And how I also hate the way it's all broken down into scattered paragraphs! But how can I link them? What else could I say that wouldn't make them even more obscure? I just don't have the courage to bring in "the little true-to-life touches." What I should be able to do is choose in terms of one clear idea of the whole and that I don't have. I just can't manage it.

Note about the *Treatise on Marriage* . . . When I refer to books that my readers are not acquainted with, I'm talking, of course, about books that haven't been published yet, or sometimes even about things that have not yet been written. At the end of my life, all the stones will be put into place, in their true order, and finally the whole edifice will be apparent. Then people will see just how carefully every part of it is fitted into the rest; nothing loose anywhere.

That last note is so annoying! It ruins everything. Why do a pirouette like that, just as I was feeling so touched, so close to you? Imilio, what game are you playing at? Why do you keep insisting you're not playing? Who's accusing you?

I'd gladly send these pages to Marie, for the words of love in them, but they would also bring home to her just how irremediable it all was. I don't find them either long-drawn-out or boring, but very moving, on the contrary.

But that doesn't mean I understand much more this time than I'd understood of *The Foreign Woman.* What's this Revelation that he's supposed to have had the first time he went to his wife's country? and that's supposed to have recurred since then? I told Emile some time ago what I thought. If they had such an excessive amount of trouble, it was more likely due to incompatibility of character. I know a lot of mixed marriages that are very happy.

A "psychotic" came in this morning, about a vague pain of some sort, a twinge or a burning feeling; he wasn't very sure. Should he change glasses? Or try dark lenses? I gave him a complete examination—nothing wrong, and his present prescription is fine. Seeing that I was about to send him away, he broke down, and finally, suffering, he told me he was "betrayed by his eyes," he didn't know where he should make them look or, rather, how to prevent them from looking anywhere they liked, because his eyes always went where he didn't want them to, "where it wasn't proper for them to go," and so he was terribly embarrassed in public. "I can't very well put my eyes in my pocket! Or scratch them out so as not to see any more! "

That wasn't my department any more. I managed to convince him to go see Niel.

The Bird

As for what happened after that, you can guess, you know it already, you've been told about it—who hasn't talked about it? But what's not true I've already told you, Doctor. It's not true that I didn't love my father. I loved him right up until the end, right up to the moment when, for the first time in my life, he looked at me differently and for the first time he backed away from me stammering, "I'm your father!" and then he turned and began to run ahead of me and shout, "Help! My son has gone crazy!" At that moment I felt something else for him—I can't tell you what it was, but it was too late, I couldn't go back by then, and he was still running ahead of me with his head thrown back and the Adam's apple sticking out and his eyes bulging, LIKE A BIRD. . . .

. . . I was playing in the courtyard of the Oukala. I was heartsick but casual at the same time the way only children can be casual even in the face of death. All the while I was jumping and marking points, I was on the look-out for my father. Did he already know? (There'd been that business about the bowl. I'll tell you about it later, if you want.) But even so I didn't see his coming, and when I heard him shout, in the midst of everyone there, it gave me a start. "That's it, play it while you can, because, in a little while, bastinado on the soles of the feet!"

That was the punishment, and the worst, the most humiliating kind. I had to take off my shoes and lie down on the sofa all by myself because, if I had resisted, I'd have received twice as many strokes, and all over the body too; then I had to wait with my feet up in the air until my father had given them their ration of strokes. So he'd been told about the whole business. So in a little while, my father would seize one foot after the other and hit it with a big square ruler that would hurt terribly because of the sharp edges. And since he gets all excited and tired after a minute, he strikes faster and faster, harder and harder, and he blames me for his being tired, as if I had insisted that he beat me, and at the end he's panting and cursing me with rage, and that hurts me more than the strokes he gives me. "May death take you! May God wipe you off the earth! You exhaust me! If you do it again, I'll break your head against the wall." At last he stops and I go sit on the floor in the corner (I can't stand up because my feet are burning and swollen) and cry.

When they heard what punishment was in store for me, the women looked at me pityingly and the children stopped playing and began to clap their hands in rhythm and all chant together,

Bina! Bina!	Bina! Bina!
Triha! Triha!	A licking! A licking!
Saqueq!	Your feet
Yeharqueq!	Will be pricking!

Then I ran toward the bedroom, throwing myself straight into the lion's jaws. But my father still had things to do outdoors. "Are you in such a big hurry?" he asked me. "Don't worry, you'll get what's coming to you."

But I went to the bedroom anyhow because I couldn't bear to hear what the children were singing or see the way the women were looking at me. The children were still chanting and beating time with their hands and their joy was audible through the walls. I'd gladly have taken them one by one and taken out an eye here, torn off an arm there and the leg of still another, the way you do with flies. I drifted around the room, furiously kicking the sofa, the laundry basket, even the wall, so that the whitewash flaked off from it. The door opened; I rushed toward it. No, it was Noucha, who had come to cheer me up. She offered to play with me.

"Leave me, girl," I said disdainfully, and spat toward the mirror.

It was then that I noticed the birdcage-trap. There were two birds inside, as it happened; usually I ate the second one some time during the day. My aunt had given me that cage in return for an errand I'd done for her. It had two compartments: in the lower one you put a bird and in the upper one a lure of some sort. Attracted by the captive bird, other birds come to eat the bait and the door of the cage closes on them. That way I eat the older of the two boarders and keep the new one, and so on. This one—luckily for him—was a nasty little thing; he was scrawny and his neck didn't have any feathers. He disgusted me a little and that's why I didn't eat him right away but instead used him several times without being able to bring myself to sacrifice him.

The idea occurred to me right away. I put my hand into the cage. The bird struggled a bit but it was a very small cage and he had no chance of escaping. I just opened my fingers and closed them down around him like a net. I could feel him, alive and warm, in the hollow of my hand and I thought, all it would take is just a slight squeeze and that would be enough to choke him. Only his tiny head stuck out and he kept turning that head this way and that to look at me, terrified, first with one eye and then with the other. But that's not what my idea was. Nouch', who was all excited too, was jumping up and down. "Oooh! Oooh! What are you going to do?"

"You'll see, girl."

I held the bird under the wings, like that, the way you hold on to a chicken to keep it from moving or flying away. It was hard because I didn't have much room, but my hands were smaller in those days. Then I tipped his head back onto his wings, the way I'd seen the chicken-slaughterer do, and with the thumb and index finger of the same hand that was holding on under the wings I tried to seize his crest. That was even harder, because he had a tiny little crest, but my fingers were tiny too. He was more and more terrified and jerked his head right and left, which complicated things for me. Maybe he was beginning to realize what I was going to do to him. Finally I managed to get a firm hold on enough skin, with those two fingers, to immobilize his head. That way, his neck was exposed and when I squeezed, his eyes were covered completely by the drawn eyelids. Then at last he tucked his feet under him and stopped moving. He looked as though he was already dead, or resigned.

I took my knife and held it open in the other hand, an old penknife, with the blade broken right in the middle. It didn't have any cutting edge any more but I could still use it to whittle wood and make holes for marbles. Suddenly I remembered that there was still something else to be done. So I placed the knife between my teeth with the edge outward; that was the way the slaughterer did—he put the knife in his mouth so as to have his hands free again. Carefully, I plucked the taut little neck; it was pink and blue underneath. Then I held onto my knife again and ran the blade along the nail of the thumb that was holding the bird, right near his throat. My knife didn't need to be checked that way, but it was part of the job.

Horrified and maybe delighted too, Noucha hugs her cheeks in her hands and tries to look away but she can't. She jumps up and down and squeals.

"Oooh! Oooh! What are you going to do, Bina, what are you going to do?"

At that point, I don't know whether I still want to go on but I'm proud of seeing the way Noucha is beside herself and her eyes bulge out. I guess I feel a little bit sick. My hand trembles but I draw the knife across his throat—once, twice. Right away, I let go of him.

Now, the bird isn't quite dead. I haven't done my job right. Instead of dropping to the floor like a stone, he begins to fly around the room. He strikes his head frantically against the wall. His little skull hits it hard and taps sharply against the whitewash each time. Minute drops of blood fall wherever he goes, as if announcing a rain of blood.

After a while he finds the window, flies out clumsily and disappears. I don't know whether he went and died farther away.

I felt very relieved at not seeing him fly around the room any more, above our heads, with his throat open and that blood falling from it like dew, but, in spite of everything, I wasn't sorry.

When my father came back he didn't understand at first what had happened. Since I refused to answer, he questioned Noucha, who told him everything. Then, strangely, he didn't say anything; his face went pale the way it does when he is furious but I sensed that it wasn't anger that made it pale. His nostrils were not flared but pinched, and he kept turning his head back and forth, something like the bird in my hand a little while ago. At last he said to me, but without raising his voice this time:

"Go take your shoes off and lie down on the sofa."

I got my licking, of course, and the children chanted all over again, but that didn't matter, because I'd already gotten back at him.

"No, I'm not sorry about anything. You'd like me to say that I was wrong, I'd lost my head. No. No, Doctor, I wasn't crazy. I'm going to tell you something else. If I began to be sorry, if I wasn't convinced that what I did, I did purposely, then that would mean

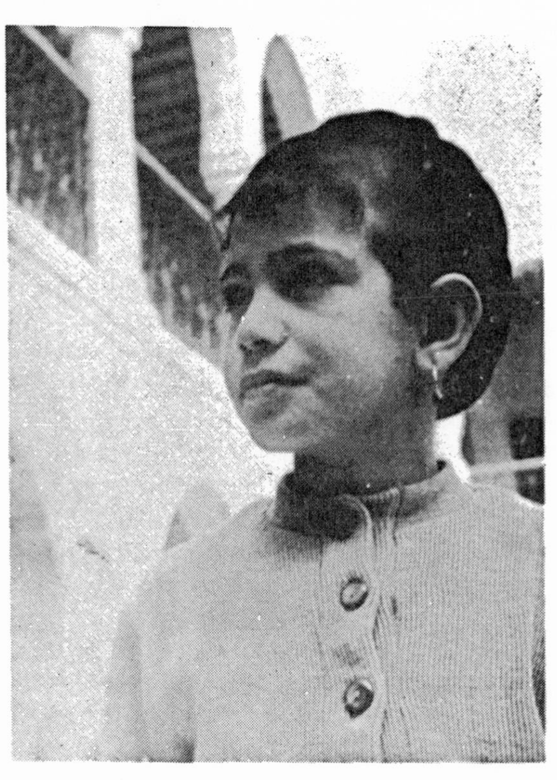

that what I did doesn't count, nothing's changed. But that's just it: things had to change.

"Afterwards, maybe I lost my head, but while I was doing it no, I swear to you, I knew perfectly well what I was doing. Never, not even when I grabbed the scissors, when I rushed at my father, not even while . . . never at any time did I tell myself I mustn't do it, not even when he was running ahead of me with his head thrown back and the Adam's apple sticking out, LIKE A BIRD.

"And I was chasing him
And he was losing blood and yelling
And I was chasing him oh! I was chasing him

"Tell me the story of the bowl, Bina," the doctor said gently. "Forget your father. You promised me you'd tell me the story. Tell me."

"No, Doctor, I can't, not today, that's enough for this time. . . . Afterwards they kept me in the hospital for two months and I don't remember much any more, I must say. In fact that's why they acquitted me. Doctor Niel told the court that my sister wasn't very sound either, and that we hadn't had a mother and above all, he said, he was sure I would never do it again. Which is certainly true; why would I? So I was acquitted. But I swear to you I wasn't the least bit out of my mind when I did what I did. It had been coming for a long time. I had to do it."

All right, so it was our father's sickness that made me decide to be an eye specialist. I was still wondering what I should specialize in when I received the letter announcing that our father had a glaucoma. Then, a few days later, an extraordinary coincidence—I really got to know Dr. Cuénot, my future supervisor. I'd just come back from vacation. In the summertime, I forgot everything; I played soccer, went swimming, and spent all my time in the sun. When I got back to college, I was black as a Negro. At the end of a lecture, I asked Cuénot a question, and he marveled at the color of my skin. Where did I come from? Who was I? I introduced myself. His eyes gleamed with a mixture of goodness and the scientific interest of a scholar.

"Go into ophthalmology, my boy! You'll be helping your country! Think of trachoma!"

From then on, he would remind me of it every time he ran

into me in the hall. "Don't forget trachoma!" he would say anxiously, persuasively.

He said trachoma, and I heard glaucoma. So I went into ophthalmology for this poor country's sake, it's true, but especially for our father's sake.

I couldn't do anything more for him, and I wasn't looking for thanks. But Emile wasn't wrong. Each of us did try to get back at our father and get rid of him as best he could.

The day before I went away on vacation for the first time—I had just gotten married and was very proud to go away with a pretty wife, and my doctor's degree in my pocket—he sent for me. Acting very mysterious, he placed several ancient silver coins from this country in my hand. Coming from him, at least, it was quite a present, worth a lot, in sentiment and in money too. He had received this treasure from his own father and had completed the collection. I couldn't see why he was suddenly making me a present of it, but he didn't say anything and I didn't ask any questions.

The day after we arrived at the Lido in Venice, I caught a bad throat infection that kept me in bed for several days. I couldn't help thinking about those coins again. Had he been trying to give me my share of an inheritance? In any case, I had found it strangely unpleasant.

When we came back home, I looked everywhere in our luggage for that tainted present and couldn't find it. I wasn't sorry, even though they were beautiful coins.

I've been mistaken again. Perhaps, in the long run, what Imilio is undertaking is an effort to restore health.

Uncle Makhlouf—3

(Project Concerning Colors, for Uncle Makhlouf's Benefit)

After Uncle has served me coffee, I'll ask him, as natural as anything:

"Uncle Makhlouf, can you tell me again what will happen when the Messiah comes?"

He will look eager and for a minute he'll stop making his great wheel turn.

"When the Messiah comes, all the people will be gathered on the land of Canaan. Then a great feast will be held, where the female of the Leviathan and the male Behemoth will be eaten.

"For as fish will be served the female of the Leviathan himself, who, as we know, is so big that he can swallow another fish weighing several hundred pounds, that the waters of the earth could be carried on his back, and that once the Eternal had created the Leviathan and his female, he realized that all creation would be endangered by the multiplication of these monsters. That is why God decided to kill the female and salt her away to keep until the feast of the Messiah.

"As meat will be served the flesh of the bull Behemoth who, as we know, is so enormous that each day he eats the hay of a thousand mountains, and that once the Eternal had created Behemoth and his female, he realized that all creation would be endangered by the multiplication of these monsters. That is why God decided to kill the female. . . . But be careful! It is said that God did not salt the female of Behemoth."

"Why not her too? Why only the female of the Leviathan?"

"Because salt meat might not be good to eat, especially after such a long time—at any rate, not as good as salt fish, and unworthy of a meal to celebrate the coming of the Messiah.

"That is why it is said that at the feast of the Messiah, the female Leviathan and the male Behemoth will be eaten. . . ."

I'll let Uncle talk all he wants and then I'll say:

"All that isn't written, is it, Uncle?"

That's when he'll take a different tone. He'll stop floating in delicious revery and talking in time with the turning wheel. He will become precise and a little bit solemn. His face will be that of a wise man.

"No, it is only said. This is what is written:

> "Say to the daughter of Zion,
> Now your savior has come.
> Now wages are with Him
> And retribution goes before Him."

Finally, I will ask him,

"How do you *interpret* that? Do wages and retribution mean material possessions only? or especially? Should we understand that the only good to come out of the coming of the Messiah will be the pleasures of the Feast?"

Then Uncle will patiently explain to me that no, that isn't what it means. He will quote from several interpretations of several Sages who emphasize quite the contrary, the moral and spiritual significance of the event. The Messiah means the reign of peace, for all men on earth. . . .

Only then, at last, will I come to my System—oh, so indirectly! so prudently, at first.

"The exciting thing," I'll say, "is the way your tone of voice and your face change depending on whether you're telling me about the Feast of the Messiah or quoting the Bible or giving me the interpretations. That look of rejoicing you have when you describe the details of this monumental meal. . . ."

"That is because the moment of the Haggadah is not the moment of the Halakah."

"That's just what I mean, Uncle. But how would you express that look of yours, the one that shows me, because I am looking at you, that you are rejoicing as you talk? Or the way your voice sounds so happy and reveals your joy to me, because I am listening to you? None of that can be expressed in writing."

Then, finally, finally I will suggest the system of colors to him. Wouldn't it be convenient to color a passage from the Haggadah differently from a passage from the Halakah or a passage from the book of Chronicles? The rose color used for the Halakah would be the equivalent of the dreamy-smile tone. The black or gray of the book of Chronicles would be the sign of seriousness, the way your voice goes neutral when you are listing facts. And isn't it obvious that when you are interpreting, offering a meditation on something, or arguing, then you need still another color?

But this roundabout way may not turn out to be the best way with Uncle. If he discovers what I'm up to, the discussion will be ended immediately and I'll have to wait some more and begin all over again the following week.

Another tactic: start with a problem. That always interests him. A question like: what is Prophecy?

"Arise, go to Nineveh, that great city, and cry against it; for their wickedness is come up before me."

In this way God orders Jonah to go and announce to the people of Nineveh that he is going to destroy their city.

Obviously this is not a Chronicle since these are facts that are yet to come; they're not true yet. In fact they are so far from being true facts as yet that Jonah refuses to obey. Far from going to Nineveh, he does the opposite:

"But Jonah rose up to flee unto Tarshish from the presence of the Lord, and went down to Joppa: and he found a ship going to Tarshish: so he paid the fare thereof and went down into it. . . ."

Is it fiction then? No, not at all, because the prophet will be obliged to go to Nineveh against his will:

"But the Lord sent out a great wind into the sea, and there was a mighty tempest in the sea, so that the ship was like to be broken. Then the mariners were afraid . . . so they took up Jonah, and cast him forth into the sea. . . . Now the Lord had prepared a great fish to swallow up Jonah. . . ."

Thus, what was predicted comes to pass. Jonah is vomited out by the fish and goes to speak to the people of Nineveh, as God wishes him to do. So, prophecy is a *foreseeing*. It comes true later; it is not true immediately.

At this point, Uncle will probably think he is winning and will use the same arguments as the last time.

"You see, the uncertainty is within yourself, because you do not see the whole; for you, there is a before and an after. But the Lord has already foreseen everything, even Jonah's hesitation and his submission. Prophecy is *already* truth."

But this time it is I who will win once and for all.

"No, dear Uncle, that's just it. God changes his mind. At the last moment he decides not to destroy Nineveh. That is what angers Jonah. You see? You have to make a distinction between what is prophesied and what is done, not out of impertinence to God but precisely because we human beings cannot penetrate the veritable intentions of the Lord."

That will be my secret weapon.

That way, without seeming to at all, I will at least have forced him to recognize that there is a problem—there are degrees and shades of truth. How can you make allowance for them?

Now, I have an idea (I will go on to say carelessly) that would make it possible to express the degrees of truth. Oh, it's a very modest idea! just a matter of technique really (emphasize that, avoid upsetting Uncle once again) that leaves the Text completely intact. After all the idea is to express the Text better because, after all, the truth is the truth.

Now of course it is often impossible to separate the different levels within life, and even within thought. And as a matter of fact, I don't want to separate them, far from it: the separation makes me suffer. I simply want to *distinguish* between them. And in order to do that, wouldn't it be a good thing to choose a few additional signs that would make it possible to render the Texts in their infinite richness? Besides, aren't the typographical arrangements that Uncle is used to already an effort in that direction? Etc., etc. . . .

Then and only then, if I haven't run aground by that time, will I explain my idea in detail.

And what if I fail—I mean, fail once and for all? No, that's not possible . . . I'd rather not think about it. If I do fail, what shall I do? Begin over and over again. I have to. I must manage to straighten things out. What makes Uncle so tough is that he expects help from the outside; that's what he's offering me all the time, like M., when you come right down to it. As far as I'm concerned, that would be dodging the issue. I don't expect anything from anyone, not even from God, if he exists.

Why didn't I realize that earlier? Why didn't I guess what Emile was getting at, above and beyond that demonstration to Uncle? Now it's clear that he wasn't just trying to persuade Uncle, and it wasn't just the Haggadah and the Halakah that were involved. The whole thing is a code that's valid for Emile too. The idea had already vaguely crossed my mind; I wondered why he changed ink so often—he seemed to be dipping his pen first in one inkwell and then in another. Now I feel certain those different colors are not just a matter of chance.

Maybe that's the end of my difficulties. I'm going to reread a few pages in the light of that particular lamp.

Besides, it appeals to me, as a game.

I'm also delighted to see Emile get the better of Uncle, but—careful! He does it only in his imagination—in other words, in rose?

So, a distinction to be made between:

The book of Chronicles
The Haggadah
The Halakah

CHRONICLES	HAGGADAH	HALAKAH
Every shade and degree of *ascertained truth* = *facts*	All the embroidery of *imagination* = *fiction*	All the *Commentaries* = meditation
Past facts = History Present facts = experience, science	Starting with truth = Apologues Pure fiction = from anecdotes to legends	From *Opinion* down to *Decision*
(e.g.: Kings) Color: BLACK	(e.g.: hassidism) Color: ROSE	(e.g.: Haskala) Color: PURPLE (Here of course one color is not enough, the views are so divergent. E.g.: a vow = green?)

Baïsa

People come to the shop to tell me how sorry they are, only two months later, as if nothing had happened. I listen to them soberly, with the dignity of a son who has lost his father, and not once has any of them dared to judge the matter in any other light.

Every morning I get up at half past five so as to be at the shop by half past six; it's not so difficult when you're your own boss. I am the boss now, and I must set an example for Baïsa. The first day he asked me:

"What time tomorrow?"

I answered:

"Seven, as usual."

The next day, at seven o'clock, he was not there. I sat down in the boss's seat and right away I began to work. The first few days, I hadn't wanted to occupy my father's empty chair; but then I had to concede that it was the best place for keeping an eye on my workman. I looked at the time again; it was already half past seven and Baïsa still wasn't there. I went and hung my watch on the nail where my father hung his because, that way, you don't have to pull it out of your fob pocket every time. That was when I noticed that I had trouble making out the hands of it at that distance. I suppose the eyes get into bad habits from staring at the leather and the thread so closely.

Baïsa arrived at eight o'clock, with his eyes still red and his eyebrows all bushy.

"Sleep deceived me," he said. "You can understand that."

His knowing smile angered me more than his lateness did. I didn't answer. Baïsa took off his coat, folded it inside out and wrapped it up in a bit of clean burlap. Then he put on his beret and his old work jacket and at last he sat down. He cracked his knuckles, then asked:

"Has the coffee man been by?"

"Yes," I said abruptly.

Baïsa got up again.

"I've got to have my coffee, otherwise what happened to my uncle will happen to me," he said jokingly. "Know what happened to my uncle?"

"That's enough," I said, "you've wasted enough time. You'll wait till he comes by again."

He looked at me, hesitating.

"What? I can't roll my cigarette? We're in prison? You're joking?"

I didn't answer. He sat down and went on grumbling.

"That's life for you. The son acts worse than the father! Not once in twenty years did your father (God keep his soul) keep me from having my coffee!"

I was a little ashamed; Baïsa was my father's age, he'd known me ever since I was a baby. But I was the boss. Just then, luckily for both of us, the coffee man came down the street again. Baïsa hailed him immediately.

"Ah, that's good, I won't do what my uncle did! What about you, do you want a coffee?"

Usually I didn't have any, but it was cold and I wanted one, and most of all I had a feeling I ought to say yes.

"Well then, two coffees, as usual!" Baïsa ordered.

We had our coffee, and Baïsa rolled a cigarette and licked it carefully before lighting it.

"I'm going to tell you what happened to my uncle. . . ."

I had to listen to him, annoyed though I was. He didn't have any responsibilities, of course. The work needed doing urgently; we were already very far behind and new orders were likely to come in. Also I had to go to Bodineau's and order more supplies. I won't have time for music for a long time; the only advantage is, I'll be able to buy a new lute; anyhow I don't want to play at family celebrations any more, it wouldn't be worthy of a man who's his own boss. Just at that point in my thoughts, Baïsa cut in with:

"Yesterday, at Mazouz' place . . ."

"Shut up, phonograph!"

It just slipped out—I didn't mean to, I didn't want to offend him. But he got angry.

"The little rat! Look how he gives himself a long tail and great big whiskers! He hopes people will take him for a lion!"

That was too much. Immediately I said what had to be said.

"Baïsa, if it doesn't suit you here, you can look somewhere else."

He was taken aback. He sighed.

"You were just waiting for your father to die to show how mean you could be."

Finally he stopped talking and we worked in silence. About eleven o'clock, Qatoussa went by and signaled to me without stopping. I knew at a glance where he was going: he was shaven and combed, and he had a bouquet of jasmine over each ear. I called to him. He came, but reluctantly; maybe he was embarrassed because I was in mourning. I stepped out into the street so that Baïsa couldn't hear.

"Listen, Qatoussa, I need you."

He didn't understand.

"Well, the thing is . . . I'm busy."

"I know it, I know it! You think I'm blind? I see where you're going all right. That's just it: can you wait till noon? I'd like to go with you."

He smiled, a big friendly grin.

"Sure, sure! You're a man now. I'll wait for you till evening if I have to."

"No," I said, "I don't want to wait any longer. Only, come back at noon. I can't leave Baïsa alone. At noon he'll go and have lunch and I'll close up the shop."

At noon on the dot, Baïsa began to get restless on his chair. I was glad to see he hadn't dared get up by himself. I sent him out to lunch because I didn't want him to see Qatoussa again. A minute later my friend arrived and we went to the rue Baian together. He led me to the door of a Moorish woman dressed as a Spanish lady.

"This is Carmen. She'll be very nice to you, won't you, Carmen?" And for the woman's benefit, he added, "You're lucky. I'm giving you a real virgin."

That wasn't quite true, because of Kakoucha, but it wasn't completely wrong either. I went into the little cell, and I did what I had to do, and I could. And I wasn't even surprised; I knew I could.

That afternoon, Ghozala's father, Hmainou, also came to see me to express his sympathies.

"So, now you're the boss."

"Yes, I'm the boss."

He stood hesitantly on the threshold.

"You know, Ghozala—Ghozala's very sad about what happened, and she's been wondering . . ."

"Ghozala's a woman," I said, "and women have to learn not to talk too much."

"I know, my son; I told her so at the time, heaven is my witness. I defended you like my son."

"I'm not anybody's son. I don't have a father any more."

"Do as you like," he said, "do as you like."

"Yes, I'll do as I like. I can, now."

"Yes, you can."

"Well then, leave me alone, and let me think."

"I'm leaving you alone."

And he left, filled with anxiety. But I didn't feel like giving him any more reassurance than that, not him nor Ghozala either. First I have to take care of the shop; one thing at a time. I'll also have to see Menana, the matchmaker, again about Noucha. I'll ask her to sound out Moumou's father discreetly even though I reproach Moumou a little for not having tried to overcome my father's veto—that seems to show that he wasn't much of a man. But I have to do it for Noucha's sake, for her health, because I'm her big brother, her father almost.

(Every Saturday, even in winter, he takes Noucha out for a walk, usually along the beach. In winter it's even better; there isn't anybody, and the humidity and the grayness of the sky don't bother them—on the contrary. They love everything about the sea, always have, since they were children.

He gives her his arm so that she won't stumble over the dikes that hold in the sand, and slowly they walk along the edge of the water. Somebody seeing them from a distance might take them for two lovers. In fun, and with extravagant gestures, he gives her mock princely presents—glass pebbles, cuttle-bones, bits of wood that the water has worked into bizarre shapes, or those pieces of tar-stained agglomerated cork that are used to protect the ropes of boats and that condense all their smells—salt, iodine, rotting seaweed, caulking tar—surprisingly into so small a volume. And so he manages to make her smile a little, but such a poor little smile that it breaks his heart. But he hopes that in time she will become well again and then she will be willing to let herself be married.)

Then it was twilight, and suddenly night.

"Baïsa," I ordered, "light the lamp."

Baïsa puts down his work, stands up, stretches his long arms, and then takes down the heavy oil lamp that hangs from the ceiling.

"Aha! The glass is dirty. If I don't wipe it, it'll smoke."

He goes to get a rag. From where I am sitting I can't tell whether the glass is really dirty. It's true, I don't see very well from a distance any more. I take my father's metal-rimmed glasses and slip them onto my nose: I knew it! Baïsa never misses a chance to dawdle; the glass isn't all that dirty.

Holding the glass between his knees, Baïsa wipes it endlessly with the rag; then he turns it inside out and goes on making that to-and-fro movement. My father was right. Tomorrow I'll have it out with him once and for all. If he continues, I'll fire him and take on a younger worker; no, a helper, not a workman. It's hard to make a man obey when he's older than you are. A helper will work more than Baïsa does and will demand less, without arguing.

Baïsa still hasn't finished cleaning that stupid glass.

"Give me that," I said, "it'll be closing time and you still won't be done."

"Lord, I was afraid!" he said, raising his head. "I thought I was seeing your father all of a sudden. Did you know that once . . ."

"Tell me about it tomorrow," I cut him off, "that is, if you can be here at seven sharp."

But he was not wrong because, as I was saying that to him, I had a strange feeling myself: I seemed to recognize the voice of my father in my own voice.

What color? Rose, of course.

Now I can't help asking myself that question with every passage I read. The results are amazing. It's not just a game.

A newspaper article, a politician's speech, all on the same page—it would take a rainbow! What a demystification!

This morning I wired to Marie-Suzanne, who's spending a few days at Ain-Draham with the children, "I love you in red."

Our Mother

(Additional Notes)

I haven't been fair to our father. "How did she manage to live with him for forty years?" Might better say, how did he manage to live with her for forty years? He must have really needed her help! The most astonishing thing about it is that he wasn't destroyed earlier—although, when you think of what was left of him . . . Blindness, asthma, fits of anxiety that made him choke and then, the finishing touches (in every way)—the discovery of drugs and that state of stupefaction continually bludgeoning the blood vessels in the brain until they ruptured, hemiplegia and that horrible death rattle that went on for two days and nights, not quite unconscious, convulsively, gratefully squeezing the hand that was left in his.

When it was her turn to become ill, and seriously ill, with Parkinson's disease, what happened? By some miracle or other, instead of collapsing and growing ugly and old, she began to get younger, I swear she did! She even began to lose the few wrinkles she had and so her forehead was smooth again, her cheeks and temples intact, her eyes dizzying, of course; and those lips that didn't even need to change, because her mouth had always been a little tight but large, full and red. And so for all time, she bequeathed us her face as it had looked at twenty. It was already familiar to us from some photographs taken at the time of her marriage, when she wasn't quite a child any longer and yet not quite a woman.

Or when, with the muscles of the larynx already affected, and despite the tremendous effort it put her to, she began to call, desperately, insistently, for henna, first of all, for her palms and the soles of her feet, then for cloves, and fennel, and even kohl for her eyes—recalling, summing up her entire universe, and mine! I couldn't understand her, not because the "shushing" sound of her voice was hardly audible by then but because I could no longer guess the movement of her lips, and the words she spoke awoke only a fainter and fainter echo in me. She was a hardy plant stubbornly defending its own poor life. At last she would become childishly furious with me and the whole world and herself, and finally with her tiny hand that was already so close to being skeletal, she would slap herself in rage.

That was before the day when the sea became hostile to me, for it happened one day that I, I of all people! grew afraid of the sea, afraid to go into it alone, afraid to feel its heavy swell beneath my feet, and then I couldn't sleep any more on the wide-spaced plank floor of the *ritounda,** especially at night, when you couldn't make out the sea at all—a blurred beast, eternally sleepless, barely drowsing, daydreaming, moaning, slapping the stilts holding up the hut that it barely tolerates and could carry away with one shrug if it suddenly took a whim to.

The veritable haunt of Lilith
Is in the depths of the sea

What would have become of us without her? But what became of us with her! Her way of waiting up on the balcony—without sleeping (or so she said; can it have been true?), sitting on an uncomfortable chair, not even a chaise longue, as if she wanted to add to her own misery—every single time we were late coming in, from the time we began to go out until we had left home for good; which spoiled all our evenings and made us cut them short, bothered by the idea that she was waiting up on that balcony of hers, waiting in the cold, drowsing on her chair; and the same nonsense began all over again as soon as we had come back from a trip, and our protests ("You don't mean to say that you waited up all night when I was thousands of miles away!") fell on a deaf ear. Thousands of miles didn't mean a thing to her; she'd never been farther away than La Goulette, a distance of ten miles. Beyond La Goulette, I imagine she went to sleep, as the rite would have no more effect. Result? Jacquot can't travel anywhere or even go out in the street without being accompanied. And Kalla, Kalla! And what about myself? I do hate traveling. . . .

What would have become of us without her? We'd have become normal people, maybe.

*** Platform built on stilts directly over the water (publisher's note).**

At first I listened to him tenderly and marveled.

The women in our country are very good mothers. They are never reluctant about giving. I saw Tuma, who had a baby of her own, suckle Aldinga, a child of five who had eaten canned meat and jam all day long in our kitchen. No woman will refuse her milk to a child, or even just her breast for him to play with. That is why not only is frustration unknown but, even more important, the child begins his life in a happy state of collective mothering.

Then, in the same voice, he added:

Yet these very good mothers eat their children—every other one. Even a child Aldinga's age could be eaten. The mothers kill the youngest ones and the fathers, the bigger ones. The father hits the child on the head, then steps away; then he comes back and hits him again until he dies, and finally he gives him to the mother. For it is interesting to note that the fathers do not eat the children. It is only the women who feast on them. They even give each other presents, exchanging the cooked flesh of their respective children. It would appear that the fathers kill out of obedience to a principle, while the women do so because they are hungry, and, specifically, because they are hungry for the meat of babies.

Sea, mother, manifold, voracious sea-mother.

Shall I describe that horrible evening when we were awakened to do immediate battle with the monster? The attacking sea—tentacular, countless, unaccountably furious—right up to the thresholds of the houses for a century in my childish memory, two nights and two days when we all had to fight and fight without stopping. Brooms, pails, towels . . . ah, how laughable we were, compared with the sea! How can the Dutch live all their lives long behind those dikes, knowing that the beast hurls itself heavily against them?

One day I overdid my playing with the sea and became literally lost in it; all my landmarks were jumbled and in the even half-light, I didn't know where the sky ended and death began.

What I have described in *The Foreign Woman* is false. I let her go without making a scene or putting up any resistance. She did not slap me, I did not slap her back; she was not pregnant and had not decided to get an abortion. I dramatized the situation because I was afraid the reader would not understand the way the heroes behaved. It wasn't exactly a lie. So many couples all around us were really destroying, killing one another! But in our own case, nothing happened, nothing at all. Nothing but an impossibility—the terrible, intense fear I felt, my panic on discovering that I could no longer solve the problem of her existence within my own, that I would never be able to solve it.

The enemy was within the walls. I had appealed to him for help against my own people, and now I couldn't tolerate those occupying troops any longer.

The only scene that is true is the one by the lake, where the oleanders were stiff with dust. But she didn't say those horrible things to me that I said she did; she did not hurl "Coward!" at me as her last word. Her last words, which she murmured in a voice so neutral that I hardly heard it and it seemed to be as much a complaint as a reproach, were:

"I am not your mother."

As he runs after his father, Bina shouts with rage:

"Kalla, Kalla, what about Kalla!"

"It was your mother who sent me to the ruins, I swear it was! She sent me there!"

I was so dumbfounded I nearly stopped still, and my anger would have gone out of me if I hadn't said to myself, He's lying! Lying to save his life! But later on I often thought of what he'd said. What if he wasn't lying? What if it was our mother who was guilty?

Those pages have obviously been put in the wrong places. Maybe I did it? Are they more of the chapter on "The Father"? Or a version that was rejected? Up until now, I had the impression that Bina's mother had died in childbirth, and, also, Bina's sister was called Noucha. Confusion with Kalla?

To tell the truth, I'm beginning to wonder if any of that matters at all; maybe what seems to be disorderliness really comes from the fact that I don't know the rules of the game, rules of life really —Emile's methodical attempt (yes, I mean methodical) to put his thoughts in order. Maybe this disorder is the order that my brother wanted.

And that photograph of our mother! Only two days ago, if I hadn't read that "project concerning colors," I'd have reacted differently. I'd have said to myself, "Now what's this all about? It's a fine photograph, all right, but it's just more showing-off. I knew about that picture too, and I've been told the story of it any number of times."

The only true thing in it is our mother's beauty—the beauty of a wild doll, compared with the mediocre plainness of her sisters—and perhaps Imilio, who was in her womb, because the fact is she was pregnant, which explains the water-jug (to hide her stomach). The photograph, taken in Bedouin clothing, was the whim of a pregnant woman. Nobody dressed that way any more. Possibly her grandfather still wore the jebba and the cedria, and, even so, he sometimes borrowed his son's jackets. These sumptuous clothes must have belonged to the photographer, and he lent them to his clients.

Why show this photograph as being typical of our mother? Isn't that a way of distorting the truth, by stretching it in one direction, especially a direction that became less familiar to us every day and (why not say it?) that we liked least of all?

But I'm just beginning to understand Emile, by seeing through his plot.

I could add something myself, for that matter.

One day our mother questioned Imilio. She put on that fake air of complicity which, she thought, would allow her to elicit the type of confession that no one ever makes to anyone, and, paradoxically, she did it in front of everyone, as if all she had to do was lower her voice and there would be an impenetrable wall separating herself from all the others.

"But Imilio, my son, tell me the truth. Why did you marry a foreign woman?"

This was a question of such gravity for him, and for us as well, that no one had dared to ask him even indirectly. To my amazement, he answered without hesitating and did it so seriously, uttering something so absurd, that for an instant I had the impression they were both clowns.

"Because foreign women don't get big behinds after they've been married a year."

Whereupon our mother, still whispering but perfectly audible to everyone, answered:

"You are wrong, my son. Women who have big behinds have clear souls." Then, sighing unexpectedly and slapping her own behind, she added, "I'm not talking about myself. Mine's practically empty—I'm like your wife."

Emile smiled at last.

"Yes, Mother, you're outdoing yourself today: you've just spoken two truths in one."

Then there was the grandmother who was paralyzed and had been living in the warmth of her bed for thirty years, rising like yeast, floating above the bed, above the room itself, that she had not left once in all those thirty years. She gave us fabulous imaginary presents: "Here, hold out your hand; this is for you." And we children had to pretend we were dazzled, when that faded hand dropped emptiness onto our open hands.

But however that may be, I still don't see why he had to inflict Parkinson's disease on our poor mother, because of course she never had that awful disease, not any more than our father is already dead. Unless Emile was captivated by the picture of our mother at twenty. But that business about slapping herself is plausible. She must have done that from time to time, half angry and half putting on an act.

What an enormous distance there is between women and ourselves in this poor country. They still belong to the "Dark Ages," while we are being violently pulled toward . . . toward what?

Emile pretended to be frightened by it and I pretended to laugh about it. I took our mother for a puppet, and he took her for a witch. Which of us was right? Who is our mother?

Drugs

The sweetish, sugary smell begins to infiltrate everything. It becomes a permanent fixture—in the curtains, in the least little scrap of cloth, in the pieces of leather, where it mingles with the acrid smell of tannin, spreading in any nook or corner as soon as you open the door, as if someone had just come there to hide in the dark and smoke (which may be the case), maybe settling into the stone itself soon. It fits in with the atmosphere of the house, tall and skinny, so narrow at the bottom and so squeezed in by the other ramshackle houses that even though the light hits the terrace violently, the ground floor is humid and almost dark. I have no trouble believing that the *jinn* take hashish before playing their silly, cruel pranks. . . . (Let's stop this kind of literature, or else that big clot of a Marcel is going to scold me. But still, to use Niel's language, why couldn't the *jinn* be the subconscious?)

Mahmoud starts earlier and earlier. Before, he didn't smoke his first cigarette until after his nap, and he didn't even do it every day. The only time that I had to put up with his dazed look and his incredible absent-mindedness was at the evening meal; then he would go down to finish off his evening at Khemaïs' place, where he had a few last puffs. And at least then he did it in secret, avoiding my questions or begging off, feigning to advise me to smoke myself, to cure a toothache and the sorrows of the heart, or in order to work better, since that's all I care about, he says; and he's right.

Now, it's as if both of us had taken off our masks. As soon as he gets up he goes blissfully about the house; his eyes look toward some invisible horizon and his gestures are slow and fuzzy. When he's carrying a tray or any heavy object, I avoid calling him or speaking too loudly because I know that my voice will be magnified endlessly as it crosses the enormous void that drugs have created between the world and himself. And yet, inefficient as he is,

I find myself respecting him, handling that cheap happiness of his with caution. His work suffers from it, but is that really what annoys me? Why do I say "cheap"? What happiness isn't, for that matter? Does it depend on the means used and on how much it costs? I would pay more; so what? I'm already paying infinitely more, as a matter of fact! and am I any better off than he is?

I'd talked to Dr. Niel about it, since his servant also smokes. He advised me to go have a look at the rue du Foie, where the poorest people get their shots in doorways and the amount of liquid they have injected depends on the amount of money they've got; and there too, of course, like anywhere else, there's a racket, with the racketeers sometimes putting distilled water in the syringes or selling chalk for heroin. In this country, who doesn't smoke? Everybody—rich or poor, intellectuals or street porters—runs after those few rare moments of release; it's so understandable. Wouldn't any one of us, once he had discovered the drug that suited him, give himself over to it eagerly? All you have to do is pay the price—a hangover, or humiliation; there's no such thing as happiness free of charge. "Take even me," said Niel. "Now I like to drink . . . Oh, don't try to say it's not true. Everybody talks about it and I know it, don't you worry."

Certain Eskimos, who are too poor and too far away from civilization to obtain any of the known drugs, have discovered that they need only boil a certain sort of lichen and that gives them the kind of drink they're looking for. And not only that but they have also found that some of the strength of this peculiar tea is still intact even after the drinker has imbibed it for the first time, and that much of its virtue was still to be found in the urine. Since moreover this lichen was extremely rare and had to be used as sparingly as possible, it is easy to guess what came next: drinking bouts followed by urinating sessions.

Just imagine what it must be like. The men gather around a pot where the miraculous lichen is brewing. A cup is handed around and each man drinks in turn. Then they are still.

After a while, one of them gets up and goes to urinate in the pot, then another does the same, then another. Once everyone has had his turn, it's left to brew again. Then the cup is handed around once more, and so on.

After doing this three or four times, of course, they have to stop, because the urine tea doesn't have any narcotic qualities left. But the men don't need it any more. They're in a happy coma by that time.

That gave me an opportunity to answer Dr. Niel by outlining my little philosophy of drugs. Now, everybody takes drugs—rich or poor, intelligent or dumb. What does that prove? This is what it proves. That it's not ignorance, or the material sort of poverty that drives men to drink, smoke, or give themselves shots. The one thing that constitutes the grandeur and the originality of man is consciousness, and he finds his consciousness unbearable. So everyone chooses the drug that induces what he wants—euphoria, a dazed state, hallucinations—the way he wants it. Otherwise, no one could bear his own existence. My father didn't find any peace until he discovered those miracle drugs (that I have always turned my back on and continue to refuse to allow myself. How long will I keep that up? The world of inner harmony—the only one that makes the other world harmonious and bearable)—that very silent man discovering that other silence, the silence of death. I said to Dr. Niel: Isn't there something disturbing about the fact that man is the only creature in all of nature to get drunk and take drugs and stubbornly attempt to blunt the reflexes that he has acquired with so much difficulty through the centuries-long process of biological maturing? The only one to dull his senses, whereas even at their best they're inferior to the senses of the other animals? The only one to destroy his adaptation, precarious as it already is, by destroying his best weapon—his one and only specialized tool—namely, that acute perception of himself and the world, that consciousness it has taken him so long to acquire. . . .

Niel's answer: Whoa! That's the romantic writer talking! You're completely wrong; animals also take drugs. Certain ants go looking for certain fleas on whose bodies they find a euphoria-inducing substance; monkeys love alcohol (they do resemble us, that's true); and elephants make their own! Yes, that's right, they make their own alcohol.

THE DRUNKEN FOREST

Every year at the same time, the animals eat huge quantities of a small berry found in the tropical forests and soon, because the fruit decomposes in their stomachs, forming alcohol and sugar, they are drunk. For several hours, a most extraordinary scene takes place. Although the elephants are usually very well behaved, they now tear up trees or try to stand on only one leg.

But these amusing consequences are not the only ones. The whole natural order is obliterated by the drug. All of those reflexes that have been slowly developed over the centuries—mistrust, slyness, wisdom—are forgotten, leaving each one at the mercy of all.

What vengeance and murder would be possible, if it weren't that all of the animals are gripped by this frenzy together, so that all the forest is drunk at the same time.

I don't see what's any more reassuring about that, I retorted. Does that mean that all life is anxiety and torment? That my father isn't an exception? since everyone, including the animals, has a taste for death. Life, an awkward little effort, quickly falling back into nothingness . . .

What color? Black of course, unfortunately!

I don't feel like playing this game, Emile, not for your sake or mine either. I don't like this at all.

Things are happening fast—oh, just details, but so meaningful! Harder and harder to overlook, and God knows how hard I've tried to play it all down, not see what's going on. Starting next year at school, all the seventh grade classes will be conducted in Arabic. We're not sure there'll be room for Jeantou at the French lycée. Rather limply, I must say, I began rehashing my usual argument: since we're going to be living in this country, why shouldn't the children have the local kind of schooling, get their education in Arabic, etc. Marie-Suzanne rebelled immediately: "Absolutely out of the question!" Why should we do any differently from their own middle class? They're in a great hurry to get their children registered at the French lycée. Which is true; paradoxically, the French schools here have never been so sought after. And all the while I was talking and accusing Marie-Suzanne of being narrow-minded and selfish, I realized that I was beginning to need convincing myself.

At the same time, nothing seems to have changed. The Palace invited me to a reception for heads of departments, which took place in the famous hall of clocks. It was the first time I'd ever entered it. Extraordinary place, I must say—clocks everywhere, all sizes, all shapes, all colors, made out of every kind of material, and they were all over the walls and the furniture and on specially built stands. "A huge phallic fair," Niel reported to me once, when he'd been called to the Palace for a consultation and seen the room. Niel told me that the Sovereign was also interested in watches and medicines. His watch collection is considerable, the experts say, and some of the items in it are worth a great deal. The medicines are more of a mystery. He keeps ordering them from all over the world. What does he do with them?

As we arrived we were all lined up on two rows of chairs with their backs to the wall, waiting for the Sovereign to come in. It seems the Bey is holding more and more receptions of this kind—probably knows he won't be there much longer. This time he had decided to invite all the heads of all the different trades and professions, and that's why I was there.

Surprised to see Mzali there already—at his ease, smiling, whispering with his neighbors, sure of himself. Instinctively my eyes searched the room and, sure enough, he was the only Assistant who'd been invited. Just in case I'd had any doubts . . . He came toward me and we shook hands, and he murmured something I didn't catch. I was about to ask him to repeat it when the Bey entered the room. We all stood up and remained standing from then on. The Sovereign however sat down, and the ceremony began immediately. It consisted mostly of each head of department being presented to the Bey by a Chamberlain-General with huge black whiskers and countless decorations, and each man kissing the Bey's hand before returning to his place. From time to time, just as a man was preparing to kiss his hand, the Sovereign would suddenly turn it palm up, as an indication of his paternal affection —which he never did, they say, with a non-Moslem. There are limits to how liberal a Sovereign can be. Sometimes, for no apparent reason, the Chamberlain-General went to take a decoration from a chest which was placed on a chair and placed the ribbon of it around the neck of the newly honored man. Except for holding out his hand, the Bey did not budge an inch all that time and didn't even open his mouth. When it was all over, the last man had been presented and the last one decorated, he got up and went out of the room, followed by his Chamberlain-General with the tremendous whiskers.

What got into me then that made me go over to Mzali and ask him:

"What did you want to tell me a minute ago?"

He smiled that pleasant smile of his and answered without the slightest hesitation:

"I said you should have worn a *chechia.*"

I'm not very good at thinking of a quick comeback, and, anyhow, how could I have answered him? I looked at the people around me and, sure enough, they were all wearing one. In fact, there's another effort to be made, since I do want to understand everything and everyone. The *chechia* is not just a religious symbol; it is more of a sign of national gratitude. If I want to stay here and fit into this nation, why shouldn't I wear one too? Maybe Mzali wasn't being the least bit ironic, at least not deliberately. Maybe he still saw me as head of a department? But, then, how could I see myself with a *chechia?*

THE FOUR THURSDAYS

First Thursday

Thursdays were the only time he could come, since Thursday was the one day he was completely free. He would take the train Wednesday evening and travel part of the night, arriving at my place about eleven in the morning; I would have him stay for lunch and then he would leave at about four to catch his train back and be at school the next day. I don't believe he saw anyone else but me; he would go from the central train station to the Tunis-Goulette-Marsa line, from the TGM to my place, and from my place to the central station. He dozed on the hard seats of the Compagnie Fermière railway coaches two nights in a row. Meanwhile, from eleven in the morning until four in the afternoon, we talked. He talked, especially.

It didn't go on for very long, actually. Four sessions—four Thursdays.

I hadn't seen him for years. I'd heard that he had come back and had asked for a job as schoolmaster in the south. He had not yet got his degree in philosophy but since he did have a certain number of credits, he could have taught as an assistant teacher, at least, especially here. And why go so far away? A lot of teachers think they'll be able to stand it. Result? Every year, right in the middle of the school year, the education authorities have to repatriate emergency cases—that have had nervous breakdowns. Some of those teachers resign overnight, by telegram. Niel tells me that the authorities are so used to these cases of sudden panic that it doesn't pay any attention to a breach of contract of that sort. It just does whatever it can to find an opening somewhere else for the poor fellow who's lost his footing.

I ran into him by accident, at the opening of an exhibition at the Dante Alighieri. He'd been back for three months. Why hadn't he come to see me? Of course I hadn't forgotten him—the best pupil I'd ever had! No, that wasn't it; he hadn't been afraid I would feel indifferent toward him. Well then, was he angry with me? There could be surprising fluctuations, as I had often discovered, in the pupil-teacher relationship. No, not exactly. At the time, I didn't pay much attention to the way he put it. What was he doing now? Why had he accepted that post, and under such conditions? No, he hadn't merely accepted it; he'd asked for it himself. Anyhow, when was he coming to see me? Soon, he answered, without hesitation; yes, he'd already taken that decision.

Hostilities began immediately. What other name could you give the relationship between us during those four Thursdays? It was an effort to settle accounts. I tried to fire back at him as little as possible, just enough to defend myself a little when I was being a bit too hard pressed; in the beginning I did it to keep the conversation going, to help him out—or so I thought; then I did it so that he would open up and tell me the rest, about himself and about me. But toward the end I was almost silent, wanting him to stop talking and go away and leave me alone at last! But whereas in the beginning he had asked me the first questions, in a neutral way, as if he wanted to make sure I was prepared to listen to him, after a very short while he didn't need my help or even my approval any more in order to keep going. It was obvious that he had worked out ahead of time everything he wanted to say to me. He had practiced it, and probably even rehearsed the wording of it, as if he were preparing to plead in a courtroom or make a speech. Maybe the only reason he had come back from Europe was to harangue me and force the results of his research on me.

He would sit in the big wicker armchair that I offer my visitors, which encourages them to stay, which I sometimes regret, and as he sat there comfortably, just opposite me, he would talk and talk, and talk, except occasionally when he looked out the window, turning his profile to me, and at those times he wouldn't say anything, as if he didn't want to talk except when he was looking me straight in the eyes. At first I was struck by how ugly he was—uglier even than he used to be, it seemed to me, with that outsized nose, bonier than ever, the kinky hair, the gawky limbs that stuck out from the armchair and writhed around. But soon I began to forget his ugliness and became captivated, fascinated by his irony and passion, and sometimes I even found him very handsome. I began to admire him and feel proud of having had such a pupil because, after all, hadn't I contributed, even if only a tiny bit, to the intelligence and forcefulness of a mind that was so rigorous and so vehement at the same time?

I simply cannot remember in detail all of the conversation we had in those four sessions, and it would be silly even to try to. Perhaps, from the very beginning, I didn't want what he told me to stick in my mind and would actually have hurried to forget it all if I could have. The first time, I did try to jot down a few notes after he'd gone, but it was no use. There was too much of it and it was all too tumultuous; although right from the beginning I had the feeling that he knew where he was going and he'd even worked out a sort of plan, so as not to lose his train of thought and so that he could manage to say everything but at the same time—the way it is when passion or the whirlwind of thoughts puts pressure on you—he also had to say everything all at once, spill it all out in order to get some relief. So that whereas at the end of each session I was incapable of summarizing all that had been undertaken or expressing it articulately, nonetheless I had the unmistakable impression that the day's work had been done, one great portion of the edifice marked for demolition had been torn down, just as the plan called for; and when the four Thursdays were over, I had the feeling that we had finished the demolition, everything had been leveled off, and, as a matter of fact, he never came again. Never. Of course not.

Immediately I asked him the same question, the one that really had me wondering and he had answered so evasively. Why had he asked for a job in a place that was so far away, so remote from everything?

"So far from whom? So remote from what? . . . Anyhow, I wanted to be alone."

"But maybe you won't be able to bear it."

"Then that will mean that life is unbearable."

I tried to kid him. I told him he must be infected by poor quality logic, and the proof was that he was drawing too broad a conclusion from premises that were too narrow. If he couldn't bear loneliness, that didn't mean that life as a whole was bitter. A woman's presence, even just one . . . In this way, I pretended at first to want to make our conversations a little bit playful. He cured me of that very quickly, very simply, by not answering, not taking his cue whenever I began to talk that way. He would look out the window.

Partly out of politeness, still, and partly in fun, I asked him if he was still writing, so as to suggest that that might keep him busy far away in that propitious desert of his. He pulled out his billfold and drew from it a folded sheet of paper (so he had prepared that too?) and held it out to me. A poem.

Steps
Sidesteps
Am I
Communing
Am I
Opaque
Hugged by my skin
Am I
Who am I
Voice without echo

Oh to die

I told him it wasn't bad, a modest bit of understatement that meant it was good and I liked it pretty well. He informed me calmly that he was pleased with it, actually, but he wasn't writing any more. Ah, why not? Because it was "an expression," the expression of "something else" and that it was that "something else" that interested him and he didn't want to spend his time on purely formal things that end up filling the mind completely. Which is what almost always happens to writers as they develop. He gave me a stern look, or so I thought. Inevitably literature becomes an exercise that becomes more and more of a void. Whereas in the beginning it is an attempt to succeed in situating certain problems correctly, once the writer has glimpsed—merely glimpsed—those problems, he grows afraid and stops short at problems of form. . . . Anyhow, never mind, not now, he didn't feel like talking about literature. . . . We'll come back to it.

(We'll come back to it! So there was an outline plan for our talks and I hadn't any say in it.)

"What I was interested in here, in this—this poem, since it

is a poem, was my body. What exactly is my relationship to my body, taken as a whole first of all, then to some particular part of my body, like my eyes, for instance. . . . This problem was revealed to me in the course of a specific experience—a real Revelation (you can take the word any way you like), that I shall never forget." (He stared toward the window; I had the feeling he was overwhelmed with anxiety, but it was so fleeting.) ". . . In Strasbourg. I too have what you call a 'mixed marriage,' you know. Marriage is one of our few chances to dispel loneliness—you've certainly repeated that often enough! And at the same time, the only things about marriage that you've described are the failures, the difficulties, the unhappiness. . . . And why is that? Because your own marriage was mixed! Haha! What marriage isn't, after all? The truth is that in spite of what you've claimed, you have realized that marriage is impossible and that in all honesty, you cannot accept any marriage. So there again, you have dodged the conclusion and preferred to hide the failure of your own 'mixed' marriage behind that pretext."

That was very indiscreet and overly aggressive. Already I was barely holding myself back from hurting him in turn; I couldn't help flinging at him, "Are you speaking for yourself?"

He snickered.

"What if I am? You're going to have to say that to me quite a number of times. So what? Am I not your favorite disciple? Am I not, in a great many ways, what you wanted me to become? But there is one difference between us. Personally, once I've discovered that I can't stand certain things any more, I refuse to shut them out of my mind or make a travesty of them. In other words, it wasn't that I married my wife, Jeanine, and then began to suffer—because I didn't like her style of cooking, or because she made the bed in a certain way (you didn't know I'd read you so closely, did you?) or because she was a 'foreign woman.' Sure, that was part of it; I don't like food cooked in butter either, and I too find eiderdown quilts unbearable. . . . But, above all, I married Jeanine because I wanted a foreign woman, because I'd become a foreigner to myself. . . . Let me tell you what happened in Strasbourg."

"We had decided to make the trip chiefly so that I could meet her family; I'd never seen any of them, except for a lightning glimpse of her father, who'd merely said he was resigned to our marriage because paternal authority didn't exist any more in that country, and an uncle who was relieved when he saw I wasn't quite black, since with him all people who came from beyond the Mediterranean were lumped together in one big biological obscurity. And besides it was Christmastime, the vacation, and in Strasbourg we would have a place to stay and something to eat—you know how scarce everything was at that time—and we were hungry, so hungry sometimes that we got dizzy as we pored over our books and the letters danced in front of our eyes.

"When you're that age, you can't do anything without showing off and squandering all your energies. We decided to get there by hitch-hiking, without stopping to think how far it was, or how cold and hungry we would be. I'm not going to go into details about everything I did; the picturesque angle ceased to be of interest to me long ago. All I'll say is that, after eating ice-cold potatoes and a bit of fruit and a little sausage, camping out more often than not, and making love avidly each time we stopped, we arrived in a state of exhaustion. So I'm not overlooking the 'physiological' explanations, as you can see.

"Or the 'sociological' explanations either, in case that's what you want to know. The people I found in Strasbourg were very decent people, but they came from another planet. A universe of gothic Catholicism. There were several Gods in every bedroom, made out of wood or plaster, painted or carved or woven, plus crucifixes, bleeding hearts and flaming hearts. Above all, in addition to the grayness and the damp that characterize those regions, there was an oppressive atmosphere, that I learned the cause of later—a rather genuine family misfortune. It had brought each of them in turn to the verge of a nervous breakdown and plunged them all into an accusing silence—yes, that's it, as if every one of them was being accused by all the others. And, besides, they spoke German! Oh, they made efforts for my sake, all right. By that I mean that they spoke German only among themselves, but I had to stand there like an idiot walled in by his own stupidity and wait till someone deigned to speak to me from time to time.

"Like all the young people in those days who had not suffered directly from the war, I had objected to any global condemnation of Germany and the Germans, because you had to think of the future, you had to trust each and every people, even if its leaders had been monsters and even if the majority of that people had listened to those leaders. Again and again, I would say, 'What

History has done, History can undo' (by the way, you must recognize that principle—it echoes what you taught us). As if History with a capital H had anything to do with it once that irritating strangeness had closed in on me and I felt as though I was submersed and drowning in icy water. Anyhow, so much for the 'objective conditions.' I hope I've devoted enough time to them and you won't take me up on them later, since I have supplied you with them myself. And now let's get down to what happened.

"One afternoon I was lying on the living room sofa, that was covered with brown velvet, of course, because apart from brown, no other color was allowed to disturb the neurasthenic quality of that light and the pinkish sameness of those ungainly stone buildings visible from the window. So, I was lying on the sofa and vaguely thinking about what I was going to do when we got back home, when suddenly a question occurred to me and something became clear to me so forcefully, so violently and upsettingly that I literally had to get up and walk about so as to shake myself. How can I express what I discovered, exactly? Oh, I've thought about it a great deal since, but nothing is altogether satisfactory, no one formula would be adequate. It would take a swarm of speeches and explanations and images, but then we'd be way off the track since it was a single impression to begin with. I'm going to try to make a comparison anyhow.

"Have you ever had an odd feeling as you shave? asked yourself a question before your own face in the mirror? Not—let me make this clear—some vague academic question, not a literary game about the mirror or the mirror image that is not identical, reflecting your double but where the left is on the right, etc. No, no, not that. I mean, have you ever asked yourself, with sudden anguish, who is that man in front of you, who must be you but whom you're not quite sure of recognizing any more. If you haven't, then try it, sincerely, strongly. Look at yourself in the mirror tomorrow morning, for instance, as you shave. It will quickly become unbearable to you. Don't tell me you're used to looking at yourself, even complacently. It's not true, you're always thinking of something else—what you're going to be doing in a little while, or what you did yesterday, or no matter what besides yourself, outside of yourself. You're not really looking at yourself. Your eyes are sliding over the mirror, over a bit of cheek or chin, over the image of a bit of cheek or the image of a bit of chin, the image of a hand holding the image of a razor. You're not looking at yourself, at you yourself, as a whole, as you really are. . . . If you actually did it, if you really looked for yourself, you might find yourself, perhaps, or rather, no, you would find a stranger, and fear would come over you. I'll bet you a thousand to one that if that revelation were made to you and if that impression lasted, then your shaving sessions would become a daily torture. You've discovered that you're unknown to yourself, the person in front of you is unknown, and although you thought you knew him, that was only because of a long-standing absent-minded habit, a refusal to put the problem to yourself, a problem you've never tried to face squarely. . . . I want to make this clear. What I'm talking about is not merely an idea, an idea like any other—interesting but immaterial, transparent, something you get rid of or forget immediately afterwards. What I mean is a sort of dizziness on the brink of an unbridgeable chasm, the ultimate intuition of a fundamental truth.

"Is that clear? Does my comparison suggest anything to you? I'm afraid that if you haven't had that revelation, or at least part of it, yourself, you can't even glimpse what I'm talking about. I must move ahead.

"Now extend that experience to the entire body, the entire being, then to everything that exists. I had become a riddle to myself, and soon the whole world was to become a riddle. . . . No, that's not quite it; I hadn't become one. I had grasped it all at once and at the same time I found out that I had always been a riddle, only I hadn't realized it until then and I simply needed time to understand the full extent of my discovery. I was living with myself and with the world in a sort of truce, that could have lasted forever, I suppose, if I had managed to maintain the balance between frivolity, half-sleep, and escape that is the lot of most people. What I found unbelievable, now that I had awakened, was that I had been able to live that way for such a long time and hadn't seen it earlier, hadn't felt what a fluke my life and my person were and how extraordinarily flimsy the whole construction was.

"Are you following me a little better? I can't do any more. . . . At any rate, it had come home to me at the same time that I could never again go on living as I had before and that I would never again be able to dodge that throbbing, unbearable issue. And in fact I've never been freed of it since. Sometimes I forget it for an instant, or even for a brief period, but I never forget it completely, and I always come back to it as to the problem which is central to my existence. The most painful, most frightening problem.

"Because, as you already realize, of course, it was a terrifying discovery and, no matter how important it is, it hasn't made me either proud or happy. Think of the overwhelming strangeness that a human face can cause when it is looked at in that way! At the theater one evening, suddenly the people, the lights, the customary flutter over an ordinary ritual—everything seemed so strange to me, so external, to the point of panic. . . . Even though I now look on that experience as a decisive vision, the prerequisite to any serious philosophy, on second thought I believe that if I had the choice . . . oh well, never mind, I don't know. For most people, in any case, it's just as well things are that way—that lack of attention to themselves, their own bodies, the way their minds operate. Look, here, obviously we couldn't have been put together any other way. No, I mean that, really, physiologically; could we have lived if we hadn't had eyes to direct their gaze way beyond ourselves? Just imagine what would have happened if we were able to look at ourselves, with our own eyes, I mean, so that everybody could see himself. . . . O.K., that doesn't seem clear. (Had my lips moved? Had I looked as though I was about to interrupt him?) But for me it's obvious; it's all part of the same intuition. Let's stop there for the time being. I must admit it's a hard idea to get a hold of.

"Anyhow, the conclusion was inescapable: from now on, everything had to be re-examined and rebuilt with that in mind. All that had to be integrated, or else. . . .

"Once we got back from Strasbourg I decided to make my wife convert to 'my' religion, though not right away, and without forcing her, of course. I was looking for the right time, some sort of gimmick, and I found it: when our son was born. It was explained to me that legally speaking, he was not my son, since at that time we were still subject to the *Statut Personnel.* I told Jeanine the facts of the matter in a detached, deliberately indifferent way. We either had to accept this legal situation, and all its consequences, or else she had to be converted. She agreed immediately. I'd been expecting more resistance. For her all it involved was a mere formality, or so she thought at the time. For me, it was crucial—an attempt to glue a few pieces back together again.

"And what was the outcome? Not only did I not glue anything together at all but it also began to undermine the couple that I had invested so much hope in, and Jeanine as well. She told me how she heard her father sobbing in the back of the temple while the ceremony was going on. A kind of hallucination, of course, since her parents didn't come; they stayed in Strasbourg. I think she never forgave me, no matter what she said to the contrary. . . .

"But after all, my dear master, haven't you done the same thing, by any chance? (I did not answer.) Oh, don't bother answering; I don't really need to know. Let's get back to the main thing. I don't think we can ever overcome that fundamental astonishment, or ever regain that unity. . . . Did I say regain? No, not regain it, because we've never had it except during that very first indiscriminate stage when we're infants or embryos. As soon as awareness emerges in a baby, he is astonished by his own hand, his own foot, and the way they move, astonished by that body that sometimes obeys him but more often functions without him. The baby's even astonished by that obedience, and he's right. We spend our life forgetting, trying not to think about that fundamental anxiety, trying to glue the pieces back together. . . ."

(I didn't like that at all. Was I really worried about him, or was I just trying to ward off the uneasiness he irresistibly made me feel or get revenge for the anxiety he was thrusting on me? Vague recollections of the psychopathology manual came to mind, and I said to myself that this business about the body, and about difficulties in relating to one's own body—none of that augured very well. I tried to suggest this to him, picking my way carefully, as you have to with cases of that sort, the way they'd taught us in that long-ago hospital training period that we had to have credit for in order to take the *agrégation* competitive exam. . . .)

He burst out laughing, a laugh that seemed so good-natured, so healthy and adolescent that it threw me off balance. I was almost disappointed; I'd almost have been reassured by pained, "sardonic" laughter. At least I'd have known where I stood as far as I personally was concerned.

"You're wondering whether I've gone crazy? Don't apologize, I was expecting you to think just that; you're not the first. The ineffable Education Director had the same question put to Niel because I would not accept his help and refused everything; I even refused to leave. He'd have felt better if I'd resigned; tough luck for me. He would have liked me to apply to be sent back to France 'and placed at the disposition of the French government.' To be sent back to France! At the disposition of the government! The French government! I told him that I couldn't be sent 'back' because I'd never *left,* because I was born here. And as for being placed at the disposition of anything whatever! . . . Don't you want to know what Niel's answer was? You've already guessed, haven't you? and that makes you more bewildered than ever! Maybe you even wish he hadn't? You'd have preferred him to say I was at least a little bit crazy, wouldn't you? He should have diagnosed what is cautiously called a nervous breakdown these days, shouldn't he? Well, he didn't. Nothing of the sort. Niel talked with me in his office for an hour. My behavior wasn't abnormal; I'd never gouged out anyone's eyes, I wasn't even strongly tempted to do it. I don't attack myself and I hadn't any intention to; and if I were to do it one day, I'd do it calmly, premeditatedly. No doctor would have committed me to an asylum, not even to get the authorities out of a predicament. And, in the end, Niel concluded—he's a decent man and a conscientious doctor, even if he does drink a little—'You're as sane as I am.' Which I didn't think was very flattering."

Well, Niel's wrong; the boy is unbalanced! Psychiatrists won't pay any attention to you unless you go around throwing stones at people's heads. But there's also such a thing as demented ideas, the kind that prevent a man from living. Poor Emile, I couldn't help feeling uneasy myself just reading these last few pages; what must you have suffered, living through what you describe with this unbalanced boy!

Second Thursday

The following Thursday, the session was shorter. Not that that was any advantage for me; on the contrary. For a while I thought he wasn't coming any more and I was somewhat relieved, I must admit. I was already in the process of setting a single place at table for lunch, when I saw him coming up the street, his whole body springing forward—first the head, then the shoulders, and then the rest—like a camel; in fact I couldn't help thinking that he was as supple and as powerfully ugly as a camel, and as awesomely stubborn. He raised his head, with its frizzy bush of hair, and smiled timidly, respectfully. I noticed how young he still was, yet I was already finding him very impressive.

It's not that he ever acted disrespectfully to me; in fact I was moved and embarrassed by his deferential manners. He still called me "sir," as if we were still at the lycée, or at least "my dear master," when he wanted to be ironic. The only thing was, as soon as he opened his mouth, he became implacable.

I set out another plate, and we lunched almost in silence. He did not apologize for coming just in time for lunch, as if I could not have done otherwise than to wait for him. He vaguely explained that, for once, he'd had to see somebody in town—as if it were clearly understood from now on that we had to go on having these talks; and in fact he began to talk again as soon as he was seated in the armchair and I was making the coffee.

It was even more horrible than the Thursday before. I didn't think we could go any further—but we did. Yet he began more calmly. He even seemed to be taking a conciliatory attitude.

"I didn't tell you Niel's verdict so as to convince you; I'm not altogether convinced by it myself. Niel does his job, which is to reassure, and channel off the excessive manifestations of disorder. You can go on thinking that I'm not of sound mind and that a normal man doesn't ask himself that kind of question. I'm quite willing to go along with the idea that

"Perhaps it is just
As the personality gives way
That you discover
The Absolute."

(There it is: the Absolute! I'd been expecting something of the sort. The Absolute! Whereas I still maintain that what we've really got here is a case of physical and psychical collapse. The boy is insane, and that's all there is to it.)

"I'm simply trying to say that maybe we're not talking about the same level. Let me ask you a question, humbly."

(Humble! So he was humble, was he? That was too much. I'd been in too much of a hurry to think he hadn't any weapons. He looked at me steadily, the way you kneel down to steady your rifle and aim better.)

"You think I'm sick? Or getting sick? Perhaps; but do you think I'm getting sick because I'm discovering these things, or that I'm discovering these things because I'm getting sick? Honestly now, are you sure you can answer that one?

"That's just to let you know that in any case, I'm not being the least bit indulgent with myself, or with the sickness, if there is any. I'm not sure of anything where that's concerned, but what I am sure of is that my ideas are not absurd. They can't be absurd simply because we haven't the strength to examine them! Aren't those questions the only real ones? The ultimate questions, that the philosophers and the founders of religions and the scientists who haven't let themselves get bogged down in details have asked themselves. Sickness or no sickness, once you've discovered that, everything else becomes mere anecdote, tabloid stuff. . . .

"Did you know my brother Alain? He wasn't your pupil but Dunan's instead, your enemy's . . . well, in our high school Manicheism, he was your enemy. You represented free thought and progress, the sciences, and the philosophy of light. Dunan was the henchman of spiritualism, a backward believer in the hazy glimmer-and-shadow of intuition; his entire course was based on Bergson! Anyhow, maybe it was Dunan's influence, but Alain began to lean in that direction. . . . We argued more and more hotly. He exasperated me and I must have irritated him profoundly, even though he pretended to treat me with benevolent condescension—the believers' version of charitable disdain. And in fact Alain soon became a believer, one hundred percent and a practicing one at that, twenty-four hours a day. He couldn't make a single gesture without praying first; he read and re-read the so-called sacred books; he even changed physically, right under my eyes and, worse than that, he changed everything around him, the atmosphere of the whole house, our own relationship, our parents, who were only too thrilled at seeing their son embrace religion again. It reassured them about him and about themselves, and it gave us all a link with tradition, and heaven too. . . . An unhoped-for salvation, especially when you know what Alain and I had put them through! Youth groups (usually illegal) from the age of fourteen, meetings, putting up posters, handing out tracts, and a steady stream of sarcastic remarks, of course, even at table, about anything that was even remotely connected with religion or any 'class mystification.' And suddenly there was Alain coming completely over to their side, reinstating the old order, preserving the heritage, linking past and future. They were delighted, exultant; I felt betrayed, sickened. After a while Alain and I weren't speaking to each other any more, and that went on until . . . Now, one day, it was discovered that my brother had a serious heart condition, and we had to be prepared for the worst. Had his heart trouble developed after his religious crisis or was it, as you would say, the other way around? It doesn't matter which is the right side and which is the wrong side, or how you discover the truths, whether by chance or through illness; the truths are all that count, and they're the only thing that leads to despair. . . . All of a sudden I understood my horror of anything having to do with religion, literally a sacred horror, and it's always been the same horror, for him and for me. All he had done was change tactics; whereas I continued to rebel, Alain was trying to tame the danger instead. We had sensed the same yawning gap and each of us had reacted as stupidly as the other—first together, and then separately. Both of us (except Alain maybe, toward the end) had desperately tried not to see, closing our eyes to the huge submerged mass of the iceberg. Today, at any rate, I know that a man's nobility can be measured in terms of the time he spends learning to bear the disintegration of those absolute truths. I realize that few men can face that gaze for very long, and that maybe it takes a special state. . . ."

(After all, why not? Why not assume that certain states are simply more . . . well, propitious, shall we say, to the effort of asking yourself certain questions? Philosophy, a serious illness of the soul; religion, an attempted remedy, a balm that is ineffectual but may reassure some people . . .)

". . . Death."

(I don't think he had stopped talking. I had stopped listening some while back.)

"What proof is there? Everyone thinks about it, and everyone responds in his own way, but never finds the definitive reply. Once my mother-in-law had finally got used, one way or another, to the idea that I was her son-in-law—that is, the future father of her grandchildren—she decided to grant me a great privilege. She asked me to go with her to the cemetery. Her daughter—my wife—explained that she had been taking that walk to the cemetery every day for thirty years. I thought such boldness admirable, and said that I personally would have found such an obsession with death unbearable. Her answer was that on the contrary, she did it precisely so as not to think about it, by taming death to the point where it became nothing more than a stroll in the grass among the trees. The women in our country prefer never to talk about it directly. They use allusions or symbolic gestures. They never call death by its real name; instead, they call it the red, the black, the dreadful, the perfidious. In a house where someone has died, they cover all the mirrors with white sheets. Aren't they expressing the same powerlessness and the same despair? What have the various types of philosophy or religion or art added to that? Nothing, absolutely nothing; words, sham. We talk about something else, just the way you divert the attention of a madman from the gnawing anxiety that is driving him mad. Death is the end of everything, the end of other people, the end of oneself."

(The automobile accident that killed Liliane, a friend's wife—I was a little bit in love with her—that dear head, that little nose, that mouth, that smile, all that tender body, crushed and bloody and wiped out forever! Oh, the horrified panic where you feel yourself dissolving! Who has not had at least a lightning glimpse, through the death of someone too close, of that dizzying pain that wrenches you away from yourself, that irrevocable shudder? My own unexpected sobbing when my father died . . .)

"Are you going to make a list," I said to him angrily, "of all the causes of anguish? Anyhow, you must forgive me for saying this, but it's not very original.

Death is in man as the worm is in the fruit, etc. etc.

"That's already been said, in so many ways!"

"It has indeed, even by you. Here:"

(He'd said it without the slightest irony, opening his briefcase, pulling out a thick notebook, putting it on the desk.)

"Here, I've brought you this. These are the notes I took in your classes."

(There was no denying that he was my double, a cruel and lucid double.)

"How we admired you! You were young, enthusiastic, impassioned, ironic, merciless with yourself and your colleagues and even with those great philosophers that you offered us as models just the same. 'Never admire anyone if it's going to paralyze you to do so. Any model you take is by way of a guidepost, a landmark.' You used to tell us about your hassles with the school administration and we loved to hear you ridicule any authority, any established order, any tradition that had not been reappraised and confirmed by reason. One day, the Principal's patience ran out and he said to you, 'I, sir, waited thirty years to obtain what I wanted,' and you answered, 'That's because you, sir, were asking only for little things, the ones that are demanded by too many people at once.' We used to revel in repeating that dialogue and for months afterward our own conversations would begin with 'I, sir' and go on with 'You, sir.' You didn't even have that solidarity that adults automatically have and that divides the world into two parts, either side of the laughable criterion of age, with no regard for intelligence, nobility or will. You used to describe your colleagues to us with feigned astonishment, but we saw through it, to the disdain that was just behind. They had been the greatest disappointment of your life."

(They divided their time this way: lycée in the morning, card games in the afternoon. The younger ones played tennis. The best ones, the ones who got good inspection grades and would go on to a successful career, kept up an index file. I respected them for that, until I realized it was just another sort of card game. Instead of buying printed index cards, they made them themselves, scribbled on them, then filed them and filed them over and over again. What for? For how long? From time to time, they would add a comma, or take one out of the bundle and brandish it triumphantly before their pupils and admirers. "I've got three thousand of them," they would boast.)

"A stupid milieu, without the slightest spiritual ambition, the slightest audacity—or so at least you gave us to understand. Whereas you wanted to 'get down to essentials,' and you insisted that we go along with you. You didn't say it in so many words, but how could we have helped but understand you, and follow you, all united in the same impulse? At every instant, you wanted—and I quote—

To have the most acute awareness of oneself and of one's place in the world.

"The liberals awaited you impatiently. As a young philosophy teacher who had already published several promising things, you were expected to bring much-needed reinforcements to the ideological combat that went on in our city, a little closed world all its own. From the beginning, you showed that you were going to keep your distance: no sects, not even a lay sect; no lies, not even in the name of righteousness. What was better still, your first battle was pitched against your ex-future friends. They had not realized that, whether they liked it or not, decolonization, which was imminent, would take place in the national, not the socialist, vein. The face of Justice does not always look the way you hoped it would. As for the theory whereby History asked only the questions it could answer, you dismissed it as stupid and narrow-minded and, in historical terms, false. The minds with some nobility to them have always tried to reach those limits. Your first lecture was provocation in itself—about the Cabala and the ten sephiroths. You maintained that scientists, theologians, mystics, and poets were all moved by fundamentally the same ambition. In other words, you were accusing the liberals of lacking imagination and courage!

"The believers around town began to hope, but the second

blow fell on them. It was as if you did everything you could to be alone. So, we were supposed to admire the mystics and the theologians? Ah, but just a minute now, that was all nonsense! People like that just pretended to fly by closing their eyes as they sat ensconced in their armchairs. Sick people, much of the time. You took an evil pleasure in quoting the phrase by Pierre Janet, 'Saint Theresa, patron saint of the hysterical.' 'Mystical experience.' 'Poetical experience.' Experiences of what? you would ask, and that was the whole question. Silly little personal worries blown up to Cinemascope size. Neuro-vegetative and more or less conscious difficulties masquerading as all the unhappiness in the world.

"Whereas what you wanted was a genuine, objective, double-checked stocktaking. without illusions about oneself or the world."

(Have I mentioned what admirable eyes he had?—large, black and almond-shaped. Even if he'd never opened his mouth, I ought to have read it all in his eyes, that blend of acute intelligence and cruelty, good will and despair. How well I recognized that violence, the unreplaceable, strong, and bitter taste of passion!)

"What you wanted was a science of limits, a science that went all the way to the limit itself; blandishments were a matter for the technicians. When you think how vain and boastful the scientists and the builders have become because they've managed to go as high (as high!) as 7 or 8 or 10 miles above the ground! They promise us that soon we'll be taking puny little jaunts to the suburbs of the earth—it's ludicrous! No greedy ant-like accumulation of activities like that will ever supply an answer to the genuinely important problems of human destiny."

(I was still a teacher when I was put in charge of the psycho-pedagogical laboratory. We were supposed to do everything, satisfy every need in town, give advice, dispense therapy, and do research. One result was that my own philosophy students sometimes came in to consult me. In the beginning I thought that was pretty funny and I felt proud as a young peacock of that double responsibility of mine. Complacently, I would say, "In the morning, I make them sick with anxiety, and in the afternoon, I treat them for it."

Let's reach the limits! Let's destroy the limits! What a lot of nerve! What ignorance! Didn't I overestimate my strength? The mere idea of such a trip overwhelms me. "Those puny little jaunts to the suburbs of the earth" would be simply unbearable for me. I've tried to imagine myself lost in space, without any landmarks, unable to tell which was right and which was left, which was up and which was down; and I've been filled with intolerable anguish, the way I was the day I got lost at the bottom of the sea.)

"Only, this is the thing. You did not tell us everything. I'm not blaming you since you probably didn't know yourself:

the price that would have to be paid

and

whether the attempt was feasible.

"And that—excuse me for saying this, sir—that may be the source of your boldness: the naïveté of your undertaking."

Limply, I made an effort. "You're contradicting yourself. First of all you reproach me with . . ."

He cut me off sharply.

"No, I'm not contradicting myself, and you know it perfectly well:

"That undertaking is the only worthwhile effort that consciousness can make; and

"It is impossible.

"I did not say you were wrong. Remember that, and please don't forget it again: never, at any time, have I said that you were wrong.

"On the contrary, I've come to believe that from the very beginning you were altogether right, once and for all. That's also why I've come back to see you. I've come back to do two things—to tell you that you were right, and to check whether the conclusions I now draw from that are correct."

(Yes, this young man is my double, or the double of what I once was, except that he wants to get to the very bottom of my line of thought, the very bottom of myself, in fact. My God, what am I to say to him? How can I prevent him from doing it? What arguments can I use?

If my readers only knew! Here I am, a writer, supposedly

right down to the tips of my fingers, and yet I had not the slightest intention of writing. First of all, until I was twenty-five, I fancied myself a philosopher. It took that experience at the Bibliothèque Sainte-Geneviève, on an uncomfortable bench—I've told that story already, and it's one hundred percent true. That's when I began to flee, and ever since I've been running from book to book, stubbornly refusing to poke my head out of the clouds. It took the horrible certainty I felt that day—the utter inanity of all those efforts—and what for? For how long? To understand what? The despair that suddenly came over me when I read that passage in Spinoza: one would have to stand *outside of the world* so as to see it at last from without, like God. God! A notion that's handy enough, all right, but what it really expresses is our feelings of anguish and helplessness. How could one be within and without at the same time, inside and outside of the world, the whole globe, the whole universe? If that wasn't possible, I would give up; and that's what I did. I gave up knowledge, I gave up philosophy, for good, and since then I've been fencing cautiously with those deadly, impossible ideas.)

"Do these problems exist or don't they? If they do, they're unbearable. As soon as we open our eyes, we cannot avoid them and we cannot stand to face them."

(This morning I deliberately stared, to the point of painfulness, at the sharp steel blue light of a soldering lamp that a workman was using on some pipes in a ditch. Terrifying struggle with the dreadful glacial purity of it, then a huge black blotch, as big as the flame itself, that hung before my eyes and moved wherever I moved, at the same distance from me as the flame had been. Then the blotch faded away but specks kept floating in front of my eyes, and I had a headache all afternoon.)

(That's a smart thing to do! That's how you get a lesion of the retina. The workman, of course, was not a writer hunting for romantic provocation, and he undoubtedly wore very dark, sturdy protective glasses. But why do it? Why cooperate with misfortune?)

"So, what are we to do? We are face to face with that twofold night—before our birth and after our death—that rings us in.

With the tininess of this globe that hangs in the black unending universe. With the fact that because we are put together the wrong way, we are fundamentally unable to penetrate those shadowy reaches. With our helplessness ever to understand ourselves and speak to one another accurately."

(My dismay when Marcel explained to me that because Marie's eyes were blue and mine were black, we did not and never would see the same colors! And that, contrary to common belief, bulls do not see the color red! and would get angry in just the same way before any old rag that was waved in front of their noses!)

"Don't be so dramatic," I told him (and of course, the minute I'd said it, I felt so small and ridiculous). "Since you have done me the honor of remembering my courses, remember this:

If all things on this earth were to turn into smoke, we would know them through our nostrils.

"Yes, of course I remember," he said bitterly, "I carefully made my own dictionary. But all we would know would be smoke. Nothing, nobody can guarantee that what we know even now is anything other than smoke."

Third Thursday

"My father had an old workman named Joseph who had served him for thirty years. To us he was almost one of the family. Often he would come back to the house with my father and stay to have a glass of alcohol and a meatball with us. Once my father began to drink heavily, Joseph would come home with him almost every evening and they would drink together, as if it was a continuation of their common workday. It was in our house that the accident happened. They were silently filling up, amidst general disapproval, when Joseph dropped his glass and slid heavily off his chair 'forward, onto his knees, like a camel!' My mother thought he was drunk and grumbled a little more. My father was not deceived; he knew that Joseph held his alcohol better than he did. Alarmed, he tapped Joseph on the hands, on the cheeks, and, despite my mother's sarcastic comments, asked him in a choking voice, 'What's the matter? Answer me, answer me!'

"Just then I came home and when I saw that Joseph was frothing at the mouth and seemed disjointed, I agreed with my father. 'He's definitely sick,' I told my mother; she shrugged and said, 'Sick on brandy.' What could I say in reply? A few minutes later, someone called to us from the street—my father, who had come back with a calash. I thought it would have been better to send for a doctor, to decide whether he should be moved, but everyone was treating it as a big joke—the neighbors had come running to see the show and get their word in. I was beginning to get angry but the calash was waiting and paradoxically, as is often the case in dramatic situations, I felt very distant and very remote from everything that was going on around me.

"The ride to Joseph's house was interminable. He lived in a narrow alley in that labyrinth called Little Sicily. Perhaps it was the nearness of the walls on either side that made the horses gallop frantically along the trench-like way, bouncing the large inert body that we could just barely manage to hold on the seat. When we arrived, I rushed to call his wife and prepare her for the shock.

"Do you know what her reaction was? Just the same as my mother's, and here too, the neighbors began to gather, laughing, making the same jokes and the same accusations against drunkards, and so on. I tried to make them feel some concern, tried to make his wife at least realize that they should send for a doctor. Nothing would move her; besides, she'd been resenting us for years because of those sessions at our house with my father. We almost got thrown out. It wasn't until two days later that we found out that Joseph had had a stroke which would probably leave his right side paralyzed. And in fact that's just the way it turned out, and he was almost totally dependent on his wife until he died three years later, relieving them both of a terrible burden.

"Several days after Joseph had had his stroke, I was trying to comfort my father for the loss of his long-time workman and companion in pleasure. He had undoubtedly thought he was doing the right thing when he went to get that calash; and in fact I was annoyed with myself, too. We shouldn't have given in to Joseph's wife and gone away without insisting that a doctor come immediately. Maybe if Joseph had been taken care of right then and there, he wouldn't have become a cripple. But, after all, what could we do against his wife's wishes?

"To my surprise, my father told me, irately, that I was a fool, I didn't know anything about life; didn't I understand that he'd been in such a hurry to hire a calash because he was afraid Joseph was going to die right there in our house, and it was a very good thing I hadn't insisted Joseph's wife get a doctor because if I had I'd merely have made us all look suspicious."

I don't recall how this anecdote came into the conversation. Maybe it was the first thing he told me on this particular Thursday, as a way of setting the tone, leading up to what he had decided to talk to me about.

Trying to reassure him, I told him he didn't need to feel guilty about Joseph becoming a cripple; after all, Joseph had worked for his father, not for him, and anyhow he'd done all he could. I told him we were too inclined to think we were guilty all the time and look for ways to punish ourselves. If he was disturbed, didn't this have something to do with it? Wasn't this why he had gone into voluntary exile in the South? and why he felt desperate now?

He listened to me but he looked stubbornly out the window,

his head turned away so that I couldn't see even his large bony nose. I thought his silence was a good sign; I must have hit the nail on the head. So I went on, telling him the story about the bowl and the extraordinary relief I felt afterwards when my father gave me a beating. And since he remained so exceptionally quiet, I drew nearer him as I talked and placed my hand on his shoulder.

He looked at me then, hesitantly, it seemed to me, and I had a lightning intuition that he was finally going to say to me, "That's what I've come for. Help me! Let's stop this silly struggle! I'll stop attacking you and you'll stop being on the defensive against me! Can't you see that all this is just a trick? that it's really myself I'm attacking, through you. . . ."

But when he did smile at me at last, it was an icy, almost insulting smile. Suddenly, I was overcome with feelings that were the opposite of what I had just felt for him. I was angry, furious, I almost hated him.

Now he was explaining to me calmly, assuring me that, no, I had thoroughly misunderstood the meaning of that story, it wasn't anything of the sort, he didn't feel any guiltier than his father had. This is what he was trying to say: his father was right, nobody is responsible for anybody because nobody can do anything for anybody. Better still, or worse still, every man is a cause of fear for his neighbor: Joseph's wife had taken her revenge, and she'd been punished for it.

"Once again, my dear master, all I was doing was listening to you and trying to see things in the light of your principles. And I saw. I saw that there is almost nothing we can do to protect ourselves from that collective mechanism. I merely drew the lesson from your lessons, as a good disciple should."

(Oh, no, he'd gone ahead of me long ago, possibly along the same road but I, at any rate, couldn't follow him any more. What was he going to talk about now? What dike, what refuge—in himself, in me—was he going to attack, and destroy?)

My father's hand, enclosed in the silence of his stroke, while we chatted away in one corner of his bedroom, getting more and more relaxed, almost on the verge of telling jokes, and suddenly that fit of sobbing that burst from my chest—I who had stayed so calm and distant and almost ironic, I suddenly discovered how frightening his solitude was, how irremediably he was walled in.

Why didn't I grasp that clenched and grateful hand and keep it just as long as was necessary—such a short time, as it turned out, until suddenly someone cried out in distress, "I think he's stopped breathing!" Ah, I could have hit him! May I find some peace again, if that is still possible. . . .

"In a deservedly lyrical way, you have described the anger of the victims and their discovery of violence as an irresistible and poisonous light. You have maintained that at that point, violence was inevitable and legitimate. Colonization, for instance, stirs violence, because it is violence itself, and nothing but greater violence can put an end to violence. All right.

"But why did you stop there? Why didn't you tell us *everything you were thinking*, the full extent of it, as far as you could go? Why didn't you say, violence is everywhere? Because oppression is everywhere and all power is oppressive? The victims' power and their executioners' power. Why didn't you show how former victims become flesh-eaters in turn. . . . No, that's not it; they don't become, they already were. At the same time as they were being devoured, they too were devouring whomever they could. Do you remember that extraordinary example you often used to give us, about those caterpillars that followed each other so blindly that the person conducting the experiment had succeeded in creating a closed circle of caterpillars, going around and around and around on itself, endlessly. Well, human beings are a closed circle of victims and executioners, each one torturing someone else, all at the same time or each in turn, and all with the same satisfaction and the same cynicism. And the motor that keeps this circle moving endlessly is the blind, wicked, underhanded force which is barely contained by contracts that are constantly being broken."

(Nanou hit me. I hit Nanou.

My father hit me. I hit my father.

When I threw the old chipped bowl at Nanou who had been persecuting me for so long, and when I saw my impromptu weapon revolve in the air like a disc and hit Nanou on the head, my heart beat hard with fear, because I was afraid he would die—not afraid for his sake, but because of the very regrettable consequences his death would have for me. As far as he was concerned, I'd have wished him dead with all my heart, if only death didn't mean blood and catastrophe, if only all it meant was that my tormentor would be crushed, wiped off the surface of the earth. Even when the bowl had actually struck his head and the blood gushed out and spread over his face and his clothes, and Nanou began to cry and shout in terror, and fat Foufa, his mother, arrived and also howled in terror, "Nanou, Nanou, my heart, my soul! "—even then I did not feel any pity or any regret. I was afraid and at the same time I rejoiced at seeing my tormentor ridiculous now and imploring, he who used to be so much mightier than I.

Violence or humiliation; perhaps there isn't any other way, after all.)

"All right. The only thing was, since you consented to violence, you should have described the effects of violence, and not just the effects it had on your friends and mine, the people whose cause we thought just. As if justice could keep blood from ever being anything but that warm and sticky liquid, or could keep mothers from going crazy at the sight of their children's brains blown out, or keep a man whose throat is slit from feeling the fire of the knife at his throat and the horror of his head coming loose from his body. . . . Hey, what did violence mean to you? Just a word? A pure idea? "

"A political—a sociological fact," I stammered. "Otherwise, no social action."

"Ah, there we go again, that marvelous invention of yours! As if there was such a thing as politics without metaphysics! Aseptic sociology! As if everything didn't extend over the whole of existence, as if in the last analysis, everything wasn't a matter of life or death. . . . Look here," he threw the words at me savagely, "have you ever—you yourself, if not your wife or your son—have you ever been the object of that violence of yours? Have you ever been knocked down, or wounded, or tortured? "

(Yes, once; I was wounded in the head. Only a scratch; that's why I didn't dare tell him. Afterwards, they apologized to me. They hadn't known who I was; I shouldn't have got mixed up with that demonstration, should I?)

"Have you ever carried a rifle? Do you know how to use a hand grenade? "

"Grenade? Grenade, granada, *grenade*—I know what that is," I said, still trying to joke. "That's what we call pomegranates; they grow here in this country. Yes, I know how to use grenades, I've learned—and I've even taught other people. I've even made them. . . ."

He seemed surprised and incredibly interested all of a sudden, grateful, suddenly almost humble.

"Really? You really do? You've thrown some? "

(No, I've not been tortured; no, I've not carried weapons. It's worse than that. I've taken part in violence, but in the most equivocal, the blindest, the most hypocritical way.

Ben Smaan came to see me [see *The Explosion,* an authentic story]. He reminded me of the conversations we'd had in the beginning, when things began happening. He remembered that I knew how to make hand grenades and use them. Would I be willing, despite our differences of opinion . . .

"Against whom?"

"You'll be told, just before."

"If I agree now, could I refuse later on? "

"No, then it'll be too late. You don't choose once you're where the fighting is."

"Then I'll choose now. The answer is no."

We compromised. I would make them but I would not have to use them or know whom they were going to be used against. In other words, they'll be used against anyone, no matter whom, for any kind of action, even the kinds I disapprove of.)

"No," I said, "I haven't thrown any myself."

He did not let his disappointment show—out of pity, maybe.

". . . Anyhow, excuse me for saying this, sir, that's not what counts the most. What counts is coherence. Either violence is necessary, and in that case you have to agree to its being used, and against yourself and your family too, and you have to agree to use it yourself, no matter how horrible it is; or else, what is the meaning of this necessity that doesn't lead to anything? Or you discover that nothing is worth such monstrous acts, that turn against themselves and turn into a massacre of the innocents or new types of iniquities, and in that case, how are you going to do away with the iniquities that exist already? Either you approve of violence or you use violence . . . that's the fundamental human relationship, and I might add that I haven't found any way out myself. Either . . ."

Either . . . or! Either . . . or! I'm either an honest man or a traitor! Either a hero or a coward! Either I breathe or I choke! Either I deserve to live or I die! No, I was not tortured; no, they did not pull out my nails; yes, I refused to toss hand grenades into the crowd; so I haven't done anything, I haven't said anything worthwhile; all I've done is shake up a few ideas. I haven't even existed.

I could have tried to explain why, could have tried to clear myself, but I didn't want to any more, not just out of pride, and rebellion, but mostly because I felt myself overcome by a great weariness. It was already deep inside of me, and I was fighting it with all my strength. I could still have found some specific arguments. For instance, I could have told him that I knew from the beginning—in fact I wrote, that the majority of our people would be liquidated anyhow. And that under those circumstances, I could not be as eager to fight as the others were. My heart wasn't in it, so how, why should I go on fighting, as I always had, for men who were not the least bit concerned about my people? I might have felt more committed, perhaps, if circumstances . . . But even if I had said all that to him, he still would have answered,

"That's not the point."

And, looking me straight in the eye, almost smiling, sharing the secret with me, he would have added,

"You know perfectly well that that's not the point."

Ah, but I don't know anything! I've never known anything! A last shred of modesty kept me from telling him the truth, which was simpler and more awful than anything else and would have given him complete and final victory. The truth was that my relationship with other people, and with History, was based on a misunderstanding. Did I ever seriously believe in anyone's reasonableness or goodness—including my own? Ever since I wrote those Political Essays, I've often been asked to sign manifestoes, or appeals or petitions. Naturally, I've signed them—how could I refuse? I found it reassuring to be asked, and also—why not admit it—flattering. But my fellow human beings were as disturbing to me as they were loveable. I needed them and I was afraid of them, in equal amounts.

I have on occasion been deliberately mixed up in various types of direct "action." Why did I let myself get involved? I search myself for motives and the only one I can find is curiosity, or the wish to prove to myself that I could live with other people and participate in their anger and their hopes. Because I hardly ever went out and because I saw very few people, I usually found out about things afterwards, when they were all over; or else, I would completely underestimate the importance of what was happening, so that suddenly, at the critical moment, but in the most naïve way possible, I would find myself in the midst of people with weapons who were prepared for anything or had just been cutting each other's throats, and there I would be, calmly walking around during the truce and almost wondering why the ground was red in places and why these people looked that way, and then, when I came back, my friends, first, and then my readers would hail me as a hero, marveling that I dared go right up to the doors of death, and thanking me, since I had undoubtedly been there in order to bring back munitions for them. For instance, that famous bit about going through the German lines at Hammam-Lif. The truth was that I didn't know the road was blocked. Once I came in front of the Germans, I just continued on my way, of course, amid the shellfire. I'm not any more lacking in physical courage than the next man, but what else could I do? Or that night at La Marsa when I took a woman journalist to take photographs of the Palace—just the Palace! To get a local color story! And she took photographs of the Bey's guards who had lost some of their men in a regular pitched battle just an hour before, whereas what was expected, from one moment to the next, was that the Sovereign would be deposed.

Even on literary grounds, these passages, which brought me a reputation for generosity and commitment, were originally nothing more than efforts to put things in order within myself and situate myself in the cruel and chaotic world of men. I will grant myself one virtue, however, and that is a sort of absent-minded obstinacy, an inability to keep the results of my questing to myself. During the events I am referring to, I could not understand why my friends kept warning me in whispers, "Be careful!" —until I found out that every day, in the prisons, copies of my books were being found on the inmates and seized.

I always seem to have gone through the crowd enveloped in

respect and well-wishing sympathy, whereas I had the horrified conviction that cohabitation was scarcely to be borne and I always dreaded seeing the dikes give way and the raging waters rush in through the breach.

Fourth Thursday

"Women! What are women, after all, but a bunch of poodles with colored ribbons around their necks! Looking to women for help —what an absurdity! They're the ones who need help, always asking you to pet them and adore them and protect them. How very comical it is, really, when you think that men have imagined they could find refuge with underdeveloped animals like that! Did you know that biologically speaking, women are incomplete animals. . . ."

(He made an impatient gesture with his hand, warding off a thought that might have occurred to me.)

"Now please don't go placing me in the vulgar antifeminist category, long on hair and short on ideas. I'm talking about a very serious scientific theory. The reason women don't have body hair and their skin stays smooth instead of being wrinkled is that they're halfway between children and men. Want me to prove it? Toward the end of their lives, they finally begin to look like men. . . . Well, never mind. At any rate, they're more vulnerable than we are, less well suited to the social struggle, and impervious to any metaphysics. Ah, the very idea of looking to them for help! and in matters of the gravest sort! What simpletons we are!"

"Let's just say, it's a very pleasant thing to do," I suggested.

"That's not the point—or rather, yes it is, it's exactly the point. We should admit that it's mere entertainment. Pleasure there is, certainly, but just pleasure and nothing else. As for the rest! The rest is just a laugh! When I think of all that effort, all that maneuvering—to do what? Excuse me for saying this, sir: in order to put a little bit of flesh into a little hole of flesh. . . . After all, what is a woman? If you leave out that overdone part about 'mystery' (and if you call that mystery, then everything is mystery). What is that flesh? That lukewarm cushiony fold, the same as a she-goat's, or a hen's—is that the consolation? Is that the refuge? A piece of rubber would do as well! In fact I hear they sell rubber things like that for sailors, and the Japanese use them too, even whole dummies, complete dummies—one model for men and another one for women. . . . But expect help from them? A vain hope! You want proof? All that ingenuity and persistence—to do what, in the end? To change partners. Doesn't that prove how deeply unsatisfactory that kind of search is? Because you never find what you're looking for? For several years before I met Jeanine and we got married, I used to run around a lot, one woman after another. It was my major occupation, it was what I went out in the street for, I identified the cities I went through by their women. I'd have given any sight in the world in exchange for a woman. In the Biblical sense of the word, I knew several dozen women—a little less than King Solomon did, but a little more than a sultan's harem. And now what is left to me out of all that? Not even faces. I get them mixed up. Finally, one day, I realized that one woman is just as good as any other; in other words, they're all alike. In other words, the end result of my running around was always the same. Vanity, vanity, all is vanity."

(He gave me a sharp quick look and made the same imperative gesture as he had a little while back.)

"No, I did not discover that I was a homosexual. Don't go looking for that kind of explanation. Anyhow, what would it mean if I had? That I go to bed with a man? That I would go to bed with a man? Well, what of it? I have no objection to that in principle, if that can supply me with the help I need. But from that standpoint, men and women amount to the same thing: illusion! All you have to do is close your eyes and everything becomes the same, especially during . . . When I think that you've written dozens and dozens of pages about women, and about the 'way out' that they supposedly stand for! You're not the only one, it's true; writers, and philosophers too, have spent a great deal of their time dwelling on that, instead of getting down to the bottom of the matter. Even supposing they wanted to get to the bottom! Whereas literature may be one way of not getting to the bottom. . . . But I don't want to talk about literature with you. You wouldn't be able to stand it. You wouldn't even be willing to listen to me anymore. That's the one question I cannot go into with you."

(He smiled at me—such an intelligent and complex smile! A slightly indulgent, slightly tender smile, possibly a secret-sharing smile? In any case, it meant he'd understood it all, absolutely everything. He even knew how to avoid dealing me the final blow.)

"Whereas, after all, you're not involved in all that, at least not directly. I'm the one who's involved."

"Now it's my turn to say to you, that's not the point. That's no longer the point."

I wanted to try to distract him one last time but, God, how nearly helpless we are, in the face of the obvious.

"Will you allow me to ask you some questions of a more . . . personal nature?"

He shrugged one shoulder, by way of agreement, like a sulky child. I didn't need permission.

"Do you still make love?"

"No, not for several months now. Jeanine is staying in France and as for the prostitutes . . . Oh, I haven't got anything against whores—all women are alike, as I said—and with them it's actually more convenient and more natural. I prefer them as a matter of fact. But it just doesn't appeal to me any more."

(I almost began to hope again: was he really so very sure he wasn't sick? Why didn't he go ask Niel for advice? In other words, every time he brought up a problem that couldn't be solved, I was tempted to fall back on the idea that he was sick. Which amounted to denying that there was any problem at all because I couldn't see any solution to it either.)

"Listen," I said to him, "now don't get angry again, but why not try psychoanalysis? "

(I said it just as humbly as I could, and his answer was not resentful at all.)

"Don't go thinking I've got it in for doctors. They are a bit laughable, but they do their job—they know how to disinfect a wound and put healing balm on a sore spot."

"It's like cleaning out a cellar; you get rid of the bad smells that way. . . ."

"Yes, but not for very long. Cellars fill up again and start smelling bad all over again. Anyhow doctors can't do anything about the fact that cellars exist—that the world itself, such as it is, exists. So how can we change the world, or the way we relate to it? You say I should put up with that relationship, but the fact is, the relationship is there and in the last analysis it's unacceptable. No known remedy has been effective—sex, poetry, drugs, nothing. How many times have I said to myself, do what the trees do. What does a tree do? It eats, it grows, it reproduces. But the comparison is a bad one, because a tree doesn't think; it's fixed to the ground and doesn't know it. Whereas as soon as you know it, it becomes unbearable, and especially since there is no way out."

"There are ways of improving things, through politics, for instance. . . ."

"Can't you see we're going around in circles? Once again we're leaving the question aside because we can't face it directly. This deep-seated pain, this fear, this questioning are common to all men independently of social systems, independently of History itself, perhaps. Don't smile!"

"I didn't smile."

"You smiled inwardly, because you're already familiar with that kind of reasoning. You warned us about it long ago. It's a reactionary alibi that releases us from the obligation to help other people. . . ."

"I wasn't smiling about that. I was smiling because I have spotted one contradiction, anyhow, in what you say. Isn't it contradictory to reproach me with not taking any action and at the same time to maintain that political activity doesn't get us anywhere?"

"What's contradictory about that, my dear master? If you think that political activity is a good and effective thing, then you have to go about it seriously, and if not, it's you who are contradicting yourself. Personally I think that in the long run, it doesn't do any good because there's never any end to it.

"Your friends are nearly free by now. What's the result? They're poorer than they were before, and the best ones are back in jail. They've defended their dignity, you say—is that what dignity amounts to? Poverty, prison, and further oppression! I used to know a militant nationalist, who'd invested his whole soul and every ounce of his strength in fighting the French. Once independence had come, he grew impatient for reforms that were not being made, and he went over to the opposition. His former comrades smashed his jaw and both his legs. Now he's a terror-struck invalid.

"But in spite of everything, I wouldn't want you to think I'd become a reactionary. Up until the day before I left, I kept on going to youth movement meetings. I took part in demonstrations, I sold newspapers, I put up posters. I'm not forgetting pain or poverty. When people suffer, you must alleviate their pain, and oppression is one continuous pain. I do not repudiate your teachings, as you can see.

"But what form of society or government can take that pain away? and provide us with the solution? Solution to what, for that matter? For how long? The only straightforward concept of politics, if you still take a metaphysical view of politics and don't look on it as an abject affair of personal 'success' (great God! How comical that word 'success' strikes me as being today!), would be a permanent attitude of struggle against oppression. So, you go one step further, and you realize that it's never a final, nor even an imminent, solution.

"You know the story of the mountaineer who saw some tourists straining and sweating terribly to reach some summit or other. He asked them:

" 'Once you've got up there, what do you intend to do?'

" 'Come back down again.'

" 'Well, in that case, what are you going up there for?' "

"That's a silly story," I said. "It's the getting up there that counts . . . as if you didn't know it."

"Of course I knew it, just as I knew you would think it a stupid story. But what the mountaineer said was profoundly right even so. Is it necessary to go on struggling forever? Either that or else it's the struggle in itself that interests you because it is never-ending; it always has to be resumed. Now what if I don't want to go in that direction? What if that doesn't suit me personally? If action doesn't bring me any special joy, then it's a piece of trickery, isn't it?

"Not to mention that, as I said, there is no such thing as a serious political stand that doesn't make room for death, and not just mentally but concretely. Now, if life itself is lost, what's left that has any meaning? Don't go talking to me about a meaning in terms of values, like 'mankind,' 'the supreme sacrifice,' etc. When I hear people talking about 'duty' or 'morality,' I pull out my gun—it's worse than trickery. It's an absurdity, it's a logical error. If somebody throws a paving stone and I get hit in the head, or if one of my lungs is punctured and my eyes close, what becomes of meaning as far as I'm concerned? Meaning can't exist except for other people—until it's their own turn to kick the bucket. But where I'm concerned, nothing. That's obvious, and I don't see how you're going to get around that.

"But, especially, don't go thinking this is a way of running away. Everything I'm saying here in front of you is part of a certain gesture. A gesture that's already beginning to take shape. . . ."

"What gesture?"

(My heart was beating hard as I asked him that, but he didn't answer. He went on just as if he hadn't heard me.)

"Do you know what a certain surrealist poet wrote to his friends a few days before he committed suicide?"

You are all poets, and I—I have gone the way of death.

"Ah, my own philosophy on life and death is a very simple one," I said, and my throat was tight. "You've heard it already."

When you have the possibility of living and you live, that is a happiness granted by heaven. When it comes time to die and you die, that is a happiness granted by heaven.

"Yes, and I at the time thought that was very beautiful and very powerful. But later, you see, it occurred to me to check up on your sources. They're always accurate but, once again, you stopped at a place that suited you without going on to the end. I managed to find the rest."

If you ought to die and you do not die, it is a punishment inflicted by heaven.

"Now and again, someone discovers that it is impossible to live except absent-mindedly. The truth is, you don't kill yourself for certain reasons but because you suddenly find out that there are no reasons. You discover that the disgusting animal is right there under your hand, crouching under a rock on the beach. It's overall frivolity that amounts to running away, slipping a mask over the reality of day-to-day."

"That's wrong, wrong!" I shouted. "What's natural is to live spontaneously, and that's what you call being frivolous. Look at animals! Look at babies! They don't try to strike tragic poses. . . . That's what's healthy!"

"Here we go again. I'm not healthy, I'm sick, because you don't know what to do with me. You can see perfectly well you haven't got the answer. Neither of us has an answer. At least let's ask ourselves the real questions. What I reproach writers with . . ."

(There was a long silence. During that horrible blank, I held my thoughts, the way one holds one's breath, and so did he, I think. In spite of everything, I was hoping he would not take that point up. Then suddenly, like a man diving in after closing his eyes, he said in a rush)

"I don't think I'll come back next Thursday . . . so what the hell, let's finish up. Yes, even literature. If I had been willing to run away, I might have chosen that way of doing it. . . ."

Either literature is an exploration of limits or it is no more important than the art of arranging flowers.

"Who said that? Don't try to guess," and he pointed to the file on the table. "You, once again. You said that ten years ago."

(I didn't remember having said that to them. God, the things you can say to young people, without even dreaming that they're going to take you literally!)

"And you were right, once again. Either that, or else literature is just another bit of frivolity. Oh, I've got nothing against frivolity; it's a matter of taste, and any kind of taste can be natural. No more important than flower arranging indeed, or gold-smithing. Now gold-smithing can produce some very graceful stuff. Only you can't go around saying 'We are the language specialists, we are interested only in words, and in seeing how they're arranged and how they shimmer' and at the same time claim to have the answers to all the questions and all the worries of the human race. Writers cheat. They're backing two horses at once."

(I made as if I was about to protest.)

"Yes, I know, that doesn't apply to you personally. That's why I've come back to see you. But that's just it. You, personally, should have admitted having failed. You should have clearly acknowledged that literature-cum-exploration is impossible, that literature doesn't solve everything, and instead you've grown resigned to those half-baked books that all end in the same way, with the passion of the first few pages subsiding into a sort of resigned sadness where the reader gets the impression that actually you're hiding more than you're revealing . . . when you think that in the beginning you were determined to 'tell all'! You were going to explore the limits! Transform everything! And you know it perfectly well. We both know it."

(It was as if he'd stolen my thoughts from me and compelled me to unfold them in broad daylight, with no chance of hiding behind excuses. It was only right: I had been his master, and now he referred me back to my own lessons. He became my master now, a younger one, a more strict and rigorous one—the one I had been, perhaps.

It's true that the more time went by and the more my books began to pile up, the more I got the impression that their purpose was fading away, and the more I also got the impression that I had fallen into a trap. What would I have left if I got right down to admitting that my books are not my children, or an insurance policy, or a tool for transforming society, or a means of mastering the world either?)

I used to like strolling through the streets around the District, not because of the warm presence of those hundreds of available women who were visible at every turning but because of the second-hand dealers and the inexhaustible discoveries that they also offered, of a different kind—furniture, trinkets, toys, the clothing of so many diverse peoples mingled here. . . . Arabian or Spanish tables and screens with inlaid mother-of-pearl, lamps of Murano glass, Venetian mirrors, heavy Bedouin bracelets and necklaces, Tuareg daggers bound with leather and colored strings, stuffed lizards and snakes . . . A whole disparate universe but all of it a single dream, that civil servants turned their back on as they returned at last to the reassuring and colorless life of the mother country and wondered, with regret sometimes, which life was the real life.

And so it was that one day as I was slowly strolling about, I came across a leather-bound gold-stamped book, published in 1708 "by privilege of the King," with a title that made my heart jump: *The Essential Book,* no less. Without arguing I paid the price the second-hand dealer asked—much too high a price, undoubtedly meant for haggling—and went away with my book like a thief with his loot. All the way home I was so excited that I would not allow myself to peek into it until I was safely back in my room. My disappointment was equal to my excitement: it was a book of calculations! "Essential book for accountants, notaries, attorneys, merchants, treasurers or cashiers and generally speaking for people of all social classes because in all classes one has to lend or borrow money at interest. . . ." All over every one of its pages there was nothing but columns of figures, and I checked them one after the other until I threw the book down onto the table out of rage and vexation.

But it is still there, as a reminder. Maybe its author wasn't wrong after all. Maybe it is the only kind of book that is absolutely essential. But I've never shown it to Marcel—he would laugh so.

It's true that I had thought literature would be my solution and it is also true that that's the way I managed to dodge the most terrifying questions—like, why am I what I am? Why this world? Why live? Why this woman and not another? Why have children? That's what this young man in front of me was going through. And, after all, what he'd come looking for was answers—a last attempt, because I had been his teacher and I had helped him (!) to put his questions into words. What answer could I give him, my God? I'd have had to succeed in doing my own *Essential Book.*

Clearly, *The Scorpion* was undo-able, neither done nor yet to be done. In order to do it successfully, I'd have had to make a success of leading my life. My life itself would have had to be a success, would have had to comprise at least an underlying unity linking the pieces together. But, in fact, what is my life? What is the lesson it teaches? Total failure, dispersion, and constant anxiety. Only now do I sense that all of my published work is just an unending commentary on a work to come—in the insane hope that in the end the commentary itself would constitute the work. But it's time to admit to myself that I've merely gone around and around in circles, and for all my using a different color to draw each circle I won't have come any nearer the center. Uncle Makhlouf was right again.

"And what if I finally said to you, 'Help me.' What would your answer be?"

(My God, had I heard him right? He was calling out at last just as I was realizing, just as I was admitting to myself that I couldn't do anything for him. I couldn't do anything but let him drown before my eyes. Couldn't do anything but drown with him.)

The following Thursday, as a matter of fact, he did not come. On Friday I was told that he had shot and killed himself with a pistol. Nobody understood how such a brilliant, intelligent, etc., young man could have renounced life. A year earlier his elder brother had also killed himself, but he at least had had heart trouble. Well, people concluded, there must be a secret blemish hidden somewhere in the family's background.

But your book is done! and it does have unity, and so does your life—it's the whole, everything all at once, *The Scorpion,* the Journal, the collages, and maybe even (forgive me) my own comments. . . . In fact a crazy idea has occurred to me: did that young man exist? Certainly, Y. M. did commit suicide and I knew he'd been one of your best pupils. But did you really say all that to one another? Did all that really go on between the two of you?

What I'm trying to say is, isn't this story also part of the book? Anyhow, I'll leave it in there with the rest.

My poor brother! I couldn't have stood those sessions either; just reading these pages has been unbearable for me. In the beginning I said to myself, why doesn't he throw him out? The boy's crazy. Then I said, he's not crazy, but why listen to him? What's the point of all that talking since nobody could answer him? But you're right, you had to listen to him and transcribe it; that lesson

שמירה לילד וליולדת

יאר יהוה פניו אליך ויחנך :

מהבעל שם טוב זצל״הה

בשם יהוה אלהי ישראל גדול ונורא

אליהו ז״ל היה הולך בדרך
ופגע בלילית וכל
כת דילה ואמר לה לילית
הרשעה אן את מטארה
ורשעת ורוח טומאה וכל כת
דיליך כלם טמאים הולכים ?
ותען ותאמר אדוני אליהו
אנכי הולכת לבית היולדת
פב״פ לתת לה שנת המות
ולקחת את בנה הנולד לה
לשתות את דמו ולמצוץ את
מוח עצמותיו ולהניח את
בשרו · והשיב לה אליהו ז״ל
ואמר לה בחרם עצורה תהי
את מתשרית כאבן דומם תהי
וענתה ואמרה לו אדוני למען
ה׳ תתר לי ואני אברח ·
ואשבע לך בשם ה׳ אלהי
מערכות ישרא׳ לעזוב את
דרכי הללו מהיולדת הזאת
ובנה הנולד· וכ״ז שאני רואה

או שומעת את שמותי מיד
אני אברח · ועתה אודיע לך
שמותי . וכל זמן שמזכירים
אותם לא יהיה לי וכל כת
דילי כח להרע לכנוס לבית
היולדת ומכל שכן להזיק
תשבעת אני לגלות את
שמותי לך ותגם לכותבם
ולתלות אותם של הילד או
בבית היולדת ומיד אני
בורחת ואלו הם שמותי
שטרינ״א לילי״ת אביטו
אמיזו אמירפו קקש אודם
איק פודו אילו פטרטומ״א
אבבזקט״א קלי בטנ״א תלתו
פרטשא · וכל מי שיודע
שמותי אלו וכותבם מיד אני
בורחת מן התינוק ותלה בבית
היולדת או על הילד זה הקמיע
הילד וגם אמו לא ינזקו מפני
לעולם אנו״א סס״ם :

שט״ן	קר״ע	שד״י
וסמנגלוף	וסנסוי	סנוי
יעקב ול״אה	יצחק ורבקה	אברהם ושרה

מכשפה לא תחיה
לא תחיה מכשפה
תחיה מכשפה לא

לילית וכת דילה חוץ

תחיה מכשפה לא
לא תחיה מכשפה
מכשפה לא תחיה

Imp. UZAN Père & Fils, 49, Rue des Maltais — TUNIS — Téléph. 12.34

too is part of your research and your work. And there was nothing else you could do for him. There is no such thing as the essential, because everything is essential. What is essential in life is the everyday, and you just have to be strong enough to accept that. Because he cannot accept death, he kills himself. Because he discovers that we are doomed to ultimate defeat, he rushes into it headlong, refusing to use any shock absorbers, so . . . who's the dupe? It's you who were right and Y. M. who was wrong; wisdom is exactly that: arranging the everyday. You came to that realization late, but this young man did not have the patience to wait. There was nothing else you could do. Oh, if only I had talent, I'd have written just one book and written it gladly, and I'd have called it, *No One Is Guilty!*

THE SCORPION

(continued)

The Robot

A few scattered pages left—no connection with what's gone before —I don't know where to put them, but I don't care, because by now the problem is no longer situated where I so stubbornly insisted it should be. Now I know that Imilio and myself are equally involved.

The robot. Once upon a time there was a wonderful robot, who was not a real robot but a man disguised as one. Actually one of his friends, an engineer, had camouflaged him that way so as to protect him from his powerful enemies.

This was the idea. Since, in real life, the robot was a very good chess player, he would be exhibited as an attraction and would pit his skill against anyone who wanted to challenge him.

Thanks to this ruse, his life would be out of danger and he would earn enough to support himself and his inventor.

For a while everything went very well. The engineer was very much in demand among the great ladies and the nobles of the kingdom, and he would stand behind his machine, silent and discreet, while the jerky, inexorable movements of the robot made them stare with fascination, and some repulsion. To the glee of the public, the court, and the frequenters of salons, the robot defeated the best players in the country. When he sensed that he was in danger of losing to his adversary, he used a trick move and cheated right before the spectators' eyes, but they were too busy being amused by the show to pay close attention to the way the game was played.

Now the King himself was a formidable opponent at chess, but he had always refused to play against the robot. At last one day his pride was too much for him and he ordered that the robot be brought before him.

"If he wins," he said, "I will give him a fortune, but if he loses, I will have him shot by my guards."

Naturally a crowd thronged into the grand hall of mirrors to watch the final match.

Now, this is what came to pass. The game was very close, on a heroic level. Suddenly, in the middle of it, the robot began to knock over the pieces with his jerky gestures and spoiled the game.

The King went white with rage. He ordered that the mechanical man be carried out of the gallery of mirrors and be shot by his guards immediately.

Minutes later, in the deserted courtyard, the engineer found the robot, bleeding in the agonies of death.

"What happened?" he asked him. "Why did you knock over the pieces?"

"I was losing. I knew the King was going to win."

"Why didn't you use your trick move?"

"I didn't dare cheat, because of the mirrors."

"Why didn't you at least try to play till the end?"

"Because any way you looked at it, I would lose, and I didn't want to die defeated."

His entire work was a desperate effort to see more clearly: he ruined his eyes in the process.

The haze that's thicker and thicker, more and more persistent, the specks dancing around more and more; and now those strange little flashes. I tried to think it was my dirty lenses attracting splinters of light, but it isn't—it's going on inside of me. Sometimes tempted to go and see Marcel. Never. Will I, too, soon have to find myself a great Wheel or live silent and motionless forever in an armchair? Our father, Aunt Louisa, Uncle Georges at the age of thirty—they've all gone blind, and soon it will be Uncle Makhlouf's turn. That's a lot for a single family; too many to be coincidence.

(Do you mean to say that you too needed my help? Needed me? How gladly I'd have helped you, you dear old idiot! Why "never"? Because I had to keep on being the kid brother? Well, I would have, and at the same time I'd have become your doctor, your friend, if only you'd given the slightest indication!)

I haven't told everything, that wouldn't be right. I rub my eyes the way other people bite their nails or masturbate. What a voluptuous feeling every time! I go on until they burn, until I feel the pain that pleasure inevitably turns into—then what a guilt feeling afterwards! (And what horror when I realize what I already know and try so hard to forget, namely, how terribly self-destructive I'm being.) Promising all over again not to do it any more and never keeping my promise, of course.

I knew it, I knew it but, again, why make a pact with misfortune? Why lend it a hand?

The sherbet. Those gaudy sherbets dripping with chocolate or pistachio or vanilla or strawberry but all made out of colored cardboard that ice cream vendors put in the window and that fascinated me so much that one day, despite the danger of doing it, I stole one—I who am so scrupulous, at such pains to avoid getting into trouble with the law over stupid things like that. Then back home, my heart pounding, and I staring bewildered at this object that now turned out to be so completely useless and trying to understand what it was that had carried me away: the fact that it was such a good imitation that you might not realize it was a fake or, on the contrary, the fact that it was so obviously fake at the same time as it depicted the real thing so accurately?

For me, my work is only a last resort.

The Prince.

"I would like you to be more . . . Prince," she said to me, "like before."

"Was I once?"

"I prefer you when you are cruel. Do you remember when you used to explain to us carelessly why it was a good idea to gouge out the eyes of children who were going to be musicians? You would go into the most horrible details. Or when you described how the Dutch drowned like insects behind their own dikes once the sea had broken them down? Our friends exchanged horrified looks, and even I couldn't tell whether you were joking. They must have thought, 'What a savage!' which made me feel even more thrilled. Now you couldn't even stand to listen to stories like that from somebody else. Oh, I liked you better when you were pitiless."

What did she want from me? What do they all want from

me? Are you really supposed to live at the summit of yourself all the time?

Why am I I?
That is what sometimes at night distresses me.

The shoelaces. I told my father about the unpleasant conversation I had on Thursday with the Minister of Public Health.

"After all I'm the one who set up the Department and organized it and made it what it is!"

"And you have been head of it," the Minister retorted, "and that was pretty good, wasn't it?"

I was raging mad, and I'd have answered him hotly but that I felt a strange sort of shame too and, at the same time, I resented my own feeling of shame. Here I was being suspected and forced to talk about my own merits, which was hateful enough in itself; and on top of that I had to defend myself—as if there was the slightest scrap of truth in his accusation. I certainly hadn't started the Department for the vain pleasure of being head of it! What did he take me for?

My father:

"What does he take you for? For what he thinks we are. And what are we? I'm going to tell you what we are."

And like Uncle Makhlouf, he didn't say it in so many words; he told a story.

He told me how he was coming back from the matchmaker's and from giving his consent for my sister's wedding; he was happy and he wanted to do someone some good. On his way down rue Bab-Carthagene, he met a blind man who was selling shoelaces. He didn't need any shoelaces but, then, the blind man wasn't really selling shoelaces either. It would be an act of charity, disguised as a purchase.

"How much?"

"Twenty-five centimes apiece."

He took four of them and gave the blind man a franc.

He walked a few steps away. Then he said to himself that what he had done was not exactly an act of charity, since he had bought those laces. . . . True, he did not need them but he had taken them anyhow, in exchange for his money. So he went back and without asking the blind man for anything this time, and without counting how much, he put a bit of change into his cup. —"God's share," my father thought. But his eyes were already beginning to dim and, in the universal gesture of all who have poor eyesight, his hand touched the edge of the cup to make sure that he was really putting his money into it and not dropping it outside.

The blind man seized his hand and did not let go.

"What are you doing? What are you doing?"

"I put in some money for you, ya baba."

"You put in money? Why would you put in money without asking me for any shoelaces?"

"I don't need any, ya baba; I bought some from you a few minutes ago. You must recognize my voice."

"Yes I do recognize your voice, that's just it. You bought some from me a few minutes ago, so why would you come back?"

"May God inspire you better," my father pleaded, beginning to get worried. "A few minutes ago I bought something from you but this time I just wanted to do you a kindness."

"A kindness? Why would you do me a kindness after buying the laces from me?"

A crowd was beginning to gather. The blind man still had a tight grip on my father's hand and kept attracting more people. My father was sweating, defending himself desperately. At last they let him go, but reluctantly, because they all suspected him.

"That's it, absolutely. That's exactly what's happening to me. I'll go away like a thief."

The difference. Everything means something here—the sound of a chair being moved, the cry of a child violating the silence at nap-time, the indeterminate color of a white sheet in the shadow of the louvered shutters. You don't live here any more? But you do, that's just it, so to speak; you do because of the distance, you do through difference. For instance, you don't fully appreciate the coolness of the water except when it's very hot out; or when you water the burning ground and the water comes back up to you as a light vapor; or when you go hot-bodied into the sea (but only moderately because otherwise, if your body is too hot and the water too cold, the proportion is not right and already, beyond the cruel and exquisite voluptuousness of it, you will be suffering); or when you lie down on a woman's body, your passion and the coolness of her skin make you shiver. It's the being within and without, so very near and yet so far, that makes you unceasingly discover the unreplaceable, inviolate source of life, anywhere in the world—on your tongue, the irritating coyness of fennel; watermelon, a bath from within, the coolness of it bursting in your mouth . . . Cultivate your difference if you can, it's all you have left. . . . Ah, if you only can!

The sea. In this closed rocky colorless landscape, where the houses fade into the stone, the repainted door of an old inn, and all the gladness and coolness of the sea are condensed in that streak of blue, and there you are—happy! delivered from the rockiness, breathing freely, drawn up by a voluptuous and reassuring somewhere else as if, outside the stifled heart of this country, beyond the mountain, the sea was really there close by.

Vacation. For one long week I don't see anything except what's absolutely right around me and no further than the distance in which I am confined by the glasses I wear for working. I live within a little circle and take it with me wherever I go. Then slowly I discover that my eyes can look farther away, that there are also houses, trees, and people, the landscape grows more detailed, more complicated, I see bigger and broader, all the way to the hills—yes, they really are there—all the way to the sky that opens beyond the hills.

And then I go back and with me I bring those spaces that are too wide open and that way of looking that is tuned to the horizon, and I bump into the walls, into people, cars. I guess that's what it's like to look back nostalgically on your vacation? The recollection that I can—that I could break the circle surrounding this armchair, this shelf, this sheet of paper, I could recuperate the entire world, recuperate myself?

The fish. I told Uncle the story of the shoelaces.

"Your father's gotten older," he answered. "I know him better than you do. Only twenty years ago, he'd have told you the story of the fish instead.

"When your father broke his arm as a child, our young uncle, who was beginning to earn some money and grow a moustache, decided to console him by buying him a veritable street vendor's game of chance, in the form of a box with hundreds of candies inside, each with a number, and especially a huge black fish made out of one solid piece of licorice. Its scales shimmered in the light, it had two big astonished red eyes and, around its neck was a gold ribbon with a number one marked on it.

"It was a great success. Customers could hope to win the fish with just one sou. Little children and sometimes big ones too thronged around your father, whose arm was still in a cast, and bought candy-chances from him. They all had their eye on the big prize, of course. There was such deep silence every time that all you could hear was the sound of the candy wrapper being undone and then 'Oh!'s of disappointment from all sides. Even your father was all wrapped up in the game and he was just as anxious for the result as all the others. His heart beat in time with theirs and he went 'Oh!' along with the rest of them.

"Time went by. More than half the box had been sold and still the magnificent fish lay untouched in its multicolored paper nest. Your father had acquired a sort of glory that attracted people from the neighboring districts.

"But sometimes, when he was alone, your father would buy a candy from himself and open it in the same feverish way, hoping to carry off the fish at last, and each time the outcome was disheartening. Sometimes, with the money his candy sales had brought in, he would buy himself four or five candies in a row. Then one day, he couldn't wait any longer. He opened one candy, then another, and another . . . until he'd opened them all. There wasn't any winning number. The game was fixed.

"Your father was crushed. He did not go out into the street the next day or the day after either. He looked and looked at his box stuffed with the undone paper wrappers that nearly hid the big fish with the stupid eyes. Finally he reached a decision. He chose one of the numbers at random, crossed it out with a crayon, wrote a huge 1 in place of it, and then carefully wrapped up all the candies again.

"The game started up again, just as exciting and breathtaking as before, and two days later victory went to a little boy who lived down the street."

INDUCTOR-OBJECTS
(Theory of . . .)

Build up a battery of objects, or fragments, each of which, by its smell or its color, evokes some fundamental dimension.

Peculiar to each person. Self-inductors.

For instance, mine would be:

a bit of tar-stained cork that has spent a long time in the sea; I won't come back to it.

a piece of tin—yellow, red, blue, or no color at all, actually gray light in condensed form; shiver of schoolboy mornings, danger as make-believe as it was serious; cold acid taste of the whistles we used to put together ourselves from the scraps of metal we picked up around the tinsmiths' shops, scene of untiring creativity —funnels, oil measures, holiday candlesticks.

an Italian vase, Venice or Murano, striations of dull silver and gold, specks of red and green; fragment, replica of the exuberant colors and milky lacework of those fabulous chandeliers in the homes of the poorest families, carefully sought out today by canny merchants and sold to tourists for sky-high prices. If possible, the supreme happiness: white-frilled yellow narcissus in the water, green stems visible through the precious transparency of the glass.

Leather! Any and all kinds of leather, varied, warm, strong, shielding my sleep, recalling all the moments of distress I have overcome! Oh my God, if only the world could be just leather—could become just leather once again! Leather and just possibly wood . . . that's the only concession I can make.

White pepper, a set of spices, separate or expertly mixed, the retail and the wholesale, the only collective fragrance, along with that of leathers, which is enriched by all the others and gains in moving intensity.

Amber, the yellow and the black, animal and vegetable.

With that I can go—I would like to go to the end of the world; each part of myself reconstituted at will.

A little portable homeland.

Here the pages of *The Cellar* run out. I had thought the drawer was fuller than it was because of a few bundles of paper carefully done up in string that lay in the back of it, underneath the rest. They have curious titles: *Chronicle of the Kingdom of Within, Colored Writing, Writing and Music, The Scorpion's Journal. . . .* I'll look at all that when I have time.

I put all the packets of paper back in the half-open drawer, where the sun gives them a red glow, as if it had set fire to the cellar.

So this is where Emile's effort stops, but what happened afterward? What was this the outcome of?—Marie, literature, political events, the Young Man, or his eyes? Or everything at once?

Went to see Uncle again. Not surprised to see me so often. A man of language who guesses everything without having to ask questions. There again I understand Imilio—when I come away from these conversations I feel tired but lighter, unknotted, like after a hammam. I read the last pages to him, especially the story of the robot.

"What do you think?" I asked him, apprehensively. "It's already too late, isn't it?"

To my relief, he answered without hesitation, as usual.

"No, he has not given up, and a man who wants to go on fighting has not lost yet, especially if he is willing to risk his life. One way or another, I think we'll hear from Imilio some day."

Yes, we will! I want to believe it. For his sake as much as for mine, I need to believe that Emile has not disappeared, he's convalescing somewhere, he's making another attempt to re-achieve his unity some different way, trying to come to peace with himself again, without us, since all we did, by making demands on him, was make it even more difficult for him because we didn't understand that he was desperately anxious to find peace. Why not assume he's gone to some other country and that there, rid of our problems, he is slowly straightening out his own? Perhaps he has simply gone on one of those long trips of his? He used to say that they cleansed his soul. After all, he hasn't any other burden to carry now but himself, although (he's right about this too) that burden is the heaviest.

The Abscess

The boat glides on purple water with curly white foam, in the heat of a lazy sun pleasantly cooled by the imperceptible sprinkling of the spray. A kind of happiness. Never has any departure given me such a feeling of liberation. Liberation—how ironic! Would I ever have thought it possible as little as a month ago? After all I did nearly die. THE SCORPION DOES NOT KILL HIMSELF, ALL RIGHT; BUT IN THE END, AS HE IS THRASHING AROUND, HE WOUNDS HIMSELF MORTALLY. What difference does that make? Imilio was right. For me, though, everything has been put back in its right place. I only nearly died. In that abscess all my difficulties concentrated and came to a head; I got over it; I decided to live, and to go away.

The day before, after I'd gone to see Uncle, I felt feverish and my throat bothered me. Naturally I thought it was tonsillitis; nothing visible, but I felt so listless I went to bed. By eight the next morning I had a temperature of 104°, was completely knocked out, and had trouble swallowing. Marie-Suzanne called Coscas.

"It's not tonsillitis." He made his diagnosis immediately. "An abscess in the throat, that's what it is, and pretty ugly already, that's what it is. I don't like the looks of it. It'll take the works, the whole works, that's what we'll do; penicillin etc., etc. I'll come back tomorrow morning."

The strange part of it was, I wasn't in any pain; I floated in a sort of resigned torpor, a little like when you have a liver attack, without the dizziness or the nausea. My mind wandered and whirled me away in a sort of formless but irresistible round dance, which was neither disagreeable nor upsetting. It went on and on, that's all, and I could feel myself being carried irremediably away and had no desire to resist. I must have dozed off from time to time because I would awaken with a start and the round would start up again, not really tiring, a little annoying after a while because there was no rudder, no way of controlling the boat. Something in my throat seemed to be taking up more and more room but I didn't worry about it very much up there in the clouds except maybe that I wasn't breathing so easily. Marie-Suzanne must have called Coscas again because he came very early, nine in the morning. He looked at my throat and then sat down next to my bed:

"I don't understand it at all, no I don't; hey, you should be helping me instead of daydreaming like that; it's grown incredibly bigger in just twenty-four hours, that's what it's done. . . ."

Then he began to talk about doctors who got sick; we're not sick very often but once we start, my, my, then we really have to make it worthwhile; last year, Benmussa had some trouble with his liver and of course it had to be a kind of thing that's practically unknown here; now they say that we worry about ourselves more than other people do but that's not true; we have to convince other people that we're really sick, so we go whole hog; otherwise nobody believes us, they don't want to believe us because they're afraid they'll miss us, the way a wounded general is missed, but look here old man, you don't have to prove to me that you're sick, you are sick, you really are, and I know it, so come on, help me . . .

It wasn't very clear to me what he wanted me to do; I found his gaiety artificial and insipid, he tired me. He went away. Marie-Suzanne saw him to the door and then came back to sit in front of me. Then I saw that her eyes were red. I knew that scene by heart—what had Coscas told her? Was it as serious as all that? But that was perfectly all right with me; I closed my eyes and began to drift again. On a high ridge, between the within and the without; it seemed to me that for brief instants I managed to see both sides at once; strange; not unpleasant but I had a premonition that it was not possible for any length of time. At that point Marie-Suzanne delivered her strange speech to me.

"I have to tell you something; once you're all over this, even if you stay here, I'm going to leave with the children. . . ."

I wanted to protest! This was really the right time to talk about things like that; I could hardly speak. But it was the right time, yes it was—now or never! She went on, and I'd never seen her that way, tough, without the slightest consideration for the state of exhaustion I was in, breaking in on my indifference, forcing me to set foot on the shore and keep my eyes open.

"Make up your mind. Either you stay here alone, or you come with me, with us."

It seemed to me I'd already heard that, said by someone else—or was everything getting mixed up in my head? No, it wasn't my imagination. Marie must have said it to Imilio just as furiously, and he repeated it to me.

"Marie? You think she wasn't right? When you come right down to it, you men don't see anything, you don't understand anything. But I knew; as soon as I realized that my children couldn't live here, I knew it was all over. I let you work it out for yourself and come to the same conclusion by yourself because I would not have been able to convince you. It didn't take long. Only, this is what's come out of it all. Do you know what's the matter with you? You're afraid to go away, afraid of leaving your clinic and your department and your friends and your patients. But what's happening? They're being taken away from you by force. So, you go to bed. But I'm going away anyhow, no matter what happens, so make up your mind. Make up your mind!"

Then she began to sob. Curiously enough, I was not moved. I suddenly hated her with a cold childish sort of hate—pursuing me like that, trying to make me stop and think just when I was so sick! A drunkard's notion flashed through my mind—she wanted to decide for me, take me by the hand and carry me away over the sea; I felt her strong disdainful hand pick me up like a feather; I was annoyed and hurt, she was treating me like a child. Well, nothing doing; if I lived I would go away alone, all alone, not even with the children. Maybe I would die of sadness but never mind—I would leave in an honorable and dignified way. Pity I decided so late, I could have taken them all away with me. Never mind. I closed my eyes and the waves carried me away again.

By evening I was finding it difficult to breathe; it was a little alarming to have to make such an effort, but my throat still wasn't hurting me. Even so I felt somehow sorry to die; I got emotional about my family, especially. If I survived, then we'd see; Marie-Suzanne was a good wife and the children were fine children; we would all go away together; that was a promise. Coscas appeared again, in the night—it may have been very late. I don't remember what he said to me or even whether he spoke to me. Almost all of me was far away, struggling with suitcases that wouldn't close; they fell open on the wharf and let all my possessions fall out of them in front of the customs men, who confiscated everything although I pleaded with them not to. The air was humid, impossible to breathe, I was sweating great drops of perspiration and was tormented by the September flies; doomed to die themselves, panicky, sticking to me, letting themselves get squashed against my skin rather than fly away. One of them stung me so hard that I made a terrific swipe at it; Coscas stopped my hand in mid-air: I had nearly broken the syringe. . . . I was still there, sick in bed. Too bad, I was absolutely determined now, we would leave, it was a promise, I swore it, we would get on the boat with or without suitcases, in the September heat. My mother won't wait for me all night long on the balcony any more, won't tie me to her any more with that thread of anxiety that binds me irresistibly. Let the district, the whole city burst and hurl me all over the world! or let the world finally become me! I fell asleep again without looking at Coscas. I threw my suitcases furiously in the customs men's faces. Let them keep it all, we'll leave anyhow!

When I awoke the next day light was flooding through the windows—the shutters had not been closed—and Marie-Suzanne was sleeping, fully dressed, in the armchair. My God, was it that serious? At this point I noticed that the waves weren't carrying me along any more. I closed my eyes and reopened them; no, the round dance had stopped, I wasn't drifting any more. My pyjamas were soaked but I wasn't perspiring any more. The fever had gone away. I must have slept straight through the night. I swallowed. Something still bothered me a little but I could swallow just about right. A miracle! Most of the abscess had been reabsorbed. I was thirsty. For a minute I hesitated to wake up Marie-Suzanne; then I told myself that in any case it would be better if she went to lie down, so I called to her softly. My voice was working again, without rasping any more like a clogged-up pipe, and I could breathe freely. Marie-Suzanne refused to go to bed and gave me a rapid sponge-bath, which was marvelously pleasant. I announced that I had decided we would leave at the end of the summer. She didn't say anything in reply but the way her eyes shone was eloquent enough. When Coscas came back to give me a last injection, I was reading, and he exclaimed heartily, "Commediante!" Coscas was a well-educated man, and a good doctor too. Impatient though I was, he would not let me get out of bed for two more days. But I felt quite well.

I went to see Uncle and told him what we had decided.

"And what about yourself?" I asked him. "What are you going to do?"

He answered that he was too old in any case. Then, while he was getting the coffee ready, he told me, in passing, about the time when, as a young man, he had gone to the funeral of a friend's wife. (She had died a horrible death—thrown more than ten feet up into the air by one of those incredibly swift sports cars, one of the first we had ever seen in those days, people weren't used to them yet; she hit ground again in time to be run over by the same car.) So with his eyes full of tears, Uncle had rushed to the house of the dead woman to embrace her husband, his friend. There he found a large crowd of people, of course, including the whole Baranès family right in the entrance. He didn't know them at all, but he remembered that the young woman's maiden name had in fact been Baranès. So he began to kiss them one after the other, heartfelt, affectionate kisses for each member of this cruelly bereaved family. . . .

And about how, in the midst of this kissing, he realized that each of the persons he kissed froze with embarrassment at the tears with which he was wetting them, and how it came to him in a flash that this Baranès family had nothing to do with the Baranès family of the dead woman.

"What was I supposed to do? What would you have done if you'd been in my place? Was I supposed to stop? Apologize? That would have made me even more ridiculous and might also have embarrassed them still more. So I went on boldly kissing them.

"So, I stay here, my boy. I'm too old to leave this district—my ears know every least sound in it—or this room, where my hands know every roughness of every surface. And, above all, I have my books. Here or anywhere else, I have my books, and they are my real homeland."

Now there's a solution. Uncle has his books, Imilio has his literature, and I, what do I have? My patients. Never mind the buildings, the furniture, and the apparatus (and the vanity too): other people will use them. Mzali is just waiting for it to happen. I used to wonder what I was officiating over; I officiate over pain and death. You can say mass anywhere; there are men needing to be taken care of everywhere. That may be the reason why Imilio has gone: he can write anywhere. I will go on helping men no matter what they do, what sort of men they are; I'll love them anywhere. And those I leave behind here I will go on loving, even from far away.

As I was coming back from Uncle's, I felt an irresistible need to go by the Place de la Batha again. . . . No matter how I try, every time I see that sudden gaping nothingness, it's as if I've been punched hard in the chest. . . . The day Emile turned up unexpectedly at the Dispensary, which was not like him at all, and said, very pale:

"It's starting! They're moving in on Sidi Mardoum! The bulldozer's already as far as the rue Ghermati! Whole walls have already been knocked down!"

"In the part that's not lived in, of course," I ventured.

He gave me an annoyed look—didn't I understand anything? As if that was what mattered! It was our home ground that was being knocked out of existence! But I'd understood all right, so well in fact that despite my indifference, which I thought was sincere (ah, the bulldozer has also leveled the pretty little shrine in the Casbah?), I hadn't the courage to go and see. And I too began to make detours to avoid going by there and coming on that void.

I spent the next few days getting things ready for our departure. The Dispensary, the Department, the patients. I drafted a few letters to colleagues in France who had been friendly during their visits here, especially Quilici, who had set up a group office and had told me in so many words, "We would be glad to have you join us." I'm also going to reconsider taking the *agrégation* exam again—the struggle is harder over there and you need all the ammunition you can get.

When I told Mzali the news, he hugged me—yes he did, he actually hugged me! I thought he wanted to thank me and I found that in bad taste, but no, he was moved. I couldn't bear it, though, when he said:

"So you too are abandoning us?"

I nearly got angry but, once again, I felt strangely muddled. I just answered affectionately, "Bastard." He looked at me with the eyes of a faithful dog and I'm not sure he understood. That same evening he telephoned to say he was arranging a little party in our honor; there would be two musicians and a girl singer. . . . Ah no, enough was enough!

No point in going to see the Ministry people and having them go through the same nonsense, only theirs would be less sincere and so less funny, and I would be likely to get really angry. Anyhow I know what they're all going to say—I encouraged this liberation, I worked toward it, then hardly does it begin to emerge when I'm in a hurry to weigh anchor. Wasn't I considered a "patriot" at one point? No getting around it, I will always be a traitor, the perfect traitor, the double traitor, betraying both sides. How could I explain this double truth to them, both parts true at the same time:

This country outside which, no matter where, I will be in exile.

(Did I read that in something of Emile's? Or did I say that myself? In all events, if Emile's papers were to be published one day, I would be explained at the same time.)

This country inside which I have never ceased to be in exile.

I decided not to bring anything away from the Dispensary itself other than the Phoenician masks, and just as I was about to take them down from the wall, Mahmoud indicated that he wanted them, which bewildered me. I didn't know Mahmoud was interested in the Phoenicians. All right, he can keep them; he'll put them to better use from now on than I would. He took them gratefully and seemed embarrassed, then went and hung them back on the wall where they had been.

One last visit to the Doctors' Club. A persistent rumor that I hope there are no grounds for: the government intends to take back the Club, in two stages. First stage: nationalization; second stage: handing it over to a new so-called national Conseil de l'Ordre; and somewhere in between, we would be shoved out, by the process of elimination. Why all the hypocrisy?

The Club belongs to all the doctors; we've all helped to build it and furnish it luxuriously. Since they can't just openly decree that our shares in it are null and void, they shield themselves behind some great national scheme. My colleagues are rabid, of course. "It's outright spoliation! It's another act of theft!" "All they do is raid and pillage! Look at Granada! Look at Kairouan! Even in the best of cases, they use the columns the Romans left, and stone that other people have carved! They've destroyed more than they've built—and when they do manage to put up something it's made out of stucco or plaster!" I refuse to get upset like my fellow doctors; it's none of my business any more, and no matter what happens, I do not want to give way to oversimplified reactions like that. But, good God, I can't help wondering why it is that once the victims have been freed, they become as stupidly and scandalously unjust as their ex-tyrants were?

All this while, Marie-Suzanne was going around singing. In her imagination, she had already left, and for several days she had been saying, "When we go back to France" just as naturally as you please. She was going back to France, where she had spent perhaps four or five months in her entire life, but already she was living in the future. Who was the fool who said that women dwelt in the past? The fact is that their children are the continuation, the irresistible forward projection of themselves. They're always ready to leave, to follow their husbands, and also the children they bring into the world; they don't know where those children are going to lead them but they know that life lies in that direction. Bina was right—or was it Qatoussa? I don't remember which—we men are idiots; we kill or get killed for mere words, and only women love life and survive. Young Y. M. is altogether wrong on that score.

With nostalgic amusement, I told the children the half-true, half-fabulous story of our genealogy, as mapped out by their uncle. To my surprise, they didn't find it the least bit ridiculous. Quite the contrary. Two days later my son brought me his Virgil and, without the hint of a smile, showed me a passage he had carefully circled:

For the first contest, four matched ships, the pick of all the fleet, enter, with their heavy oars. Mnestheus' keen rowers drive

خویش باز کشاده و قبه را بنا یه کرده و بالای سر فرشته یازده ارش کرده و این قبه را
بیازده سال تمام کرده اند و ان را دو ستون برنجین ساخته هر یکی بچند ارش بر سر
هر یکی ده اسیا و حوضی مسین در انجا کار کرده

قبه دیگر قبه ذهبیه در زنگبار کنیه است زیر ان صورتی طوقهای بسیار در دست
و گردن و در پیش وی درختی از هفت میوه بر ان درخت انگور و انجیر و نارنج و ترنج و
به و انار هر سال دو بار بار دهد بر سر ان درخت علاقه آهنین چون هلال زنگی حلق خود
بر ان هلال افکند و اویخته شود پیش ان صورت تا سرش یک سو افتد و تنش از دیگر

the swift Sea-Dragon, Mnestheus the Italian to be, from whose name is the MEMMIAN family.

(Virgil, *Aeneid,* V, verses 114–117)

He remarked, earnestly, "Mnestheus must be the ancestor of the Memmia family, whose name reminded the Latins of Memini, just as Mnestheus reminded Greeks of the verb, to remember *μεμτησθλι.*"

Since we're going to Europe, I'll go to see the via Memmi in Milan that is supposed to lead into via Pestalozzi, and in Venice I'll look for recent traces of the Memmo family, at least two of whom are supposed to have been Doges (the 21st and the 93rd). The Renaissance painters really existed, in any event; I've already checked. Lippo Memmi, especially, was a well-known painter, and the dictionary even shows a detail from his "Annunciation." I have not found any trace of Silvio, who went to North Africa, according to Emile, but what difference does that make? Emile's plan is clear now. And to think that I seriously wondered whether my brother wasn't out of his mind. Well, if he was, then I'm out of my mind too. These details about Memmius Gemellus should be added to my tables: tribune in 66, aedile 60, praetor in 58; he prevented Lucullus from triumphing after his campaign against Mithridates; he married one of Sylla's daughters and divorced her; great talent as orator; recognized poet. Have I already noted that Abdel Kebir el Memmi, young officer in the new army and son of the contractor who was a member of the resistance in the Sahel, was involved in the most recent plot? Anyhow, he was sentenced today: death by hanging.

And now here we are, on the gleaming white deck of a French steamship. I am stretched out on a deck chair in the shade, because even though we're halfway there, and the spray provides some protection, I am wary of the sun. This is the Mediterranean, after all.

I'm shivering. What does that mean? Too hot in the sun, cold in the shade in no time. What if I'm wrong after all? What if it was a mistake to leave? What if Uncle was right? Enough of that now; let's stop weighing pros and cons. Only Bina has stayed behind, but he's an imaginary character, and as for Uncle . . . Shivering again. I'd better cover up.

Right here, in the small suitcase my hand is holding, is all of Emile's *The Cellar.* Incredible to think that all that takes up so little room—Emile's whole life, our whole life. Imilio, my brother—to think that I tried to believe I was so very different from you, whereas I even went so far as to call my wife Marie-Suzanne because yours is named Marie, although her real name is just Suzanne! It was only our ways of responding that seemed to differ for a while. Emile hoped he would integrate through the imagination and tried to do it, while I thought it was possible only through action, but we were both experiencing the same dramatic situation. I am going to reread it all once more so as to converse with you better and understand myself better. First of all I want to glance at those last bundles done up with string that I didn't have time to look through before I got sick. Here's one.

Colored Writing

"I don't know yet whether this business of colored writing is to be taken seriously or not. . . ."

THE CELLAR

Printing all of the pieces found in *The Cellar* in one volume was out of the question. *The Scorpion* would have taken on monstrous proportions.

We will eventually bring out complete editions of the most coherent sets of pieces, that is: *The Chronicle of the Kingdom of Within, The Scorpion's Journal, Colored Writing, Music and Literature,* and *The Life and Works of Uncle Makhlouf.*

Meanwhile we have thought it might be a good idea to give a few samples of the *Chronicle*. . . . In themselves, we find, they shed a different sort of light on what the author intended.

Publisher's Note

CHRONICLE OF THE KINGDOM OF WITHIN

The Chamberlain

After the funeral and the traditional period of mourning, the King consulted me as to the choice of a new chamberlain. Should he be a philosopher or a doctor? A layman or a priest? An artist or a man of action? Or, best of all perhaps, an intimate of the Court?

What was I to understand? I could not conceal my excitement.

The office was one of considerable importance. It involves arranging the ceremonies and keeping the archives—in short, composing the face our nation would wear in the future. It was a difficult office. The King spoke to me of it with concern. It requires devoting oneself entirely to that and never again taking part in anything else.

But who would be more worthy of it than I? What else have I been doing until now? As was customary, however, I promised the King that I would give it some thought and make an investigation.

The Guards

Now I can see what those trying years must have been like for my poor mother, who lived in constant anxiety, in expectation of a recognition which in fact never came. On the contrary; the fatal decree could have been pronounced at any time. Until at last my cousin, upon succeeding his father, forgave me my birth, provided of course that I never mention it.

We were already living in this house where I remain today and where I will probably live until my death. It is built against the wall of the Royal Cemetery at the back of the grounds. In order to go out of the Palace, you have to go by the black guards, whose fang-like moustaches, enormous black eyes, and sharp-edged sabers were the terror of my childhood. I was also panicky with fear of the dead. In short, I felt cornered.

I do not even think that my uncle, the King, deliberately arranged things that way. Actually, everyone has to go by the guards in order to go out of the Palace, and the entire Palace looks out onto the Royal Cemetery. But the whole point—and it is enormous—is that you must know whether the guards are your friends and whether you are not afraid of the cemetery.

And is that not what has happened to me?

Happily for me, the significance of everything has changed at last. Today, the dead protect me; I know that no one will dare to come by way of the cemetery. And the guards salute me proudly; I suppose they must have guessed my real identity. They are obviously grateful to receive the little favors I bestow on them as I go by—a coin, a sweetmeat, a cigar—or simply to hear me compliment them on their imposing presence and their handsome moustaches. I must admit they reassure me.

And so the double danger has become my double shield. All that was needed was that the King recognize me, in a vague and secret way, it is true, and especially, that I become strong, so that my very weaknesses now contribute to my strength. Have I not, because I am isolated, become the best witness of court and kingdom?

The Unknown Just Men

Naturally, I am exempt from the obligation to work; yet am I not one of the busiest men in the kingdom?

An old tradition has it that the duration of the world depends upon thirty-six Just Men. But no one knows, not even themselves, that they have that mission, and no one must know. For if they ceased to be anonymous, they would cease to be anything, and this would have the direst consequences for the world. They are, and it is necessary that they be, unknown Just Men.

Am I not a prince myself? Cousin to a king, in any case, and possibly more? Unknown of course—it has had to be that way—but not to all, not to myself in any case. That is the only difference.

But for that very reason, do I not have to exercise constant vigilance over everything? Over my royal cousin, over matters of current importance, over my own person?

The Two Swords

I congratulated my cousin on his idea of having our soldiers carry two swords, one long and the other short.

"Splendid idea," I said to him. "They are thus equipped for fighting at a distance and for hand-to-hand combat, when too long a sword would actually be in their way; at least I assume that that is the purpose of your reform."

"Yes, it is, of course," he answered, "and that is what everyone has assumed. But to you I will confide that that is not my main purpose. The shorter sword is to be used to kill themselves the day all is lost. It is a great source of strength for a soldier to have death in reserve and immediately available."

"But they do not know it!" I exclaimed in astonishment. "Why don't you tell them?"

"No no, they mustn't know! They could not bear to have it by their side in the ordinary course of things. But you may be sure that when the time of danger comes, they will discover its use all by themselves. They will bless me then for having given them a weapon against themselves."

The Holy of Holies

The first time—and the only one, thank God—that a conqueror was able to penetrate within our city, what stupefaction when he came to the tabernacle! He had girded himself to discover that so very mysterious God of ours that we do not talk about and which all other peoples unanimously consider the source of our invincibility to date. His heart was pounding; he was expecting to see some fabulous creature, some rare animal, some unwonted object, at the very least. And what did he find, when he entered the Holy of Holies? Nothing. Absolutely nothing. A completely empty space.

That, at least, is the way the historians tell it, and we have never denied their version, for reasons that are easy to guess. But I know better than anyone else what really happened, because the High Priest is also a member of our family. A few minutes beforehand, when the High Priest was warned that the city was about to fall, he carried the Ark away to a safe place.

Thus originated all the speculation by philosophers the world over as to the nature of our God, which is essentially, according to them, an absence, a common nostalgia, the negative cement of our collective soul, the ghost of the virtues we do not possess, etc., etc. Now, I ask you. If they have talked so much about Nothing, what would they have said if there had been Something?

El Ghoul

Homecoming of our ambassador to King El Ghoul, our black cousin—actually a very distant cousin, through the Queen of Sheba, but our cousin just the same.

The ambassador is full of curious anecdotes about the black part of our family. For instance, he tells us how, every single morning, when El Ghoul wakes up, he invariably climbs onto his throne (a laundry soap crate that he has had covered with green and red felt) and how he stands on it and spits four times—once toward each cardinal point. That is his way of insulting all the powers on earth and asserting his own.

Our ambassador's mission was completely successful. He persuaded El Ghoul to send us another contingent of those magnificent black guards.

The Electric Chair

I tried to persuade my royal cousin to put a stop to a certain practice commonly used by our doctors which dishonors us and makes us ridiculous in the eyes of foreigners who are traveling through our country. Especially on market days, when peasants crowd into the town, the doctors cannot handle all the patients who come to see them in their offices. One of them—and most of the others soon followed suit—thought of having a sort of armchair made that was covered with thin sheets of metal and connected to an electric plug. The patient puts on a fireman's helmet and sits in this armchair, which the doctor then plugs in. Aside from the fact that this causes a rather astonishing sensation, I must admit (having tried it myself), merely touching the patient makes sparks fly out from him. The doctor of course charges in proportion to the gravity of the illness, the amount of time taken, and the extent of the fireworks.

As I fully realized, my royal cousin felt strangely perplexed about the whole matter. He trotted out the usual arguments. No one had ever complained. Should Authority anticipate a possible complaint when it could not even manage to remedy all of the recognized ills? Doctors did not have very many means at their disposal. For once they had found one that was not dangerous—should they be forbidden to use it? It allows a doctor to treat a good-sized crowd in a single morning—a yield whose rate the lawmaker must surely appreciate? And, finally, the patients come away feeling better, or so they think. Was that not the most important thing for a sovereign, just as it was for a doctor?

The Electric Chair

(continued)

Naturally, I rejected all these arguments and appealed to the royal dignity, saying that it must not shield such goings-on, based on trickery. Reluctantly, and after much hesitation, my cousin told me this story (which proves once again what confidence he had in me).

"After all, it is not very long since we began using electricity. It was only the father of the present king, my own uncle, who had it installed in the Palace, and it was only then that the wealthiest families in the kingdom followed suit.

"And even so," added my cousin, "my father was already old at the time . . . a detail, perhaps, but you will soon understand the significance of it.

"My father could feel himself growing weaker. You know how much emphasis he always placed upon his personal magnetism and how proud he was of his physical strength. He said it contributed to a leader's influence over the crowd. He did not know what to do to keep up the vigor that made him so fascinating and carried his subjects away—carried us all away, in fact, because he seemed to be carried away himself by some extraordinary secret source of strength.

"It may have been a happy stroke of luck, but at that point he had the idea of sticking his fingers into the dark holes of a brand new electric plug. He received such a tremendous shock that he leapt in the air like a young man and was convinced he had discovered an extraordinary source of energy which could help him recover his own energy. You know how courageous he was. Despite the pain it caused him, he subjected himself periodically to this treatment. It had such a violent effect on him, making his old heart beat and stimulating every muscle in his body to such a point that he actually had to rein in the extraordinary excitement that took hold of him.

"In time, however, it became clear that this was likely to do him more harm than good. Discreetly, we consulted the doctors, who advised strictly against this terrible remedy, and I had to take it on myself to tell the King. He would not speak to me for an entire

week thereafter. But when he realized that my only motive had been to protect his health and prolong his life, he forgave me, and we compromised. We agreed to have a special plug made with weaker current, which would be better adapted to the King's own diminishing strength.

"So I gradually weakened the strength of the current, until, toward the end, I cut it off altogether. I am sure the King noticed it, but not once before making some important decision or doing something that would require extreme effort on his part did he fail to stick his fingers into those little dark holes.

"Come," my cousin added, "come and I'll show you the plug. . . . Look, here it is. Try it, put your fingers in it. You'll see!"

I decided to end the conversation right there. Obviously I could not go against the respect he felt for the memory of his royal father. But I was sorry I had not thought of asking him just one more question. He had said, "You'll see!" I'd see what?

Sublime words spoken by this same great king.

He lived to be very old, but a bad fall from a horse sent him into a deep coma. He recovered but it left him paralyzed in one leg and one arm and subject to various other disorders, including considerable gaps in his memory.

It was while he was in the coma that went on and on, that the Council of Wise Men, acting on the advice of his doctors, placed the power in the hands of the young Prince, on a temporary basis at first, then permanently, when it became clear that the King would never be himself again. Out of respect for the noble patient and for his sensitivity, which already had to endure so much, and also—it must be admitted—out of a remnant of fear of a man who had embodied the royal majesty for so long and so well, no one dared to inform him of the Council's decision.

An extraordinary piece of play-acting was spontaneously set in motion. Since he could no longer leave his room, the ministers and important officials regularly came to see him and kept him informed of the affairs of the kingdom, just as they had done before. The King listened; with his good arm he took notes, and then he gave orders in the same old imperious way, and when he had finally spoken, there was no argument possible. Just as before, he sometimes summoned the Prime Minister in the middle of the night to tell him about an idea he had had or a decision he had come to. The only difference was that he frequently forgot these conversations . . . which, in the midst of his misfortune, was fortunate. For matters would have become very awkward if the King had remembered everything and required each person to report to him in detail, just as before, on the effects of his policy.

He lived this way for five years, handled with the most respectful caution from all sides. It was even carried to the extent of printing a fake newspaper reserved for him alone. Until a stroke affected his brain again and brought him unremittingly to the doors of death. Then it was that he uttered those admirable words. He had just recovered the faculty of speech, and he was surrounded by his children and grandchildren, his doctors and the high digni-

taries. After exchanging a wink with his colleagues, his personal physician began to reassure him, saying that he was out of danger once again.

"No, gentlemen," said the King, "you do not need to continue acting out that comedy any longer. I thank you but I do not need it any more. I know I am going to die. I was willing to pretend I was reigning, since I was unable to reign in earnest. I refuse to pretend about dying, since at last I am able to die."

And indeed he died an hour later, in the most unaffected and thoroughly dignified way.

The Red-Eye

Death of Belalouna's wife yesterday. What will become of him? Blind, he could not do without her.

Belalouna is a red-eye—that is what we call someone with this very peculiar type of blindness. The eye appears to be intact; it is just slightly red, as if there had been some visual strain, but it is brighter, more wide open, as if preserved forever, somehow, in its dazzled state.

From time to time, either through a mistake on the part of the navigator or because of a shifting sand bar, a boat may come within sight of cliffs of rock salt. The way the light glances off them is so dangerous for the eyes that as soon as the man at the wheel calls out that he has seen the prodigious fiery facets, multiplied by the sun and the water, the entire crew rushes down into the hold. But to prevent the boat from drifting rudderless and going down with all hands aboard, one sailor must remain on deck, and go blind in the process.

But it is said to be a vision of such exceptional beauty that the poor man always maintains that he does not regret his sacrifice, since his eyes closed forever on a sight that nothing would ever be able to equal. Which is undoubtedly true, although no one has ever been in a position to challenge this claim, since those who have beheld that unearthly vision have never regained their sight and the others have never been able to do even so much as glimpse it. In any case, the blind man spends the rest of his life telling the story of this astonishing adventure and describing the bewitching splendor of those few matchless minutes.

Alas, anything grows dull with time, and although those burned-out motionless pink china eyes continue to awe, the blind man himself soon becomes a bore. Luckily for Belalouna, he had his wife; to her he could repeat his story endlessly.

Out of gratitude, and so that his infirmity would not keep her from enjoying the good things of this world, he made long and frequent trips with her. And so that he would not be sacrificed once again and his devotion would bring him something more than mere fatigue, she would describe to him what she saw. "Here is a house, here is a handsome tree, here is a donkey, etc."

He grew to like this and, no matter how immeasurably rich his single memory was. I can't help wondering whether, in the end, he didn't go on those trips for his own pleasure too.

Later, when old age set in, she became paralyzed in both legs; and as soon as she began to fret, he would hasten to suggest, "Say, how would you like to go on a trip?—an imaginary one?" And immediately she would say, "Here is a house, here is a handsome tree, here is a donkey, etc."

What will become of Belalouna?

Drugs

Lalloum:

I began taking drugs some time in the 1930's. I had never taken any before. That's the one thing I regret—having discovered drugs so late.

The authorities were waging a big campaign at that time against the consumption of hashish, which had grown to alarming proportions. It was estimated that one third of the population smoked it, which decreased the country's productivity. Disapproving descriptions were circulated of the curious states brought on by this drug—a sort of permanent absent-mindedness, an inability to focus one's attention on the slightest bit of work, a light-hearted laziness, a blunting of all desire. In short, what is disdainfully termed "Oriental fatalism."

I had never smoked hashish and in fact I had always turned my back on temptations of that sort. But this time I was impressed by the extent and the severity of the anti-drugs campaign and even more impressed by the stubborn resistance of the offenders at whom it was aimed. I said to myself, if people on both sides make so much effort, they must feel it's worth their while; hashish must be something really special. I took some, and felt simply wonderful.

What they had forgotten to mention, in their polemics, was the happiness that hashish brings. I work less, that is true, but I am satisfied with what I have; I do not feel any desire, that is also true, but neither do I suffer any pain; I am withdrawn from life, but I look serenely on death. Nothing saddens me and everything gives me joy.

The Centipede

First Age Ceremony for the son of the Princess (my cousin, sister to the King).

Leaving aside the details of this occasion—the way the men get drunk and the women flutter with excitement—here is what it actually amounts to. The High Priest dons his most ceremonial robes, warms his hands, and presses his thumb against the underside of the infant's penis. A woman takes a centipede which has been caught the day before, touches the infant's forehead with it, then places it on his penis, and she holds the wriggling insect there until the child howls with irritation.

More than once I have been able to observe that the women apparently respect what the priest does and are totally indifferent to what he says. The High Priest recited the long verse explaining that the mystical object of this ceremony is to make this new life firm and strong and render its faculties as diverse as those countless insect legs.

Meanwhile the women were cackling with almost obscene laughter. They did not, it is true, understand one bit of the text, all of which was in the sacred tongue. And as always, when I listened to them, I discovered another world, completely different from the world of the Law. According to them, all of this meant just one thing. Touching the penis in that way prevented it from growing too big, at least for the time being. If this were not done, the penis would stand erect every time a woman came in sight—which, for a child that age, would cause a great many complications.

Proof? Why touch his forehead? To make him forget his penis and chase the wicked thoughts away. Why a centipede? Because one cannot be too careful—the action of a hundred legs was more powerful than the action of only one; that way the infant's penis would be lulled to sleep that much more surely.

One more, undeniable proof: the job is entrusted to a woman. Later on, we'll see . . . More cackling at this point. What a woman has done, a woman will undo. How can you blame this feminine pride? But at the same time, how can you forget that a woman is a woman?

The Couple

"Oh my beloved, how could I show you how much I love you? In another life, I would like to become your she-cat!"

"Then, in another life, I would be your tom-cat."

"In another life, I would like to become your ewe!"

"Then I would be your ram."

"In another life I would like to become your mare!"

"In another life I would be your stallion."

And so we relived all the metamorphoses in the world, Nouch' and I did.

"Tell me, Nouch', what is the greatest proof of love, for a woman?"

"That she wish to become a man, so as to understand her lover better."

"Tell me, Nouch', what is the greatest proof of love, for a man?"

"That he wish to become a woman, so as to understand his mistress better."

"Undoubtedly; but in order to appreciate our new condition fully, we would each have to remember what our present life is like."

"Stop this make-believe, you frighten me!"

The Son

The King asked for my advice on something that concerned him, of a private nature this time. Should the Second Age ceremony be organized for his son, the Prince?

"On the pretext of keeping me informed about what he does in school with his new master," the King told me, "the Prince made this strange speech to me.

" 'So,' he said, 'God made man in his own image. Mustn't we also conclude from this that God is likewise the image of man?'

"Of course I answered him severely. I told him that irreverence of that sort was very commonplace, that someone else had already said it before him; and that I myself, when I had been even younger . . .

" 'I did not want to blaspheme, Father, I promise you. I simply thought I would lead up to this other question. How is it that God has tolerated such a mediocre image of himself?'

"And still another question: don't you think that is the reason why man does not always take God seriously?

"Then he added, speaking so gravely that I cannot manage to pick out the mischievousness which is probably hidden in it:

" 'Father, I am sure that at my age you had already settled these questions. You were certainly more advanced than I was. That's normal, after all; I am only your son—your image, actually.' "

"There is no doubt about it," I said to the King. "It is time to celebrate the Prince's Second Age. That was his first genuinely impertinent remark."

Strange age even so, when he does not know yet that his father is King but already wants to make his majesty totter.

Nonetheless I urged my cousin to seek the advice of the High Priest as well. Anything having to do with God concerns him, after all. And if the power of the King is sacred, is not the nascent right of the Prince also sacred?

Other People's Children

The finest periods in our History are those when catastrophes occur. Then it is that the noblest sentiments emerge.

During the Great Famine, for instance, in order to avoid eating their own children, people exchanged them for those of their neighbors.

The Rug

It was the King himself who spoke to me about writers. He named a few, especially Meguedèche.

I strongly advised against choosing writers for a job of that sort; not that I have anything against writers, or against Meguedèche, who is certainly the most outstanding of them all. But the idea of asking a writer to write History! Do they even know which is truth and which is lies? And History pays them back the same way, all right! Oh, I could tell you a lot about that, if it was worth spending so much time on what is only a bunch of pipe-dreams, after all!

And Meguedèche himself—how many people know his own history? Here it is the way he told it to me, with all the frankness that makes him so popular.

"How did I become a writer? Simple enough. I come from a poor family, as all my readers know (it's true that he has never tried to deny it; on the contrary, in fact—as if being born poor was a virtue!). I began to work with my uncle, a small-time street-corner showman. My job consisted mostly of keeping the onlookers entertained while he was getting ready to do his act. He was slow and sad and not much of a talker, whereas I liked to gab even then. People got bored standing around while he was preparing a heavier dumbbell or pulling the sword he was supposed to swallow out of its sheath, and often they just drifted away. My uncle asked me to do the barking for him.

" 'What should I tell them?'

" 'Anything. It doesn't matter, they don't care.'

"I had an idea. I would tell them about my life—you know the kind of thing—what it's like being itinerant performers from father to son, traveling around and so on. None of it was true; no one else in our family had been a showman, and my uncle had never left the district we lived in. But I could see they were interested; they kept silent and listened. Soon I realized that listening to me amused them more than watching my uncle, and that's when I had my second idea. Since my uncle was getting jealous and unpleas-

ant and tried to cut down on my speaking time, I left him and set up on my own.

"I bought a big rug and spread it out on the market place at the same time every day. And I worked it so that at each session I told about just one episode in my life and started on another; this kept up the suspense and made sure my public would be back the next day."

(At this point Meguedèche would slip into the tone and delivery of the public storyteller, doing it so naturally that it was clear he was telling the truth. "Now then ladies and gentlemen, every one of you just toss what you can onto this rug, anything from 11 francs up, I'll begin as soon as there's 2525 francs in all, those of you who know me also know that I tell everything, including the most daring and most intimate details, and if I leave out anything, don't worry, you'll be able to guess it all right. You'll hear all there is to know about my friends and relations and even the people I've just run into by chance. In short, what with one detail leading to another, you'll know all about my entire life and whatever's missing I'll make up right here in front of you. . . . All right ladies and gentlemen, I'm beginning now, make me begin, all you have to do is throw just one little coin and clap hard to encourage me and warm up your hands.")

"So, I built up a steady, reliable set of customers.

"You can guess what happened next. One day, the Director of the Royal Library happened to go by, and stopped, and found my speech to his liking. I'd noticed him in the crowd and I outdid myself that day. He's the one who gave me the third idea of my career. Why not put my life story down in writing? Instead of selling it in just one district and having to sit there in the cold or the heat waiting for a crowd to gather, I could have it distributed throughout the country—and even elsewhere, since I have had the good fortune of being translated and having money come in from several foreign countries."

And that's how they become writers!

The Game of the Scorpion

Finally, I told my royal cousin the story—the real story—of the scorpion's death.

Contrary to what is commonly believed, the scorpion does not generally die of his own sting. Sometimes, of course, he does wound himself and suffer, and sometimes even, if he struggles a little too violently, he sticks his own stinger into his neck (or whatever corresponds to a neck) and goes completely stiff. To all appearances, he is dead.

But if you watch closely, you see him slowly regain consciousness, and after a while the scorpion that has "committed suicide" is fully recovered and pretends to go quietly away.

"Is that a tragedy?" I asked the King. "More of a comedy, I would say! And the man exhibiting him knows it perfectly well. He waits until the spectators have left, and then he grabs the scorpion and puts him away until the next show."

I was unable to convince my cousin. Maybe I shouldn't have talked in riddles like that. He informed me of his decision: he would appoint a writer anyhow.

"They like money and fame?" he said. "I find that reassuring; it will make them all the more compliant. They like to talk about themselves? Who does not? from the King himself right down to any one of his subjects! They distort the truth? Do we do any differently, all of us, all the time, from the day we are born to the day we die? They at least embellish the truth—is the pleasure they bring us a lesser good because of that?"

I yielded once again to the wisdom and authority of the Prince. I did not dare tell him that I would gladly have accepted the responsibility myself.

This book has been set on the linotype in Baskerville, Helvetica and Memphis.
The display type is Bulmer.
The composition, printing, and binding is by H. Wolff Book Manufacturing Co., New York
Designed by Jacqueline Schuman.